Praise for Ellie Alexander's Bakeshop mystery series

"Delectable." —*Portland Book Review*

"Delicious." —*RT Book Reviews*

"Quirky . . . intriguing . . . [with] recipes to make your stomach growl." —*Reader to Reader*

"This debut culinary mystery is a light soufflé of a book (with recipes) that makes a perfect mix for fans of Jenn McKinlay, Leslie Budewitz, or Jessica Beck."
—*Library Journal* on *Meet Your Baker*

"Marvelous." —*Fresh Fiction*

"Scrumptious . . . will delight fans of cozy mysteries with culinary delights." —*Night Owl Reviews*

"Clever plots, likable characters, and good food . . . Still hungry? Not to worry, because desserts abound in . . . this delectable series."
—*Mystery Scene* on *A Batter of Life and Death*

"[With] *Meet Your Baker,* Alexander weaves a tasty tale of deceit, family ties, delicious pastries, and murder."
—Edith Maxwell, author of *A Tine to Live, A Tine to Die*

"Sure to satisfy both dedicated foodies and ardent mystery lovers alike."
—Jessie Crockett, author of *Drizzled with Death*

A Cup of Holiday Fear

Ellie Alexander

St. Martin's Paperbacks

This is a work of fiction. All of the characters, organizations, and events portrayed in this novel are either products of the author's imagination or are used fictitiously.

First published in the United States by St. Martin's Paperbacks, an imprint of St. Martin's Publishing Group.

A CUP OF HOLIDAY FEAR

For information address St. Martin's Publishing Group, 120 Broadway, New York, NY 10271.

www.stmartins.com

ISBN: 978-1-250-21434-8

Our books may be purchased in bulk for promotional, educational, or business use. Please contact your local bookseller or the Macmillan Corporate and Premium Sales Department at 1-800-221-7945, ext. 5442, or by e-mail at MacmillanSpecialMarkets@macmillan.com.

Printed in the United States of America

St. Martin's Paperbacks edition / October 2019

10 9 8 7 6 5 4 3 2 1

Chapter One

They say that the holidays bring people together. Nothing could be truer in my hometown of Ashland, Oregon, which looked like a scene straight out of a picture postcard. Our Shakespearean hamlet had been decked out for the holidays with garlands of fresh evergreen boughs draped over the Elizabethan shop windows and blue and white snowflake HAPPY HOLIDAY banners dangling from antique lampposts. Torte, my family's bakeshop, was no exception. Our red brick exterior gleamed a beautiful crimson under the warm glow of golden Edison-style lights that stretched from the side of our building to the entrance to the Calle Guanajuato, a cobblestone walkway that paralleled Ashland Creek. Enormous wreaths wrapped with bright red bows hung in the bakeshop's front windows. Strings of colorful vintage bulbs dotted the roofline and would soon be illuminated along with those of every other shop, restaurant, lamppost, and tree in the plaza.

For the moment our sweet downtown shopping district sat in a dusky slumber. The sun hugged the top of the mountains, readying itself for its descent. As soon as darkness washed over the Rogue Valley, the holiday season would officially take flight. Tonight was the annual Festival of Light Parade, and I was so jittery with excitement that I almost skipped an afternoon coffee as I stepped inside Torte's front door. The dining room was packed with familiar faces. I waved to a group of women sitting in a booth near the windows. They were sharing a tray of chocolate fondue, one of our seasonal specials that we served in a ceramic fondue pot with decadent melted Belgian chocolate and an assortment of fruit, pound and sponge cakes, and handmade marshmallows.

One of the women, Wendy, a Torte regular and dear friend of Mom's, dipped a skewer stick with a fluffy square of vanilla sponge into the luscious chocolate and called out, "Juliet, we all agree that Torte is going to ruin our waistlines this holiday season."

Her friend dabbed a drip of chocolate with the edge of her napkin. "Wendy's right, but what she didn't say is that we also decided that it's totally worth it."

I chuckled as I unzipped my black parka and hung it on the coatrack next to the front door. "My apologies to your waistlines, but I'm glad you're enjoying the fondue."

"No apology needed," Wendy said, helping herself to a square marshmallow. "The holidays are about little indulgences. We'll focus on our waistlines again in January, right, ladies?"

The women laughed and clinked their skewers together in a show of solidarity.

"Good plan." I flashed them a thumbs-up and turned my attention to the twelve-foot blue spruce tree to my left.

The aroma of fresh pine and balsam made me pause for a minute and breathe in the earthy scent.

For the holidays we had accented the bakeshop with Elizabethan-style greenery. Bunches of ivy, laurel, and holly twisted with golden twinkle lights wrapped around the bay windows and had been adorned along the espresso bar and around our chalkboard menu. Sprigs of mistletoe dangled above the door. Gorgeous, aromatic wreaths made of fresh herbs like rosemary and bay hung from every window. After tonight's lighting ceremony, we planned to finish decorating the tree with hundreds of hand-decorated snowflake cookies.

Rosa, one of our more recent hires, stood on a step stool as she twisted strings of pearls onto each branch. "Is this good?" She tucked her long, dark hair behind her ears and pointed to the tree.

"It's lovely." I stepped closer and inhaled the woodsy fragrance. It mingled with the wafting scent of bread and richly brewed coffee. "It's really starting to feel like the holidays in here," I said to Rosa, noting the evergreen garland she had tied to our chalkboard menu and the poinsettias placed on each tabletop in the dining area.

I left her to the decorating and squeezed past a line of customers waiting at the espresso counter. We'd been bustling with nonstop activity for weeks. Our busy season started to ramp up the day after Halloween with customers placing orders for pumpkin, pecan, apple, and chocolate and coconut cream pies for their family Thanksgiving gatherings. Bread production tripled. Our coffee sales began to skyrocket and keeping the pastry case stocked became a daily challenge.

With Thanksgiving behind us, my team of bakers-turned-elves had been rolling out our signature sugar cookie cutouts in the shape of Christmas trees and winter stars. Rows of butter stollen, chocolate Yule logs, gingerbread spice cookies, hot chocolate petits fours, and rum fruitcake filled the pastry case. There were red and white candy-cane-striped cakes on display in glass stands and baskets of our holiday breads filling every square inch of the counter. From Hanukkah cider and jelly doughnuts and chocolate rugelach to old English figgy pudding and trifle, we were committed to making sure that our offerings were special, unique, and filled with tradition.

"Hey, boss." Andy gave me a two-finger wave from behind the counter. His cheery red apron with the Torte logo was tied around his waist and a Santa hat with a fluffy cotton ball flopped to one side of his head. "I saw you come in and thought you might need sustenance for the parade." He handed me a steaming mug with a mound of whipped cream sprinkled with crushed peppermint candies. "It's my peppermint bark mocha. Tell me what you think, because Steph is getting ready to put the holiday specials up on the chalkboard."

"I'm sure it will be great. No one could claim you're skimping on the whipped cream." I snuck a taste with my pinkie. "Did you add a dash of peppermint extract to this?"

Andy grinned. "You know it. I was thinking we could serve these with sticks of peppermint candy canes, too."

"Sounds delish." I balanced my coffee and headed downstairs to check in with my baking team.

Torte had recently undergone a major renovation, including expanding into the basement space that now housed our gorgeous state-of-the-art kitchen and cozy seating area where customers could get an up-close and personal look at our bakers in action or linger with friends in front of the atomic fireplace. Rosa had wrapped evergreen boughs and twinkle lights along the stairway railing and a second (albeit slightly smaller) Christmas tree had been placed near the seating area, awaiting decoration.

"How goes parade prep?" I asked as I stepped into the kitchen.

Sterling, my newly appointed sous-chef, stood near the wood-fired oven watching over savory flatbread that had just begun to char. Stephanie had the meticulous task of hand piping the sugar cookie cutouts with royal icing. If anyone was up to the task, it was her. At first appearance her goth style, shockingly purple hair, and heavily lined eyes made her seem aloof, but I had learned that under her reserved exterior she had a tender heart. Much like the Grinch.

One of my most recent hires, Marty, a jovial and professionally trained baker in his sixties, was stirring a vat of butternut squash soup for the upcoming lunch rush. We had prepared extra stock of all of our usual offerings along with some holiday specials for the day. Tonight's parade would draw thousands of people to the plaza. Historically it was one of the busiest days of the year. Locals and visitors would line Main Street at dusk to sing carols and watch as Santa, Mrs. Claus, and their sleigh of reindeer paraded through town until they arrived at the plaza where they would illuminate a million festive lights and kick off the official holiday season. Christmas in Ashland was nothing short of magic.

Since Torte was just a few doors down from the balcony where Santa and Mrs. Claus would flip on the lights, we planned to set up an outdoor hot chocolate and cookie station. We had made stacks of unfrosted cookies in fun holiday shapes—trees, stockings, presents, wreathes, and Santa's sleigh. Children would be invited to frost a cookie with colorful buttercream and decorate them with an assortment of shimmery sprinkles. We would offer complimentary hot chocolate and handmade peppermint marshmallows to warm people's spirits while they waited for the light show.

"Andy and I have the tables set up outside," Bethany said, interrupting my internal checklist. "Do you want to come see?"

Bethany wore a long-sleeved emerald-green T-shirt with red and white lettering that read WE WHISK YOU A MERRY CHRISTMAS. Her unruly, long curls had been tied into two ponytails with matching red and green ribbons.

"Nice shirt," Sterling noted with a smile as he removed a tray of bubbling mozzarella, salami, and tomato flatbread from the pizza oven. "Where do you find so many shirts with baking puns?" His jet-black hair had begun to grow out. It had a hint of a wave now that it fell below his ear. The naturally disheveled look suited him.

"I have my sources," Bethany bantered.

"Did you know that studies say people who use puns are smarter and wittier on average?" Marty chimed in.

"Validation!" Bethany raised her arms in triumph. "Long live the pun."

"Now look what you've done," Sterling said to Marty.

"Don't encourage her. The next thing you know we'll all be wearing matching punny T-shirts."

Marty ladled the gorgeous, creamy butternut squash soup into a waiting bowl. "Hey, you can't argue with research." He paused and shared an impish look with Bethany. "As they say, the proof is in the pudding."

Stephanie, who had remained silent, let out a groan.

Sterling rolled his eyes. "We're doomed."

I knew that the teasing was all in fun. My staff, while different, shared a mutual love of the craft of pastries and a mutual respect for each other. Mom and I prided ourselves on the fact that Torte rarely—if ever—experienced any bickering among our team. There had been one exception: Andy, our lead barista, had been less than welcoming of Sequoia, another recent hire. I had come to learn that Andy's personal life was in turmoil. He had made the decision to drop out of college and was worried that Sequoia was going to replace him. We had assured him that he would always have a place at Torte. Things between the two of them had been better ever since.

"If you guys would stop bugging me, I have real work to do, like show Jules the adorable Christmas-cookie decorating station." Bethany tossed one of her ponytails over her shoulder as I followed her out of the kitchen.

Having the bakeshop divided into two levels had allowed us to greatly expand our product line. The commercial kitchen was more than double the square footage of our old kitchen, but running up and down the stairs throughout the day to deliver fresh trays of pastries and having staff and customers on two floors provided new challenges. We had kept the royal-teal-and-red color scheme that my parents had used when they opened Torte's front doors decades ago. It felt perfect for the holiday season.

Bethany lifted a tray of Christmas puddings, cupcakes piled high with fluffy mounds of buttercream frosted to resemble snow, and raspberry and pecan kringles (a Danish pastry) that made my mouth water. "I'll drop this off upstairs before we go outside."

"Does anything else need to go up?" I asked, taking a sip of the mocha Andy had made for me. It had a wonderful balance of chocolate with hints of peppermint, but it wasn't overly sweet. He had managed to have the coffee flavor dominate, with subtle touches of mint in the background. I was impressed. It wasn't an easy task. Many coffee shops opted for overly sweet and cloying chocolate drinks with artificially flavored syrups. At Torte, we made everything by hand from natural, locally sourced ingredients.

"No." Bethany expertly maneuvered the tray. "Just this for now, but there will be lots to bring up soon."

As I glanced at the shiny Christmas puddings dotted with edible gold leaf, I felt a sense of gratitude for tradition. When my parents opened the bakeshop, they made a pact to create artisanal food baked with love and seasonality. There was something special about baking based on the season. Some of my fellow pastry chefs had succumbed to the pressure of launching their holiday lines in September. But not at Torte. We prided ourselves on savoring the flavors of every season. The beautiful Christmas puddings Bethany was carrying would only be available for the next few weeks, and I liked it that way.

Once upstairs, Bethany slid the new tray into the pastry case and received a round of oohs and ahhs from waiting customers.

"Hey, boss, what do you think of the peppermint bark mocha?" Andy asked as I went to grab my coat.

"It's heaven in a cup." I raised my half-full coffee mug in a toast.

"Awesome." Andy's sincere and youthful face lit up in a smile. His summer tan had faded, making the freckles on his cheekbones more pronounced. "I'll add it to the holiday special board. You're not going to believe what Sequoia wants to put up there." He stuck out his tongue and pointed to Sequoia, who was boxing up a pumpkin cheesecake. A month ago his reaction would have worried me, but since he and Sequoia had found a working rhythm, I knew his goofy and somewhat disgusted face was in jest.

"What?" I asked.

Sequoia handed one of our white craft pastry boxes with our blue and red fleur-de-lis logo to a customer and closed the pastry case. She had a distinctly Ashland look. Her dreadlocks were hidden beneath a navy bandana. Knotted bracelets were tied around her petite wrists. We don't have a strict dress code at Torte, but I had encouraged Sequoia to ditch her flowing peasant skirts for more practical jeans. Loose-fitting clothing or clunky jewelry isn't a good match for a crowded kitchen or the narrow space our staff had to navigate behind the pastry counter and espresso bar. Sequoia had taken my advice, in part because I think she was tired of having her tie-dyed skirts stepped on. Today she wore jeans that were covered in patches and a long-sleeved navy T-shirt under her Torte apron.

"You know, a lot of people around here celebrate winter solstice," Sequoia replied in her languid tone. "I was thinking we could do a winter solstice chai with brandy extract, star anise, cinnamon, vanilla bean, oranges, and black peppercorns. Something real earthy, you know?"

"That sounds wonderful. I'd love to try a sample." I took another drink of my coffee and set the mug in a tub under the counter.

Bethany clapped twice. "That would be so cool. I could do an Instagram post about chasing the light. Maybe we can do a whole thing about light versus dark around solstice. It's not for a couple weeks, right?"

"It's the first day of winter every year. Did you know that solstice is the turning of the sun?" Sequoia didn't wait for Bethany to respond because it was obvious by the dreamy look in Bethany's eyes that Sequoia had her full attention. "Throughout history and across nearly every culture there have been celebrations and festivals marking the return of the light. There's a huge solstice celebration here in Ashland with a bonfire at Emigrant Lake. It's an event for the whole family with face painting, music, food, and a wonderful trail of luminaries around the lake. You can follow the path of light and reflect on the past year and the year ahead."

"That sounds amazing." Bethany whipped out her phone and started scrolling. "Okay, what about something like this?" She held out a picture for me and Sequoia. "Black-and-white-dipped cookies to pair with your solstice chai—those should make some great shots for our social media and such a great story to share too—I love the idea of following a path of light. What do you think? And can I come to the solstice celebration?"

Sequoia's inner calm radiated when she smiled. Her energy wasn't as effusive as Bethany's, but it was equally inviting. "Absolutely. I'd love to have you come along."

"Hey, don't forget about my peppermint bark mochas and eggnog shooters." Andy pretended to be injured. He tossed the Santa hat he'd been wearing in Bethany's direction. "I thought you were going to get some shots for social media after you showed Jules the setup outside."

She caught the hat and handed it back to him. Her cheeks flamed as red as the felt hat. It was a common occurrence whenever Andy was around. "No worries. I am. Totally. Like we talked about this afternoon, it's going to be huge. I'm going to shoot so much footage at the tree lighting and do a massive push for your holiday drinks." She spoke so fast there wasn't time to breathe between sentences. "Anyone who comes in after the lighting and shows that they've made a purchase at any shop on the plaza is going to get twenty percent off any of our holiday drinks."

"It's cool. Don't freak. I was just messing with you." Andy raised the hat in surrender.

"Yeah, but I just want you to know that I would never say I was going to do something, like promote your amazing holiday drinks, and not follow through." Bethany's cheeks burned with color.

I took it as my cue to rescue Bethany. "Shall we go check out the cookie station?" I headed for the front door.

Sequoia flashed us a peace sign.

Andy pointed outside to the bustling plaza. A group of carolers dressed in period costumes had gathered in front of the Lithia Fountains to serenade shoppers.

"Uh, I wouldn't stand there too long if I were you, boss," Andy said, nodding at the sprig of green mistletoe above my head. "You might get smooched."

"Eeeek. Let's go, Bethany." I motioned for her to hurry, but I was too late. The door swung open and Lance, my friend and the resident artistic director at the Oregon Shakespeare Festival, swept in.

He didn't miss a beat. I guessed it was probably because Andy was still pointing at the mistletoe. Lance gasped. "To what do my wandering eyes appear? Mistletoe hanging near?" He fanned his face with one hand. "And above the fairest baker in the land." In one dancelike motion he leaned toward me and planted a kiss on my lips. Then he dipped me and proceeded to kiss both cheeks and my forehead.

"Lance, enough." I pushed him away.

"What kind of greeting is that, for your dearest friend? And at the holidays no less." He looked to Bethany for support. She chuckled.

"Holidays or not, I wasn't planning to be smothered with a wet kiss." I scowled.

He adjusted his sparkling silver tie and smoothed his black suit. "Then I might suggest you don't linger under the mistletoe. Am I right, young one?" he asked Bethany.

She pulled on a puffy red coat.

"Are you coming in or out?" I asked, opening the door again for Lance.

"I was coming to find you, darling."

"Give me five minutes. I need to check our setup for the holiday parade."

"Be careful out there. I bumped into Richard Lord on my way over and the man is on a rampage."

Great. Just what I didn't need—during the holidays or any time of the year. Richard Lord owned the run-down Merry Windsor Hotel across the street. When I returned home to Ashland, he had taken an immediate dislike to me and had tried, unsuccessfully, to put Torte out of business ever since.

"Why is he on a rampage?" I asked, reaching for my coat.

"Who knows what goes on in that man's head. He was muttering something about not getting asked to play Santa. Although why he didn't land the role is a surprise to me. He has the stomach for it, if you catch my drift." Lance nudged my waist.

"But not the disposition," I replied.

"Touché. But honestly, I might be with Mr. Lord on this one. I'm so over the parade. The holiday lighting. The magic of Ashland." Lance's voice had an unusual edge to it.

Bethany's eyes widened. "Are you being serious? The holiday lighting is literally like the best thing that happens in Ashland. In just a couple hours the plaza is going to be all lit up with beautiful lights and decorations. I can't wait. This time of year always makes me feel like a kid again."

"Sweet sentiment, kid, but I'm afraid the holidays aren't my cup of tea, as they say." He unwrapped a silver cashmere scarf tied around his neck. It matched his tie and overcoat.

I was surprised to hear that too. Lance loved drama and anything and everything that involved high production value; a million Christmas lights, traditional carolers, and an old-fashioned holiday parade sounded right up his alley.

I studied his face. "You are serious, aren't you?"

"Never more serious, darling. The holidays leave a bad taste in my mouth. I'm a full-fledged Scrooge. Usually I'm somewhere on a tropical beach with a cocktail in hand this time of year, but alas, given the recent upheaval with the board and my personal life, I'm stuck here for the duration. And to that I actually want to say bah humbug."

"Oh, you're going to love it. It's so beautiful," Bethany gushed. "I didn't realize that you've never been to the parade. Just wait, I mean, it's amazing. You will love it."

Lance cleared his throat and caught my eye.

"Can you go check on the tables?" I said to Bethany. "I see some kids who look like they're already interested in decorating." That was a half lie. There were some kids milling around the decorating stations, but there was nothing for them to do yet. We wouldn't bring the cookies, frosting, and sprinkles outside until after the parade. I wanted a minute alone with Lance.

"You bet." When she opened the door a blast of cool air hit us.

Once she was out of earshot, I patted Lance's arm. "Why don't you go get one of Andy's delicious peppermint bark mochas and find a spot to relax. I'll be back in five minutes, and then we're going to have a heart-to-heart, understood?"

"About what?"

"About your attitude. I need to warn you, Lance Rousseau, you are not getting off that easy."

"How so?"

"This is my absolute favorite time of year, and I'm not going to allow even one moment of your bah humbug attitude. When I get back, I want a smile on your face and I want you humming along to 'Jingle Bells,' understood?"

He scowled. "Juliet, I have loathed this season of supposed *merriment* since I was a kid. Well, at least since my mom died." The briefest flash of sadness passed over him.

I understood that the season could trigger painful memories. The holidays had always brought feelings of loss to the surface for me. My dad, like Lance's mom, had died when I was young. The profound grief of losing a parent had shaped me in ways I was still discovering. If there was one thing that I had learned since coming home to Ashland, it was that closing your heart doesn't protect it. It closes you off to every possibility.

"I know. I'm sorry." I reached for his hand.

Lance squared his shoulders and his emotions shifted. "Look, Juliet, I appreciate the effort, but Christmas is not my thing. You would have to work round the clock to try and convince me otherwise, and by the looks of the queues here, you don't have that kind of time."

"How wrong you are, Lance. Challenge accepted. Operation Lance Loves Christmas commences now." I pushed him toward the coffee bar.

Lance could protest as much as he wanted. The holidays were a time of joy and I was determined to help him find that magic of Christmas again.

Chapter Two

A brisk gust of air nearly blew me backward as I stepped outside onto the plaza. Ashland is nestled in the Siskiyou Mountains right on the border between Oregon and California. At an elevation of two thousand feet our Shakespearean town boasts some of the Pacific Northwest's best weather with long stretches of summer and late fall sun that fade into clear, crisp winter afternoons—perfect for skiing and snowshoeing on nearby Mount Ashland. Evening temperatures had been dipping below freezing for the past few weeks and coating the sepia-toned east hills a sparkling shade of white.

The sinking purple sun cast an almost iridescent glow on the plaza's Tudor-style buildings. For hundreds of years Ashland's plaza has been a gathering place. The natural Lithia waters had long drawn people here for healing and reflection. Now the spring-fed waters were piped into a bubbling fountain in the center of the town square. A favorite pastime for Torte staff and patrons is to watch from the windows as newcomers sample the sulfur-laced water for the first time. It's definitely an acquired taste.

City workers tested strands of lights on the lampposts to make sure the grand illumination went off smoothly. It wouldn't do to have Santa complete his countdown only to have the plaza remain plunged in darkness. Parade-goers had already claimed coveted spots on benches near the fountain and information kiosk. They were being entertained by a local children's choir singing a medley of holiday classics. Yellow caution tape marking the parade route lined both sides of Main Street. Kids dressed in heavy coats and hats pressed up against the caution tape for a front-row view. Just a couple doors down from the bakeshop I noticed the staff from Pucks Pub all wearing elf hats, setting out keg barrels with mulled spiced cider. At the flower shop, A Rose By Any Other Name, Thomas's mom was arranging materials for wreath making.

This charming scene has to sway Lance, I thought. It doesn't get more quintessential than this. However, the plaza's charm was quickly eroded by the sound of Richard Lord's booming voice.

"Hey, Juliet! I need to talk to you."

I glanced across the street to see Richard barreling toward me. He nearly knocked over a woman pushing a stroller decked out in Christmas lights in his haste. His gait was heavy, and made me think of Sasquatch.

"Listen here, Juliet, I know what you're up to and I'm going to tell you right now that you are going to lose this time."

"Nice to see you, too, Richard. Merry Christmas."

A green and red Christmas sweater with a cutout of Rudolph complete with a flashing red nose was stretched so tightly across his chest that I thought the seams might burst. "I'm not playing your little game this time. I know what's going down at the Winchester and you're not going to get your greedy hands on that property. Your mom and Mr. Shakespeare might be up there with their little peace, love, and pastry friends, but I'm on to your games." He shook his finger in my face. "I'm on to you, Juliet. You may have everyone else in town fooled with your little 'Oh, I'm so innocent' act, but not me."

"Richard, I have no idea what you're talking about." I stuck my hands into the pockets of my parka to warm them.

"Don't play dumb. The McBeths are unraveling and I've had my eye on the Winchester for years. I don't care if your mom is trying to connive her way into the McBeths' good graces just so you can sneak in there and beat me to the deal, but it's not working this time. You two already stole the basement away from me, and don't even get me started on Uva."

More and more people funneled into the plaza lugging folding chairs, blankets, and thermoses.

"Look, Richard, I don't have time for this. Like I said, I have no idea what you're talking about." I considered explaining the fact that even if the Winchester Inn was for sale, which was the first I'd heard of it, I had no interest in buying it and I knew for sure that Mom didn't either. She and the Professor had been making plans to travel more. But I didn't owe Richard anything. He couldn't harass me on the street and expect me to stand and take it.

"This isn't over, Juliet. I've got my eye on you." He gave me a hard stare.

"Have fun at your ugly-Christmas-sweater party, Richard. If there's a prize, you'll definitely win with that sweater." I turned and left him standing on the sidewalk with his mouth half open.

I zipped up my parka all the way and walked over to the far end of the plaza where Bethany and Andy had covered our outdoor tables with red tablecloths. They had strung chains of paper cutouts of gingerbread cookies around each table. There were glass jars filled with hand-made peppermint, vanilla, and chocolate marshmallows. Stacks of striped candy-cane paper cups and napkins awaited our first guests, along with warming carafes that would soon be filled with Andy's peppermint hot choco-late and spiced apple cider.

"What do you think?" Bethany asked, pointing to the nearest table where they had arranged plastic knives for spreading frosting and tins of colorful holiday sprinkles. "We kept the frosting station pretty bare so that kids will have room to decorate their cookies, but do you think we need another table?"

Torte's exterior space wasn't very large. Our bistro tables butted up between the sidewalk and curb. "No, it's fine as is. We can't block the sidewalk, so we'll try to keep the hot chocolate and cider line moving and encour-age the kids to get cozy while they work on their cookie creations." I blew into my hands to try and warm them up. "It's freezing anyway. I don't think anyone will mind be-ing in close quarters."

Bethany pointed to the tip of her nose. "I think I'm turn-ing into Rudolph. I can't feel my nose."

"That's no good, especially since I had you pegged to run the decorating station."

She rubbed her nose and cheeks. "I'm kidding. I'm not even cold. Plus, I brought a bunch of handwarmers for everyone. You can't keep me away. I've been dying to see the adorable kids frost cookies. It's going to be social media gold."

I laughed. Across the street, in the opposite direction from Richard Lord's Merry Windsor, the police office was buzzing with activity. I had always thought that the plaza police station must be the most inviting police station of all time. That was certainly true today. The station's blue and white striped awning had dozens of sparkling white snowflakes fluttering in the slight breeze. Two four-foot Christmas trees flanked the entrance, and more snowflakes had been pressed onto the windows.

"This looks great," I said to Bethany. "I'm going to run over and say hi to Thomas. Let's plan to start setting out the cookies and frosting and filling the carafes in about an hour."

Bethany returned to the bakeshop while I crossed the street. "Hey, it looks like there's going to be a parade or something?" I said to Thomas, who held a stack of plastic orange cones.

He glanced up and down Main Street where his fellow officers in uniform were clearing traffic. Then gave me a puzzled stare. "Really? I hadn't heard. Although rumor has it that Ashland does love a parade."

I appreciated our easygoing friendship. Thomas and I had dated in high school and had rekindled our friendship when I returned home. It was comforting to know that Thomas carried a piece of my history. He had known me during my awkward teen years and had stood by with steadfast support when my father died. I think he had wanted to pick back up where we had left off many years ago, but my heart wasn't free. Coming home to help Mom run Torte wasn't my only reason for returning to Ashland. I had left my husband Carlos on the ship where we had spent a decade sailing from one sun-drenched port to the next. A life at sea had fulfilled my desire for adventure, but even before I learned that Carlos had kept a life-changing secret from me, I had been searching for solid ground.

In true Thomas spirit, he hadn't tried to push me to make a choice about Carlos or my future. I appreciated the space. Being in Ashland had changed me. If Thomas had tried to push it might have led to the end of our friendship. I had come to rely on him and couldn't imagine life in Ashland without him.

Recently Thomas had seemed to take an interest in Detective Kerry, a new police officer who had joined the ranks. At first, I'd been resistant to the idea. Not because I was still harboring any feelings for Thomas (at least I didn't think I was) but because Kerry was much more tightly wound than him. I wasn't sure that Ashland was a match for her, but in the past few months I noticed her changing. Maybe it was Thomas's influence, or maybe it was Ashland.

"How's the setup going?" I rubbed my hands together. Why hadn't I thought to bring gloves?

Thomas set the cones on the sidewalk. "Not bad. We've got everything shut down on Siskiyou. You should see how many people are already lining the streets up near the start of the parade route by the library."

I glanced around us. Main Street was a mob of people

now. Paradegoers were huddled under sleeping bags and wool blankets in camp chairs. The energy in the plaza was palpable. Vendors selling light-up snow wands and glowing green Christmas-tree hats walked the route to the delight of the youngest parade viewers. Neighbors hugged each other and waved happy greetings as they squeezed into any tiny spot on the street. Across the street by the fountains the crowd had joined in singing with the choir. Nearly every shop had set up outdoor displays or had propped open their front doors to invite paradegoers inside. "If it's anything like this, I can only imagine."

Thomas waved his hand in dismissal. "This is nothing, Jules. How long has it been since you attended the Christmas parade?"

I shrugged. "A while." As I spoke my breath puffed out in front of me like little white clouds.

"Just wait. We're anticipating over twenty thousand people to pack into the plaza in the next couple hours. It's going to be a mob scene. Good thing I have my trusty badge," he teased as he pointed to the badge clipped to his blue police jacket. Thomas wisely had on a pair of thick black gloves.

I rubbed my hands together for friction. "I'm excited. I can't wait to see Santa."

Thomas groaned. "Ugh. Don't get me started with Santa."

"What? Why?" My conversation with Richard Lord came to mind.

"You know the McBeth family, right?"

"Emma and Jon, who own the Winchester Inn?"

Thomas nodded. "Yeah. They've been playing Mr. and

Mrs. Claus for going on thirty years now, but apparently there's some huge problem at the hotel and they don't know if they're going to be able to do it this year."

"That's funny timing. Lance just told me that Richard was in a huff about not getting to play Santa."

"Can you imagine? Richard Lord as Santa? We might really end up with a riot on our hands. I can see the tears now when Richard tells the poor kids that Santa isn't bringing them anything for Christmas."

"Or worse, that the only thing they are getting in their stockings is a one-night stay at the Merry Windsor," I teased.

Thomas groaned.

I looked at my watch. "Who's playing Santa? The parade is starting in less than an hour."

"I know. Don't worry. We have a backup plan." Thomas cocked his head to one side and stuck out his tongue.

"Who? You?"

"Jeez, Jules, I know we're not in high school anymore, but I haven't aged that much, have I?" Thomas looked injured. "Not me. The Professor and your mom."

"Mom and the Professor are going to dress up as Santa and Mrs. Claus?" No wonder I hadn't seen Mom at Torte—and that must have been what Richard was talking about. Although how he jumped to the conclusion that we were scheming to buy the Winchester Inn was a mystery.

"Yep. They're at the Winchester right now, making sure the costumes fit in case they have to step in."

"Neither Mom nor the Professor are exactly in Santa's age bracket either."

"I know, but the show—or parade—has to go on, and

when we got the call from the McBeths that they were likely going to have to cancel, the Professor stepped in to offer his services. The McBeths always wear wigs and makeup every year anyway and Lance sent over one of the makeup artists from OSF to help make sure they look the part."

I couldn't picture my stylish, petite mom or the tall, lanky Professor in red robes or with white hair, but then again, I lived in the land of theater where anything was possible.

Thomas picked up the cones that he had set on the sidewalk. "I should get moving. I've got to set these out. Save me something sweet, okay?"

"Deal." I left him to his work. I hoped nothing was seriously wrong at the historic hotel. The McBeth family had been actively involved in the community for decades. They donated to the school foundation and volunteered their time at park cleanups and the holiday parade. The Winchester Inn hosted a famous Dickens feast every night through Christmas Eve. The dinner was a highlight of the holiday season for many families not only in Ashland but in all of the surrounding Rogue Valley and up and down the West Coast. Visitors planned December weekend getaways to come to the Dickens feast, take in a holiday production at the Cabaret, and shop in the plaza. In fact, Mom and I had recently made reservations to the feast for our holiday staff party. I would have to stop by the hotel later and see if there was anything I could do to help.

I returned to Torte and found Lance nursing his coffee at a booth by the window. I sat down across from him.

"You'll appreciate this, I just learned a little piece of gossip for you."

Lance perked up. "Do tell."

"It sounds like Mom and the Professor might moonlight as Santa and Mrs. Claus. Now that is worth braving the cold for the parade, isn't it?"

"That hardly counts as gossip. Doug called earlier and asked if he could raid the costume shop." Lance stared at his coffee mug. His voice had lost its typical affect.

"Lance, come on. Enough of the gloom and doom. It's Christmas. People are going to parade down the street. There is literally the sweetest-sounding children's choir right outside the window. We're going to have a front-row seat to the lighting ceremony, and my mom is going to be Mrs. Claus. What's not to love?"

Before he could respond, Andy came by with a refill. "Did you just say that Mrs. C is going to be *the* Mrs. C?"

I chuckled. "I did."

Andy topped off Lance's coffee. "Dreams do come true. Forget Mrs. The Professor. Your mom is Mrs. C to me again." He handed me an empty mug. "You want some? I told Lance he should try my holiday drink special, but he went for a straight-up black cup of Joe."

"I'm fine." I waved Andy off. Once he was out of earshot, I clapped my hands together. "No more moping. You're going to come with me and clap along to the merry sounds of a small-town parade. And then I'm dragging you over to our cookie-decorating station. If anything can lift your spirits, it's adorable kids with sticky frosting fingers."

Lance recoiled. "I shudder at the thought. Sticky fingers

are not to be anywhere near Armani." He ran his hand over his tailored suit jacket.

"Fine, no cookie station, but your Armani is in no danger at the parade." I jumped to my feet and held out my hand. "Come on. It's time to spread some holiday cheer."

Chapter Three

I dragged Lance outside after we bundled up in coats, hats, and a borrowed pair of gloves I took from Torte's lost and found bin.

"This way," I said, leading Lance over to the police station where there was just enough room for the two of us to squeeze in with the crowd. We watched as dance troupes with glow sticks danced down Main Street, followed by Ashland High School's jolly marching band, and elves tossing candy canes. One of the highlights of the parade was the ski team, who were piled in the back of a pickup truck outfitted with old ski-lift chairs. The skiers threw snowballs as they rode along the route. There were horse-drawn carriages, stilt walkers, and little ballerinas dressed as sugar plum fairies.

"They are the cutest." I looped my arm through Lance's. "Seriously, you can't argue with little sugar plum fairies in tutus."

"I wouldn't even try, darling." He gave me a sideways grin.

"Isn't that Francine La Roux?" I asked, pointing to a

quartet of Dickens singers in full costume. Francine was a well-known performer, having appeared in a number of OSF productions. She was in her late sixties and looked like she had stepped straight from the pages of a Victorian novel in her burgundy velvet skirt and capelet with a white muff and matching Dickens bonnet.

"Indeed." Lance looked surprised. "Odd. You know, I had heard that she's been desperate to pick up side gigs in the off-season. This must be her quartet. You'll love their name."

"What is it?"

"Nothing but Treble." Lance cackled. "Brilliant. Isn't it? So clever. She is treble, that one." He chuckled at his own joke. "I wasn't aware that the parade was a paying job."

"It's not."

Lance blew Francine air kisses when the quartet stopped in front of us to perform a lively rendition of "Good King Wenceslas."

"Remind me to tell you more about her later," Lance said, keeping his eyes locked on Francine. I was mesmerized by their harmonies. Apparently so was the rest of the crowd. The singers were greeted with resounding applause and calls for an encore. Francine bowed toward us and then did a complete turn in the middle of Main Street to make sure she soaked in the praise from all directions. The group was about to start another song when a parade volunteer in a bright orange vest moved them along.

"Ooh, she's miffed." Lance grimaced. "I wouldn't want to be that volunteer. She's about to get an earful from Ms. La Roux."

He was right. Francine hissed at the woman in charge

of keeping the parade moving. It was a losing battle though, because the sound of sleigh bells echoed down the street. Right behind the singers came the pièce de résistance, Santa and Mrs. Claus being pulled by their reindeer in a shiny red sleigh outlined with white rope lights.

I squinted to get a better look at the big man, but it was too dark and too crowded to tell if Mom and the Professor were the ones waving happily and shouting "Ho, ho, ho."

Once Santa and Mrs. Claus made it to the end of the plaza, they ascended to the balcony of nearby Tudors restaurant and led the throng of happy revelers in a countdown. Everyone who had been standing along the start of the parade route crammed into the plaza. It was impossible to know exactly how many people had come out for the grand illumination, but if I had to guess I would say it might be all of Ashland.

As I predicted, the merry energy of the holiday parade was enough to make even Scrooge-like Lance crack a smile. I nudged Lance in the side. "Yell louder! Ten, nine, eight . . ."

He mumbled along until everyone yelled "one" and Santa illuminated downtown Ashland. A woodwind quintet serenaded the crowd from the balcony as applause erupted throughout the plaza. Millions of twinkling white, red, green, yellow, and blue lights made the trees in the plaza look like they were on fire with color. Every Shakespearean storefront had been outlined with strings of lights from the rooftop to the sidewalk. Wreaths and golden lanterns hung from the antique lampposts. Huge snowflakes and HAPPY HOLIDAYS banners stretched from one side of Main Street to the other.

"You have to admit, it's like something straight from the pages of a Dickens novel," I said to Lance, leaning my head on his shoulder.

"Yep. Charming. Absolutely charming." His tone was dry. "It makes me want to dash to the nearest shop and buy a pair of red and green striped socks and jingle bells."

I was about to scold him for his lack of cheer, but we were quickly inundated by holiday shoppers. With the lighting ceremony complete, paradegoers had begun to disperse into waiting stores and restaurants to get an early start on the holiday shopping season. Lance got pulled away by a group of adoring fans. I went to help Bethany and Rosa with the hot chocolate and cookie station. A line had already begun to form, but to my surprise I discovered Mom deftly passing out steaming cups of cider and cocoa.

"You're here." I greeted her with a kiss on the cheek.

She looked like she belonged on the slopes of Mount Ashland with her cream-colored knit hat with red pompoms and matching gloves and scarf. The light fabric made her skin glow. "Where else would I be?" she asked, using tongs to place a peppermint marshmallow on top of a mound of whipped cream.

"Rumor had it that you were going to be Mrs. Claus," I whispered, and nodded to the balcony above Tudors.

"I can't keep anything secret, can I?" She laughed and handed the paper mug to a little girl whose cheeks were splotched with green frosting. It looked as if she might have gotten as much frosting on her face as she had on the cookie she had decorated.

"Not in Ashland," I bantered back. "Put me to work. What can I do?"

Bethany flagged me with her free hand. The other held two piping bags of buttercream. "I could use another set of hands over here."

I left Mom and Rosa to the drink station and went to help Bethany.

The cookie-decorating table had only been open for a few minutes, but it already looked as if a winter storm had blown past. Sprinkles and frosting cups had been strewn everywhere. Kids with stained fingers and buttercream smudged on their faces waited in a semiorderly line for Bethany to pipe their name on their cookie and hand it to them on a paper plate.

"So much for my styled photo shoot." Bethany sighed. "This is a disaster."

"Or maybe you could call it organized chaos," I offered, reaching for a bag of pale purple buttercream. "I think you should take some photos of real life. Rarely is anything in life staged against a perfect background. I know that our customers love to see messy faces and frosting masterpieces, just as much as any of your gorgeously styled shots. This is the holidays with youngsters, right?"

A twinge of sadness came over me. I knew that many women in their thirties began to get baby crazy, but that phase seemed to have skipped me. Lately I had been wondering what it might be like to have a family. Maybe it was being home in Ashland and feeling grounded for the first time in a decade. Or it could have been having Ramiro, Carlos's son, here for a long visit. He and I had found an easy rapport and I had enjoyed having his youthful energy around. I wasn't dwelling on it, but it had been in the back of my mind.

Bethany passed a gingerbread cutout with enough frosting and sprinkles to cover ten sheet cakes to a little boy.
"Good point, Jules. Sometimes I get too caught up in perfection when it comes to my pictures. But some of our
most popular posts have been baking fails."

"See, there you go." I bent closer to a girl wearing a
handmade elf hat. "Would you like your name on your
cookie?" She nodded shyly and passed me her plate. Unlike the little boy before her, she had used restraint in her
decorating. Her stocking cookie was frosted with pale
pink and yellow buttercream with a row of pearl balls
along the tip of the toe and top. "What's your name?"

She bit her bottom lip and looked up at her mom, who
was waiting nearby.

"Go ahead, tell her your name." Her mom encouraged
her, then she placed her hand over the side of her cheek.
"We're working on getting more comfortable talking to
new people."

I smiled at the mom and then leaned closer to the girl. "I
love your cookie-decorating skills, especially how you've
embellished your stocking with these dainty pearls. This
is too pretty to eat. I think we might need to hire you at
the bakeshop. What do you think? Would you want to
come be a decorator one day?"

The girl's eyes widened. She nodded and grinned at her
mom.

"Okay, when you're old enough, I want you to come work
with us, and in the meantime, keep practicing at home."

"Can I, Mom?" She spoke for the first time. "Can I?"

Her mom nodded. "When you're old enough, but like
the nice lady said, we'll have to do more practice baking at

home." To us she said, "She has loved baking ever since she could walk or talk."

"Yay!" The shyness had evaporated. She pointed to a specific spot on her cookie. "Can you put my name right there? In purple, please. My name is Maya. Spelled with a *m*."

"You got it, Maya, spelled with an *m*." I proceeded to show her how to hold the piping bag and let her practice on another cookie.

After they left it was a blur of pudgy hands and toothless smiles as kids of all ages came to decorate cookies. I stayed warm by constantly running inside to refill piping bags and bring out new stacks of cookies. As I brought out the last tray of peppermint marshmallows, I bumped into the man of the hour—Santa.

"Santa, can I get you a cup of cocoa and a plate of cookies?" I asked, motioning to the cookie station where a throng of frosting-covered kids were shaking sprinkles and licking their fingers.

"Ho, ho, ho! I never turn down a plate of cookies." Santa rubbed his belly. "What do you say, Mrs. Claus?" He put his arm around his wife. "Shall we stop for some holiday cheer before we make our way to greet the kids?"

Mrs. Claus eyed the hot chocolate. "I would love a cup of your peppermint cocoa. Torte's handmade marshmallows are one of my favorite Christmas traditions."

We walked together toward the drink station where Rosa was filling cups with hot chocolate. I lowered my voice. "It's good to see you both. I had heard that there was a problem at the Winchester and you might not be able to make it to the parade."

Jon, aka Santa, frowned. "Nothing could keep us from the parade. It's the very best thing about Ashland during the holidays, except for our Dickens feast, isn't that right, Emma?"

Emma nodded in agreement. We reached the drink table. Mom's face lit up when she saw them. "You both made it!" She hugged them both.

"I'm sorry to have dragged you into the earlier mess, Helen."

Mom shook her head. "Don't give it a thought. Doug and I were ready to help."

Emma was careful to keep her voice low. "In all the confusion with . . ." She trailed off. "Well, in any event I forgot to mention that I saw a reservation for Torte on the books this morning," Emma said, taking a cup of hot chocolate.

Mom looked around us to make sure there weren't any young, listening ears. Most of the kids had moved on to the toy shop down the street where a troupe of dancers were performing part of the *Nutcracker*. "We just booked our tickets. We had to get in our reservation right away because I heard this might be the last feast after the sale."

"No, no, no." Jon mimicked his Santa greeting, but shook his head. "No, don't worry. Nothing will change. It's all been spelled out in the contract with the new owner. The Winchester as we know it and our wonderful Dickens feast will continue for generations to come. The sale isn't public news yet, but the new owner is thrilled and so excited about the feast. She'll be here for a week to watch how we pull off the magic later this month. That's a hard-kept secret, as I'm sure you well know." He winked.

"Cami, the new owner, is from L.A. and has never experienced a small-town Christmas like this. She's already fallen in love with the inn, but after she sees it at Christmas and gets to experience the feast, we might have to pack our bags sooner, right, Emma? We could be heading to Barbados by the new year if everything goes according to plan."

Emma's face clouded. She looked like she wanted to say more, but Jon pulled her away. "Come on, Mrs. Claus, the kids are waiting. We better get to the Black Swan Theater."

Every year after the lighting ceremony, kids would gather at the theater for a turn to sit on Santa's lap. Happy elves would usher them inside the theater, which had been transformed by OSF volunteers to resemble Santa's workshop at the North Pole. I had many memories of waiting in line with a candy cane and my wish list in hand. I was glad that the tradition continued and that it sounded like the Dickens feast would as well, but I couldn't shake the feeling that there was more to the story. Something about Jon's brush-off and the look of worry on Emma's face made me wonder if something was amiss at the Winchester.

Chapter Four

The next two weeks were a blur of activity. Torte was a constant sea of holiday baking. Along with our regular clientele and tourists visiting for the holidays, December was also the season of company parties. That meant that every day we were producing tray after tray of custom cookie assortments, coconut snowball cakes, red velvet petits fours, and cranberry gingerbread cheesecakes. I barely had time to breathe, let alone shop for anyone on my list. Not that I was complaining. The joy of getting to be part of our friends' and local business owners' holiday celebrations filled me with delight. I loved seeing the look of excitement on customers' faces when we set up a gorgeous cakescape of winter desserts in the dazzling banquet rooms at Ashland Springs Hotel or sold individually packaged whimsical cookie cutouts of deer, porcupine, and black bears with sprigs of red holly berries at the holiday artisan market. One of my favorite projects had been making dozens of ugly-Christmas-sweater cookies for Pucks Pub's holiday trivia night party.

I thought about delivering a box of the adorable ugly

sweaters to Richard Lord after our run-in the night of the parade, but this was the season of giving and there was no need to inflame an already volatile Richard Lord.

In addition to the frenzy at the bakeshop there were events around town nearly every night—caroling on the plaza, a gingerbread-castle competition, craft fairs, the poinsettia festival at the greenhouses, the Grinch on stage at the Cabaret Theater, wreath-making workshops, sleigh rides on Mount Ashland, and so much more. I tried to squeeze everything in. I wanted to experience all that the Rogue Valley had to offer and thus far had done a good job of immersing myself in the holidays. There was just one problem—Carlos. No matter how much I compartmentalized and attempted to slow the dull ache of missing him, I couldn't. It made me appreciate Lance's struggles with the season. This was a time when you should be surrounded by the people you love. At least I could take comfort in the fact that I had Mom, the Professor, and my team who had become my Ashland family.

By the time the evening of our staff party at the Winchester Inn rolled around, I was more than ready for a night off. We finished the last of the special orders by late afternoon. I sent everyone home to change and flipped the sign on the front door to CLOSED. Then I did a final walk-through to make sure Torte was spotless and ready for another marathon baking day tomorrow.

As I secured the basement doors, I noticed that my jeans were dusted in flour and spattered with jam. That wouldn't do for our celebration. The Dickens feast was a fancy affair that required something slightly nicer than my baking jeans. I needed to call Lance to remind him that he had promised to be my "date" for the dinner celebration. He had agreed under duress when I gave him a sob story about not wanting to be the only member of the team sitting solo. That wasn't entirely true. I don't mind being alone; in fact, I've welcomed my time of solitude in Ashland. It had given me a chance to linger in the past for a while. To think about how losing my father and venturing far from home could have been part of the reason I fell for Carlos so fast. I had made him my safe harbor, and that wasn't fair to either of us. Instead my return home was teaching me how to become my own port of safety. To learn how to lean on myself and trust my instincts. Unfortunately, these past months of soul-searching hadn't dampened the spark I still felt whenever I heard Carlos's voice or glanced at the picture of the two of us that I kept on my bedside table. The question of what was next loomed heavy on my head.

Stop it, Jules, I said out loud to the empty kitchen. There was no point in dwelling on the future. I had a party to get to and a phone call to make.

The real reason I wanted Lance to come to our staff party was to keep his spirits high. Thus far I had succeeded in dragging him to a holiday happy hour at the Green Goblin. But that was easy. I had him at the word "martini." Convincing him to join us for Torte's end-of-the-year bash had involved stroking his ego. I had explained that not only would I look pathetic to my young staff if I was dateless, but I had also reminded him what an integral role he had played during the bakeshop's renovation. That wasn't untrue. If it hadn't been for Lance, Torte would have likely never expanded. He had helped secure us grant funding and pushed through city legislation for low-interest small business improvement loans.

I checked the lock one last time and called Lance. "We're still on for tonight, right?" I asked as I balanced the phone between my ear and shoulder.

"Darling, I wouldn't leave you in the lurch, but I can't promise that I'm going to sing along to any Christmas carols, understood?"

"Absolutely. Although, I have heard that the quartet is phenomenal. I think Francine La Roux is performing."

"Not to take anything away from Francine but her star has been sinking lately, if you know what I mean."

"No." I walked upstairs to get my coat and purse.

"I'll explain later. If I know you, you're probably still at the bakeshop wearing a pair of boring jeans and a layer of flour. Part of this deal is that you glam up tonight, yes?"

Was Lance spying on me? Had he planted a hidden camera in the garland or the Christmas tree?

"Shall I pick you up a little before seven?"

"Perfect. See you then." I hung up and hurried home to change. I had been saving a dress I found at the fall sidewalk sales for the occasion. It was a short-sleeved elegant chiffon dress in forest green with a matching belt. The dress had a scoop neckline and hit just below my knees. Since most of my time is usually spent in a hot kitchen, I rarely have reason to wear anything flirty and fun. For the Dickens feast I planned to pair the dress with silver jewelry and matching silver ballet flats. I've always been tall and lanky, which is great when it comes to reaching bags of flour on high shelves, but not so great when it comes to towering over dates. The flats were a practical choice as

well. Ashland is very hilly. A walk in any direction from
the plaza requires a jaunt uphill. The Winchester was no
exception. The property encompassed almost half a block
at the top of a steep hill. I didn't want to risk twisting an
ankle on our way to dinner.

After a quick shower my skin felt refreshed. I blew my
long blond hair dry and used a flat iron to create loose
waves. Next, I dusted my cheeks with powder, applied a
light silver eyeshadow, mascara, and a pale pink lip gloss
with a hint of shimmer. I stood back to study my appearance in the mirror. Not bad, Jules. My silver jewelry and
touches of makeup gave my face a radiance that I hadn't
had since the start of the busy season. I had a feeling Lance
would approve.

He arrived at my place promptly. "Juliet, you are a vision. An angelic vision. See what a little makeup and hair
can do. My God, would you please, please take me up on
my offer of gracing OSF's stage?" He kissed both cheeks
three times and handed me a wrist corsage made with
three cream-colored roses, sprigs of rosemary, and red berries.

"This is beautiful, Lance. You didn't need to bring me
a corsage." I slid the dainty flowers on my wrist. Then I
planted a kiss on his cheek.

"Darling, it's nothing. I might not love the holidays, but
I'm quite offended that you would think I would arrive for
a date empty-handed. You of all people should know that
I take my gentlemanly duties seriously." He gave me a
half bow to prove his point.

I looped my arm through his. "I knew you couldn't stay
a Scrooge forever."

"Ha. You shouldn't get your hopes up." He waited while I grabbed my wrap and coat. "You do, however, look exquisite. What a shame your Latin love isn't here to see you. Green is definitely your color."

"Thanks. You look quite debonair yourself. I'm going to have to keep a tight grip on you tonight. Otherwise someone might try to snatch you away." He looked as dashing as ever in a well-cut black suit with a classic black tie and crisp white shirt.

Lance threw one hand to his forehead. "That will be the day. If only there were anyone in Ashland worth turning an eye toward."

We walked up Main Street. A group of teenagers had steamed up the front windows at the Pie in the Sky pizza shop. Couples dined by candlelight at the many restaurants along the corridor and shoppers toting wrapped packages and bags strolled from shop to shop.

"How can you not love this?" I said to Lance as we passed by a toy shop. The front-window display had scenes from each of the Twelve Days of Christmas, including an ornate partridge hanging from a pear tree. Every shop window along Main Street had been decked out for the holidays. The chamber was running a Walking in a Window Wonderland contest for downtown businesses. Visitors voted on their favorite window display throughout December and one winner would be crowned at the end of the season. My favorite was the yarn shop where spools of green, white, and red yarn had been stacked in the shape of trees with felt stars attached to the top.

Lance paused and stared at a fanciful display of wine bottles intertwined with grape lights at one of the downtown tasting rooms. "Yes, yes, I get it. It would appear that I would be over the moon for the drama of the holiday, but you have to remember, Juliet, that the holidays in my house—after my mother died—were not a time of joy and light."

I squeezed his arm. "I know. I understand. It must have been hard to lose your mom and then to feel so disconnected from your brother and father." Recently I had learned of Lance's past. His mother had inspired his passion for the arts. When she died Lance was left with his father, who owned a major logging company. His father loved Lance but didn't know how to connect with his theater-loving son. While Lance's brother thrived in the family business, Lance struggled to find his place. Eventually he left for good and pursued his dreams at art school and then at various theaters throughout the world. In some ways our stories were similar. We had both grown up in the Rogue Valley, left it behind in search of grander vistas, but eventually found our way home.

Lance's eyes misted. I felt a lump tightening in the back of my throat. "We're quite the pair, aren't we? Are we just destined to be hopeless romantics?" I asked Lance.

"No." Lance snapped his fingers and shook his head. "I will not accept your pity tonight. I intend to put on my best face and knock back a few martinis. I promised myself I would be on my best behavior. You, Juliet Montague Cap-shaw, are my best friend, and if this whole holiday shindig is important to you, then you can bet your very last dollar that I'm going to show you the time of your life tonight."

"Aw, Lance, what would I do without you." I leaned into his shoulder.

"Die, darling. You would absolutely die, and don't you forget it." He kissed the top of my head and we continued on.

The Winchester Inn sat at the top of Second Street with a main house and three smaller cottages. Painted in a rich cream with blue and maroon trim, the three-story Victorian house looked straight out of a fairy tale with flickering white lights and candles glowing from each of the windows. The boutique hotel was once home to the region's first hospital. Its tiered English gardens were aglow with lighted grapevine deer figurines and ornaments the size of small pumpkins adorning the trees.

In the main house there were two dining rooms, an award-winning bar, and guest suites. Each of the cottages offered guests private balconies, soaking tubs, and gas fireplaces.

"All right. Fine. It's stunning. The white and gold lights perfectly capture the Victorian architecture," Lance said as we walked up the redbrick pathway to the restaurant. Black lanterns with fake candles illuminated the walkway.

Childhood memories flooded me as Lance and I joined the line of guests waiting outside. Since my parents had been good friends with the McBeths, I had spent many days exploring the inn. Nate, the McBeths' son, and I had gone all the way through school together, and I remember parties at the Winchester where Nate would show me and Thomas and our group of friends the historical property's hidden secrets, like the butler's pantry next to the kitchen and the library upstairs where Nate used to insist there was a bookcase that led to a secret passageway. Sadly we never discovered the passageway, despite our attempts to pull book after book off the shelves in hopes of revealing a hidden room.

In school, we'd taken a number of walking field trips to the inn to learn about Ashland's history. Nate and I hadn't kept in touch since graduating from high school, but I always enjoyed bumping into him and his wife and two young children at events around town.

The Winchester originally served as a private family home back in the late 1800s, but then was quickly converted into the Rogue Valley's first hospital. In pioneer times the inn housed doctors' offices, but if anyone was in need of long-term convalescing they were required to bring their own staff. In the early 1900s the Victorian mansion was moved from its original location on Main Street up to the top of the hill on Second Street. Old photographs showed the house being dragged up the steep hillside with a single horse and a winch.

According to Nate the inn was haunted. He used to tell us ghost stories about hearing screams in the middle of the night when there were no guests booked and how if you listened carefully you could hear the sound of thundering footsteps in the upstairs hallways.

There were rumors that staff and guests throughout the years bumped into friendly apparitions in the upstairs hallways and basement wine cellar. When Emma and Jon bought the property in the 1980s it was in a state of utter disrepair. My parents had launched Torte into the world around the same time that the McBeths purchased the Winchester. Ashland in those years wasn't the thriving tourist mecca it is today. Many shops along the plaza had been left vacant with the collapse of the timber industry. Buildings had been boarded up and abandoned. The Oregon Shakespeare Festival continued to draw theater lovers to the region, but the plaza had been in desperate need of a makeover.

According to Mom, it was both a good and a scary time to start a business. My parents and the McBeths were able to negotiate great deals on their respective properties, but they also took a risk by investing in a struggling economy. Fortunately the gamble paid off for Torte and the Winchester. The Dickens feast had been going strong for thirty-five years and from the looks of the long line queuing up on the pathway it didn't show any signs of stopping.

"Did you ever hear how the feast got started?" I asked Lance as the line moved closer to the front porch. I wished I had worn boots instead of ballet flats. My toes started to tingle in the frosting evening air. The sky above was starless and I wondered if it finally might snow. Weather forecasters had been predicting that we were due for a dumping, but so far none of their dire winter storm warnings had come to fruition.

"No. Do tell." Lance stared at the upstairs window where we could make out the silhouette of someone wearing a top hat and cape.

"As you know, my mom and Emma have been good friends for years and years. Emma has told the story dozens of times about how she got roped into attending a chamber of commerce meeting while she and Jon were renovating the hotel. The chamber was trying to brainstorm ideas on how to get people to come to Ashland when the theater went dark for the season."

I paused and fastened the top button on my coat. Were

those tiny flakes of snow drifting down from the sky? I blinked twice. "Lance, look, is that snow?"

Lance stuck out one gloved hand. An icy white flake landed on the black leather. "How quintessential."

"Snow at the Dickens feast, you can't script this." I lifted my face to the sky and let the tiny flakes land on my forehead.

"Fine. It's lovely, but it's going to ruin your shoes, darling." He pointed to my silver flats. The snow was wispy, but it was already starting to stick to the brick pathway.

I punched him in the arm. "It's snowing at Christmas."

"It's your toes. Don't complain if you end up with frostbite." He nodded to his expensive black loafers. "You should have opted for function over fashion like moi."

"Yeah, right." I flicked him with my finger.

He rubbed his arm in mock pain. "You were telling me the story about the feast."

"If the snow sticks be prepared for an epic snowball battle on the way home." I made a fist to show that I was ready for a fight. "Anyway, back to the Dickens feast. Emma and Jon were working around the clock to get the inn open. They had to tear everything down to the studs. In fact, one of the stories I remember from childhood is about how they found a skeleton of a dead cat in one of the walls."

"Gruesome." Lance faked a gasp. "Not holiday material, Jules."

"Sorry, but it's true. They were in their twenties, just like my parents. Rebuilding the inn was a labor of blood, sweat, and tears. They did all the work themselves, from salvaging bricks from the original chimneys to building the very walkway we're standing on to hand painting the ornate ceilings in the dining rooms and installing new molding in every room in the inn." I paused and brushed a snowflake from the tip of my nose. "No one thought they would make it. In fact they might not have if it weren't for the Dickens feast."

The line inched forward. No one appeared to mind waiting in the falling snow. A group of young girls in party dresses were twirling in a circle nearby, trying to catch snowflakes on their tongues.

"It was Mom who convinced Emma to do a holiday feast. They had joined the chamber of commerce together and everyone was at a loss about how to increase winter tourism. Mom suggested a holiday tree lighting and decorating cookies with Santa. She and my dad were also in the middle of renovations and Torte wasn't open for business, but they had the brilliant idea to do a sidewalk holiday party. Your predecessor at OSF offered up Santa and elf costumes. Dad agreed to play Santa. The idea snowballed from there. Someone suggested a parade. The president of the chamber asked if any of the hotels or B and Bs would consider hosting a holiday brunch or dinner. No one volunteered, so Mom nominated Emma. She promised that she and Dad would help and made a compelling argument that hosting a holiday dinner would be great promotion for the Winchester."

"That sounds like Helen."

"I know. Saying no to her is nearly impossible." I chuckled. We stepped onto the front porch. It was almost our turn to hand over our tickets and go inside. "Emma and Jon thought about it and came up with the idea for a

Dickens feast given the Winchester's Victorian architecture. That first year Dad played Santa and Jon dressed up as Scrooge. It was such a success that they've been doing it every year since, every night in December through Christmas Eve."

"It's a sweet story, darling, but I'm still not convinced." Lance slid to the side to make room for me to go inside in front of him.

"Just wait until they serve the first course—Stilton cheese and onion soup. I'll have you converted in no time."

Little did I know that very shortly our festive dinner would turn into a holiday nightmare.

Chapter Five

"Welcome to the Dickens feast," Emma, dressed in her fur-lined Mrs. Claus red robes, greeted us in the foyer. There was a set of walnut stairs directly in front of us that led to the guest rooms on the third floor. To the left was the main dining room and to the right the banquet room. "Scrooge will take your tickets and coats." She nodded to the man dressed as Scrooge standing next to her. I recognized Scrooge as Jon and Emma's son, Nate, even under layers of white makeup and wearing a white nightshirt and cap. He was shorter than me by a few inches, with sandy-brown hair that had begun to recede.

"Bah humbug, they can put their coats in the coat check themselves," Nate said, shuffling toward us. "You're all adults, aren't you? There's money to be made and time is wasting, toss your coats on the floor and get to work."

"You might have to hire him," I said to Lance. "He's good."

I remembered Mom telling me that when Jon had dressed as Scrooge that first year my dad had had to go to each table and tell them that the inn was short-staffed and the only person they could hire was Ebenezer Scrooge. Even though he was in costume they didn't want any of the guests to mistake Scrooge for a terrible waiter. The guests had loved the tongue-in-cheek banter and commentary from Scrooge. I was glad to see that Nate was continuing the tradition.

Since we had such a large party Emma led us to the banquet room. Large sash-windows looked out into the gardens. The chocolate-brown walls with matching dark chocolate wainscoting were decorated with paper-white birch trees, snowflakes, strings of twinkling lights, and red carnation birds. Two long tables were draped with white organza tablecloths, silver snowflakes, and glowing golden lanterns. Red poinsettia garlands intertwined with more lights framed the windows. There were three smaller tables against the opposite wall that would seat two to four people each.

"What do you think?" Emma asked. "Will this work for your staff?"

"It's perfect. Even better than I remember from my childhood."

She forced a smile. "I'm so glad to hear that. The evening is off to a rocky start and I could use some good news."

I wanted to ask why, but Scrooge limped into the banquet room. "Mrs. Claus, they need you in the kitchen."

Emma left. Nate caught my eye. "Oh, hey Juliet. Good to see you." Staying in character he walked with an exaggerated hunch and greeted me with a hug. "Fair warning: Scrooge can get pretty testy with the guests, so you might want to warn your staff to be on their best behavior."

"Will do." I laughed as he arched one shoulder dramatically and made his exit.

"Isn't it beautiful?" I turned to Lance, as I took off my wrap and placed it on the back of my chair.

"I can't argue with the elegance, that's for sure." He took the seat next to me. We were the first to arrive.

I placed the name cards Stephanie had made for our team around the table while Lance reviewed the cocktail menu.

"Decisions. Decisions. Should I have a House Made Hot Buttered Rum, a Down the Chimney Sparkler, or a Home for the Holidays cocktail?"

"Those all sound delish. What's in the sparkler?" I sat next to Lance and picked up my menu. The bubbly cocktail was made with sparkling wine, royal orange bourbon, and three kinds of bitters.

"Eggnog is a pass. Why anyone would want to drink egg-laced milk is a mystery to me." Lance made a gagging sound. "The Home for the Holidays sounds divine. It's made with maraschino liqueur. Sophisticated and sweet, just like me."

"Sometimes you are too much, but I do like the enthusiasm." I nodded to the wine and champagne glasses on the table. "Plus, if memory serves, the wine and champagne will be flowing all evening."

"Now you're speaking my holiday language, darling."

I took another look at the menu and could hardly contain my taste buds. The six-course meal included a vegetable relish plate, Yorkshire pudding with wild mushrooms, Stilton cheese and onion soup, salad, prime rib or Christmas goose, and a spiced rum and pear trifle. If there was one thing that I knew about Lance, it was that he loved anything with opulence. Tonight's dinner was sure to sway him.

Soon the team began arriving. First to join us was Stephanie and Sterling. They looked quite striking together. Steph wore a strapless purple satin party dress with dark black tights, knee-high black boots, and a matching black leather ribbon tied in her violet hair. A black-studded choker finished off her outfit. Sterling wore black skinny jeans and an ugly Christmas sweater that was almost too stylish to be called "ugly." It was a beige V-neck with forest-green trim. There were three Christmas deer with hipster beards, glasses, and scarves and the words: EAT, DRINK, AND BE UGLY.

"That is classic," I said to Sterling as they found their spots at the table. "And, Steph, you look gorgeous."

She shot me her signature scowl, but when Lance agreed with me she cracked the slightest hint of a smile. I watched as she looked at the place card next to her and scowled. She picked up the place card along with the one next to Sterling and switched them to the opposite end of the table.

Andy arrived next with a date. "Happy Christmas, boss! This is my date, Amber." He introduced me to the young woman attached to his hip. She was in her early twenties with long, sleek platinum-blond hair and aqua-blue eyeshadow. Her eyebrows were adorned with tiny blue and silver gems, and her sequined skirt barely covered her backside.

"Glad you could join us." I offered her my hand. Each of her fingernails had matching rhinestones.

"Yeah, thanks for the invite. I've never been somewhere like this. My family usually hits up Taco Bell or Micky D's for dinner."

I had told my staff that everyone was welcome to bring a plus-one.

Bethany walked in as I started to ask Andy's date how they had met. "Hey, everyone. Merry Christmas. This is my . . ." She paused in mid-sentence when she spotted Andy pulling out a chair for Amber. "My . . . date, Ben."

Her date shot her a strange look. He bore a strong resemblance to Bethany with his reddish-brown hair and freckles. She fluffed her knee-length black cocktail dress and batted her eyes at Ben.

Steph patted the empty chair beside her. "I saved you a seat, Bethany."

I held back a smile. As always Stephanie's stoic exterior didn't reveal her true nature. She knew, like the rest of us, that Bethany had a crush on Andy, and by reserving a space at the end of the table for her friend, Andy and his date were pushed near us.

Andy removed his suit jacket and looked miffed. "Hey, I was going to sit next to Sterling."

Stephanie shrugged. "Your name is down at the other end by Marty and Sequoia."

Soon Mom, the Professor, Sequoia and her date, Rosa and her husband, and Marty arrived. Happy banter filled the banquet room as we joked about workers' compensation for holiday baking.

"I'm not sure I'll ever be able to bend my fingers again," Bethany said, intentionally contorting her hands into funky shapes. "So much piping work."

Steph showed off her deep purple nail polish. "I feel your pain. I couldn't get off the pastel pink food dye I was using to pipe those vintage ornament cookies last night, so I had to cover it with the darkest polish I had. No way was I about to walk around with girly pink nails."

Marty flexed one arm. "The pro of dough work is building muscle, but I have to agree with you two, my arms could go for a nice deep-tissue massage."

He paused as Emma showed a woman and two men to one of the smaller tables. "This is your table for the evening, Cami. We have Tim, our most seasoned member of the team and wine steward, as well as our son Nate, taking care of everyone in the banquet room tonight. You'll be in good hands and in good company." She motioned to our table. "Your neighbors for the feast are the staff at Ashland's best bakeshop, Torte."

"Fine. Fine." Cami dismissed Emma by reaching into her leather purse, taking out a cell phone, and starting to make a call.

"Oh, sorry." Emma bit her bottom lip as she spoke. "You must not have seen the signs posted in the foyer. We ask guests to please refrain from using any electronic devices during the Dickens feast. We want you to be completely swept away by the charm of yesteryear, and the food and music we have lined up is sure to keep you entertained. I'd be happy to keep your phone safe in my office for you."

Part of the magic of the Dickens feast was the entertainment. The Victorian quartet we'd seen at the parade, Nothing but Treble led by Francine La Roux, would serenade both dining rooms. Throughout the night the carolers, Santa, and Scrooge would rotate in and out, offering jokes and songs. During the dessert course, Santa would bring everyone a present to culminate the evening.

Cami clutched her phone as if it were a child about to be ripped from her arms. "What? You want my phone? No. No, no, that's not happening."

"You're welcome to keep it. That's fine. We just ask that you turn it off completely during dinner service."

"That's not happening either." Cami looked to the men seated across from her and rolled her eyes. To Emma, she said, "We're in Oregon. I've eaten at some of the most exclusive restaurants in L.A. and never, never has anyone asked me to turn off my phone."

Emma's face blanched.

"It's sweet that you think this place is charming," Cami said in a condescending tone. "But honey, there's a big difference between charming and outdated."

I thought Emma might burst into tears. Instead she dug her teeth into her lip and turned to hurry out of the dining room.

Lance whistled. "She's a gem."

If memory served me correctly Jon and Emma had said that the buyer who was taking over the Winchester was from L.A. and named Cami. I wondered if the sale had fallen through, because Cami certainly didn't appear to be caught up in the Winchester's spell.

I returned my attention to our table as my team swapped stories from some of our favorite memories of the year. One customer had consistently given my staff headaches—Richard Lord.

"Why does he come in anyway?" Andy asked. "His

orders are always ridiculous and loaded with sugar. Once he made me triple the amount of chocolate in his mocha and add a quarter cup of our house-made vanilla syrup. Just looking at that gut bomb made me sick to my stomach."

"He only comes in to try and steal our ideas," Sterling replied.

"We should start a secret Richard Lord menu," Bethany offered. "Make the most terrible drinks and tell him that they're selling like crazy."

"Yeah, or we could spike his coffee with bacon grease and claim it's the new trend." Andy stood to give Bethany an air-five across the table. She halfheartedly returned the gesture and then proceeded to bat her eyes at her date.

Sterling placed his arm on the back of Stephanie's chair. "I think we're on to something here. If bacon grease coffee shows up on the Merry Windsor menu after Richard tries it at Torte we'll have hard evidence that he only lurks around the bakeshop to try and pilfer our ideas."

It was good to be away from the "office" and get to dish about our work and personal lives.

Our waiter, Tim, dressed in a black tux, circulated the room filling glasses with champagne and sparkling cider. While he poured bubbly champagne into my glass he said, "If you need anything tonight, don't hesitate to ask. I'm here for your every need."

I overheard him repeat the same service-oriented sentiment to Cami, who ignored his offer and typed away on her phone.

Mom and the Professor were the last to arrive. Mom had always been a stunner, but since marrying the Professor her happiness radiated through every pore. Tonight, she had tucked one side of her shoulder-length bob back with a pearl barrette. Her almond-shaped eyes were highlighted with a cream and maroon shadow. She wore a velvet maroon dress cut off the shoulders. The Professor had mirrored her style with a dark green velvet smoking jacket. Not many men could pull off the look. But the Professor appeared completely at ease and right at home at the Victorian-inspired feast.

"Sorry we're late. We got to catching up with Santa and Mrs. Claus." Mom glanced around the table. "Everyone looks so wonderful." She and the Professor greeted everyone and then took their seats next to Lance and me.

Mom leaned over while Andy was recounting his most epic coffee fails and whispered, "Isn't this perfect, honey? It's so fun to see the staff together."

"I know. Maybe we need to do a quarterly staff party. Everyone works so hard."

"Yes, they do, and you know why?" She raised one brow.

"Why?"

"Because they love you."

I waved her off. "Mom, don't get all mushy."

The Professor cleared his throat. "Did someone call Helen mushy?" His arm rested on her shoulder.

"Guilty as charged." Mom blushed. Her rosy cheeks glowed with the candlelight. "You know me, Doug, the holidays make me teary with joy. I'm so lucky to have you, and Juliet, and this wonderful staff."

The Professor kissed the top of her head. "My dearest Helen, do not apologize. Your warm heart is one of the most endearing things about you. It reminds me of a quote, 'Christmas is the day that holds all time together.'"

"That's not Shakespeare, is it?' I asked.

The Professor shook his head. "Indeed, it is not. Those words come from the poet Alexander Smith. The Bard said very little about Christmas. Only three passages in all of his works make any reference to the holiday. Many say he was the first Scrooge."

Lance raised his cocktail glass. "Cheers to that."

I kicked him under the table.

"Kidding."

"Shakespeare wasn't a Christmas fan?" I took a sip of my champagne. The tiny bubbles made my nose feel fuzzy.

"No. Although who's to say he wouldn't have been if he were to have experienced something as elaborate as this." He tipped his head toward the Christmas tree. "But it's more likely that Shakespeare's stance on the holiday was simply lost in translation. It wasn't until the Victorian era that Christmas as we know it came to be. In the Bard's time Christmas celebrations like tonight's simply didn't happen. Christmas was merely a twelve-day festival of pageants. The Bard was most definitely not a pageant fan."

"Pageants?" Lance perked up.

"Yes, in *The Taming of the Shrew* he makes quite a direct statement on the awful acting 'gambols' one was subjected to during the Christmas pageants."

Lance drummed his fingers on the table. "Ohhh, I'm beginning to think we might need to revive this concept. A hideous Christmas pageant with a page boy. I can see it now."

The Professor laughed.

"I had no idea that Christmas wasn't a big deal in Tudor times." I took another sip of my champagne.

"No. You can thank Mr. Charles Dickens for our merriment this evening. But no credit is due to the Bard. Easter would have been a time for Christian celebrations, but not this fair holiday."

The conversation shifted as Tim and Scrooge, aka Nate, delivered the first course—relish plates.

"Here, take it." Nate nearly dropped the relish plate in the Professor's lap. "I hope you enjoy this undigested bit of beef, blot of mustard, bit of cheese, and fragment of an underdone potato."

"Why thank you, good sir." The Professor played along, placing a marinated carrot stick back on the plate.

"Bah humbug to you." Nate, in his slippers and cap, shuffled over to Cami's table. "If you ask me, you miserable bunch don't deserve so much as a lump of coal."

Tim followed him with a tray and started placing relish plates around the table. "Don't bother with this one, Scrooge. She's glued to her device."

Cami didn't flinch. Her face glowed blue from her cell phone screen.

"Oh! but *she* was a tight-fisted hand at the grindstone! a squeezing, wrenching, grasping, scraping, clutching, covetous, old sinner!" Nate quoted Dickens. "Only cares about money, doesn't she?"

"That is the truth." Tim lifted the tray above his head. Before he left the dining room, I saw him give Cami a stare that sent a tingle up my arm. Working in the service industry likely meant that he had had to deal with his fair share of "Camis" throughout the years.

"You should be boiled in your own pudding," Nate said with a fake spat to Cami. Then addressed the entire room. "Eat up because that's the next course."

"Are you going to make a speech?" Mom asked me, biting into a plump cherry tomato.

"I thought you were," I whispered back.

Mom dabbed the corner of her eyes with the Professor's red silk handkerchief. "I'm already tearing up just thinking about expressing my thanks. Can you start and then I'll chime in?"

At least I knew I came by my emotions honestly. "Of course." I squeezed Mom's hand, which now had a sparkling antique wedding band on her ring finger.

I stood and dinged my fork on my champagne glass to get everyone's attention. "Before the next course arrives, I want to take a minute to express my deepest gratitude. This has been quite a year at Torte and we could not have done it without you."

Mom stood and seconded my words. "Juliet is right." She blinked back tears. "We are so lucky to have you all not only as staff but as our family."

"Aw, Mrs. C. Torte is the best place on the planet to work." Andy raised his glass in a toast. "We all agree, right, guys?"

Everyone cheered and toasted Mom and me.

I was about to continue with my speech when a loud crash erupted behind us. Tim had dropped a tray of mini Yorkshire puddings. Ramekins shattered and the beautifully puffed puddings splattered on the floor.

"Oh no! I'm sorry. I'm so, so sorry." He apologized profusely.

Tim dropped to his knees to begin scooping up the mess.

"Imbecile! Look what you've done." Cami freed her phone from her clutches for the first time all evening and jumped up. One of the mushroom puddings had splattered on her black skirt.

Tim scrambled to pick up broken pieces of the ramekins. Cami kicked one of them and sent it shattering into the nearby baseboard. "This skirt is ruined! Ruined because of your idiocy. You'll be getting a bill for my dry cleaning. Oh, and you're fired."

Tim placed a broken piece of the ramekin on the tray. "You can't fire me."

"I just did." Cami grabbed a napkin and stormed out of the dining room.

"Darling, you didn't mention we were going to be treated to dinner theater." Lance rubbed his hands together.

Tim left the mess on the floor and ran after her. I was pretty sure none of what we had just witnessed had anything to do with dinner theater.

Chapter Six

A few minutes later an entire team of staff returned with towels and extra trays of Yorkshire puddings. Santa and Mrs. Claus delivered bottles of wine and the hot-from-the-oven puddings.

Mom caught Emma's arm on the way out. "Is everything okay?"

Emma knelt next to us and kept her voice low. "It's a disaster, Helen. I don't know what to do." She buried her face in the sleeve of her red robe.

"Tell us what we can do. We'll help, won't we, Juliet?"

"Yes. Absolutely."

"No. You're here with your staff to celebrate. I'll figure it out. Don't worry. It's just that everything is falling apart tonight. Nate and Jon are fighting. Tim is furious and refusing to continue service in here. Nate took off and I can't find him. We are booked to capacity, which means there are eighty dinners to serve and now I'm short on Yorkshire puddings, so the head chef is scrambling to see what else he can pull together."

I knew the level of choreography that went into hosting a dinner like this. The kitchen staff would have been prepping since this morning. There was a tight window to prepare, plate, and deliver each course to half of the diners while the other half were being entertained by festive carols or Santa's stand-up shtick. Then they would orchestrate the same thing all over again for the rest of the diners, course after course. The fact that Emma was even upright was impressive. I couldn't believe the McBeths put themselves through so much stress every night for the duration of the holiday season.

"Are you sure there's nothing we can do?" Mom asked. I could tell that she was concerned about Emma.

"No. Please enjoy your time with your staff." Emma paused and glanced at the table behind us. "You can do me one favor though. Keep your eye on that table, especially Cami, the woman whose face doesn't move."

I gave a subtle glance at the table. Cami had returned, wearing a new charcoal-gray skirt. As before, she paid no attention to the conversation around her, but rather scrolled through her phone. The Dickens feast was meant to be a community affair. Emma and Jon had created an atmosphere designed for conversation, not for people to veg out like zombies on screens.

"Who is she?" Mom asked. "She's been rude all evening."

"That's Cami." Emma knelt beside the table so no one else could hear. "She's in town with two of her business partners from Southern Cal and she's been a nightmare. Everyone on my staff is terrified of her. That's why I assigned Nate to this room. I figured he could handle it, but now with him and Jon fighting I don't have a choice. I'm going to have to send one of my regular waitstaff in and I'm sure she's going to complain about every course."

"We've had a handful of customers like that at Torte," Mom tried to reassure her friend. "Don't worry about it. We'll keep an eye out and let you know if things get dicey, but it's Christmas and this meal is famed. I'm sure there won't be a single complaint."

"I wish." Emma sighed and stood. "Thanks for everything. The only good thing about tonight is that you're here. At least I don't have to brace for impact against any negativity from you."

"Never." Mom pointed to the kitchen. "I know my way around your kitchen. If you change your mind and want help, please come and get me."

Emma looked relieved. "No, I won't do that to you, but what I might do is ditch these skirts. I think the feast is going to have to go on without Mrs. Claus tonight. I have to be able to stay nimble, especially if I need to go help cook."

"Good plan." Mom patted her knee. "You're a pro, Emma. Remember that first year when guests had to climb over Sheetrock and power tools to get to the dining room?"

The memory made Emma laugh. "I do. That was something, wasn't it? We were so young and naïve. Why did we think we could put on a dinner like this when there was still exposed plumbing in the walls?"

"Because I forced you." Mom winked. "We were resourceful. We hung butcher paper with hand-cut snowflakes to cover the gaping holes in the Sheetrock. People thought it was whimsical. Little did they know what it was hiding."

Emma's mood had lightened. Mom's calming aura had that effect.

"Jon and I used to joke that our only motto was 'don't go broke.' I can't believe we didn't. We had no idea what we were doing in those early years."

"None of us did, but look at us now." Mom motioned to Torte's staff, who were none the wiser that there was even the slightest hiccup in dinner service.

"Thanks for the pep talk." Emma stood. "I feel better. I'm going to go change, and then I should go check in with the chef."

"Okay, but please do come and get us if you need anything." Mom gave a subtle nod in Cami's direction, not that it mattered; Cami's face was aglow from her phone screen. "We'll keep an eye out for anything unusual."

Emma left. I felt bad for her. There was nothing worse than being short-staffed on a busy night in the kitchen, but unfortunately that came with the territory. In my years in culinary school and at sea, there had been numerous times when a chef, waiter, or dishwasher had stormed off in a huff. As Lance would say, "the show must go on." Hopefully the rest of Emma's staff would rise to the occasion.

My focus returned to our table where Andy was doting on his date and Bethany looked like she was about to cry. I decided this was a good time for a distraction.

"Everyone, can I get your attention for a sec?" I stood.

"Another speech, boss?" Andy groaned. "I can't stand this much mushy stuff in one night."

"No. I'm not going to give another speech, but I do have a little party game for us while we wait for the next course."

Stephanie's brow furrowed.

"Don't worry, it's not even a real game. I just thought

we could go around the table and share what we're wishing for this holiday season. For those of you who are new to
the Dickens feast, at some point later—probably around
the dessert course—Santa is going to come by the table
with a gift for each of us."

"Yay! Gifts." Bethany clapped.

"I thought it would be fun to compare our real wishes
with the ones Santa will soon deliver. I'll start. I'm wishing for another year like this one at Torte and hoping that
all of you stay."

Lance went next. "I'm wishing for another martini
or a patron to donate a few million dollars to dome the
Elizabethan theater. One more summer of wildfire smoke
might sink us." He swirled his empty cocktail glass. "I'll
take the million or a martini—whichever comes first."

Andy wished for a trip to one of the coffee farms where
Torte's beans originated from. Marty for a new rolling pin.
Apparently, his favorite rolling pin had broken recently.
Sequoia wanted to teach a forest bathing class. When
asked for more details she explained that forest bathing
was a modern term for meditating in the woods. Bethany
wanted a set of custom backdrops for her photography.
Sterling was contemplating a new tattoo. Rosa shared that
she had asked her husband for a set of vintage pie plates.
Stephanie tried to pass.

"No way. No passes allowed." Andy shook his index
finger at her. "You have to want something."

She shrugged. "No, I don't."

He wouldn't let it go. "Come on, you must want something."

"I'm not really into stuff."

"It doesn't have to be stuff. You could say you want world peace."

"Fine. I want world peace." Stephanie folded her arms across her chest.

"That's cheating."

"I know something she wants," Bethany said with a sly grin.

"What?" Andy had her full attention now.

"Don't you wish you knew?" Bethany made a zipping motion across her lips. "I'll never tell."

Stephanie twisted the choker around her neck.

Andy looked to me for support. "Boss, some help here? They're breaking the rules."

"There are no rules." I watched as Sterling leaned in and whispered something in Stephanie's ear. Her face remained neutral. I wasn't sure if Bethany really knew one of Steph's secrets or if she was trying to get Andy's attention. The two of them had grown close. Often, I would find them deep in conversation while they worked in unison rolling out fondant cutouts for custom wedding cakes. It made me happy to know that they had developed a bond.

Mom came to the rescue. "I'll go next. I really do want world peace. And more than anything I want the best for all of you." She patted the Professor's knee. "Doug and I are filled with happiness and that is my wish for each and every one of you. Torte has been my life since Juliet was young and not a day goes by that I'm not filled with the deepest gratitude for expanding that life to include all of you. Torte is more than a bakeshop. It's a safe haven for many of our customers and that is a testament to your hard work and to truly pouring your hearts into everything we bake." She placed her hand over her chest. "There aren't enough words to express my thanks."

The Professor pressed his hands together in thanks. "I could not agree more. As the Bard says, 'It is not in the stars that hold our destiny but in ourselves.' May this holiday season and coming new year fulfill your every dream and destiny."

"Hear, hear!" Lance raised his newly filled martini glass as the Victorian carolers came into the dining room singing "Ding Dong Merrily on High." They were led by Francine La Roux. The quartet included another woman, about half Francine's age, who wore a dress, muff, and bonnet like Francine's but in deep navy. Two men, one holding a harmonica and the other a set of vintage sleigh bells, boomed out the lyrics to the upbeat carol in deep baritone voices. Between the Winchester's décor and their black top hats and capes I felt as if I had actually been transported back in time.

Everyone at our table swayed and clapped along. Cami and her counterparts didn't even try to lower their voices. They rudely maintained their conversation to the obvious frustration of Francine.

"She doesn't look pleased," I whispered to Lance. Francine hit the final note of the song while staring Cami down.

Lance turned to look over his shoulder and pressed his finger to his lips. "Shush, please," he said to Cami. "The rest of us are trying to enjoy this delightful entertainment."

Cami shot him a nasty glare, but Lance's scolding worked. She stopped talking and resumed scrolling on her phone.

The quartet got in tune for their next song with a harmonica. Not a fork clinked, or a whisper was uttered while the quartet serenaded us with a medley of Victorian-era classics. I didn't recognize any of the songs, but Francine's beautiful harmonies captivated me.

Applause erupted when they finished the first set, with one exception—Cami. Cami was still glued to her phone and apparently oblivious to the fact that she was in the presence of one of the greatest opera singers in the region.

The quartet huddled together for a minute and scoured their songbooks. I assumed that they were trying to decide what to sing next.

"It appears we have an impromptu change in tonight's set list," Lance noted.

"Why do you say that?"

He rolled his eyes. "Darling, Please. Someone as professional and experienced as Francine has orchestrated every song choice. I'm guessing she wasn't expecting to have yours truly in the audience tonight and has decided that since she's performing for a celebrity that it's time for a show-stopping number."

"I love that you refer to yourself as a celebrity."

He lifted his martini glass. "If the shoe fits, darling."

Lance was mistaken though. I quickly realized the change in the set list didn't have anything to do with him, but rather everything to do with Cami. Francine was clearly not happy that she didn't have the rapt attention of everyone in the audience. The carolers made their way toward Cami's table, and Francine addressed the room.

"We've given you a selection of some of the best

Dickens-era songs and now we'd like to bring you to our modern era with a new favorite—'Text Me Merry Christmas.'"

Everyone chuckled.

"Shall we?" Francine made eye contact with her fellow singers, then she reached over and snatched Cami's cell phone straight from her hands. "As our name states we're Nothing but Treble and you are in for treble tonight."

The quartet began belting a punny tune about texting Merry Christmas, as Cami fumed. She flew to her feet.

"Give me my phone."

Francine pretended not to hear her. She sang louder, keeping a tight grasp on Cami's phone.

"Seriously. Give me the phone. Right now."

A wide smile spread on Francine's face as she continued to sing:

Text me Merry Christmas
Make my holiday complete
Though you're far from me
Say you'll brb
That's a text I'll never delete
Choose just the right emoji
One that makes me lol
And if you text me something naughty
I promise I won't tell.

Listening to the carolers in full Victorian costumes singing about emojis had the dining room in tears of laughter. Even Stephanie cracked a grin.

However, Cami flared her nostrils and planted her heels

firmly on the carpet. Her unsuccessful attempts to recover her phone from Francine's clutches had her reaching for a steak knife.

She held the knife up like a weapon. "Give me my phone this instant or I will kill you."

Francine looked taken aback.

Cami stepped closer. She made a stabbing motion in the air. "The phone. Now."

Lance got ready to intervene.

The quartet sang on.

"One more warning, and if you don't hand me my phone, I'm dead serious that I will cut you."

Chapter Seven

A collective gasp sounded in the dining room as Francine and Cami stood head-to-head. They were a mismatch. Francine was nearly twice Cami's size in height and girth. But Cami appeared to be serious about potentially stabbing Francine. She had a death grip on the steak knife.

Hand over the phone, I screamed in my head. Why was Francine antagonizing Cami? She obviously had no sense of humor.

The last chords of the song finished. Cami lunged forward with the knife. Francine tossed the phone at Cami.

Cami caught the phone with her free hand. Then she whipped around and stabbed the knife into the tabletop. "This place is a freaking joke." She tapped her phone and then held it out for everyone in the dining room to see. "You know what this is? This is a contract with a local bulldozer. I hope you enjoy this ridiculous, corny feast because it's the last of its kind. The second I take ownership of this hellhole, I'm tearing it down."

The news wasn't exactly shocking given her sullen attitude throughout the evening, but I couldn't reconcile Jon and Emma's claim that she loved the hotel and had been swept up in its charm. She was going to level the Winchester? Could that even be legal? The inn was on the National Register of Historic Places.

"Merry Christmas," Lance said in a sarcastic tone. "This is making my family look like something from a Norman Rockwell painting."

"Cami is going to tear down the inn and cancel the Dickens feast?" I tried to make sense of what had just happened. "I don't understand why Jon and Emma said that Cami planned to keep everything exactly as is, if her plan was to bulldoze the Winchester."

Lance shrugged and pointed to Cami who was yelling at one of the waitstaff to get her a shot of whiskey. "Perhaps something was lost in translation. Or, they intentionally lied to get through one last holiday season. Think about it, darling, if they had told their staff Cami's true intentions, what are the odds that anyone would stick around?"

He had a point, but why would Emma and Jon have lied to me?

As if on cue, Emma came into the dining room. She had changed from her Mrs. Claus costume into a pair of slacks and a black sweater. Tim followed behind her with the dinner course. "Serve Torte first," she instructed him. "I'll take care of the other table."

I got the sense that she was protecting Tim from another confrontation with Cami by positioning herself between them as a physical barrier.

One of the men in the quartet blew a short note on the harmonica. Emma shook her head and grabbed Francine's arm. "The other room is ready for you," Emma said to Francine. They shared a look I couldn't decipher.

Francine stepped forward and took a long bow. "You've been a most receptive audience. We will take our leave while you enjoy dinner and return for dessert." With that she swept out of the room, followed closely by her fellow singers.

I tried to push Cami's plans of destroying the inn to the back of my mind as we tucked into the Christmas roast with chestnut stuffing, heirloom vegetables, and herbed mashed potatoes. Andy and Marty kept the conversation flowing and a constant rotation of waiters kept the wine flowing. I wondered if Emma had gone out and recruited help from the streets.

Mom was quieter than usual.

"Are you okay?" I asked, resting my fork on my plate. The rich meal was delicious, but I had to save some space for the dessert course.

"I'm worried about Emma." She glanced to the reception area. I could hear the carolers in the other dining room and what sounded like an argument in the kitchen.

"Do you hear that?"

Mom shook her head. Between the happy chatter and hum of the old radiator heaters the room muffled the sound of angry voices.

"I think someone's fighting in the kitchen."

"Should we go check on Emma?" Mom asked.

"No. You stay. Finish your dinner." I noted her half-eaten plate. "I'll go."

She started to protest, but I had already pushed back my chair and excused myself from the group. The reception area was vacant except for rows of full coatracks and a basket of cell phones. A wall of windows gave me a prime view of the other dining room where the carolers were finishing up their second set. I knew that meant that dinner would be served next and we were due for a palate-cleansing granita before dessert. The main dining room was equally festive in décor with a huge Christmas tree bearing bunches of bright red cranberries and pine-cones dusted with shimmering white glitter.

A narrow hallway divided the mansion in half. To my left an ornate staircase led to guest rooms upstairs. If I followed it straight I would end up at the kitchen in the back of the house where another set of stairs (without guest access) went down into the wine cellar and laundry facilities in the basement.

I followed the sound of shouting to the industrial kitchen. Emma stood at the front of the kitchen wielding a wooden spoon in one hand. "I don't care who did what or why you did it, but this night is already a disaster and I can't take any more. Whoever did it, step forward. You will not be punished, but if someone doesn't own up to this everyone is going to be in trouble."

The kitchen staff were silent.

What was Emma upset about?

Emma banged the wooden spoon on the door frame.

One of the sous-chefs dropped a dinner plate.

Things really were in utter chaos. I hadn't seen a kitchen like this since I had been hired to temporarily fill in for the head pastry chef on *The Amour of the Seas.*

"Emma, can I help?" I touched her shoulder.

She jumped and whipped around, holding the wooden

spoon in front of her face like a weapon. "Oh, Juliet." She placed her hand over her heart and exhaled. "I'm sorry. You startled me, I didn't hear you."

"It's my fault. I snuck up on you." I kept my tone even and calm.

Emma dropped the wooden spoon on the nearby countertop. "I'm sorry you have to see us in such disarray. I swear the Winchester's kitchen usually runs as smooth as butter, but not tonight. Have you ever had a dinner service where everything has gone wrong?" She didn't wait for me to answer. "Well, no, of course you haven't. You don't do dinner service, but you must have had a bad day in the bakeshop, right?"

"Absolutely." I tried to comfort her. "I don't think there's any escaping having a bad day every now and then in this business." I went on to tell her about a time when I had accidentally swapped salt for sugar in an entire batch of cookies for a corporate order. Fortunately, I had tasted a cookie before boxing them up for delivery. But nonetheless I had to dump dozens of cookies and start all over.

"Thanks for the pep talk." Emma held a finger up for a minute and addressed her kitchen staff. "Please finish plating and get the dinner course out to dining room number one. The waitstaff will be clearing dining two and I want granitas delivered to them asap. Understood?"

The head chef gave her a salute. "We're nearly ready for service. No problem."

"Fine. We'll discuss the ornament incident later."

She motioned for me to follow her into the reception area.

"Ornament incident?" I asked.

"Yes." She folded a gray wig and cap resting on the reception desk that I assumed had been part of her costume. "As if having Nate storm out, having to scramble to come up with something to replace the Yorkshire puddings, and being over twenty minutes behind on service wasn't enough, now I have a major issue to deal with in the cellar."

"What's that?" I glanced into the dining room to check on my staff. They were laughing and completely oblivious to turmoil behind the scenes.

Emma waited for a guest to walk past on her way to the restroom. She spoke so low I could barely hear her. "As you know, Jon will be delivering special gifts to each guest soon."

"Right. I just had a bit of fun with that." I told her about my wish game.

She tried to smile. "I'm afraid Santa might not be able to grant any wishes tonight."

"Why?"

"The first issue is that we've fallen way behind on our timeline. Losing Nate and the Yorkshire puddings pushed back dinner service to the first dining room. Our schedule is so tight and usually runs like clockwork. A five-minute delay at the beginning of service can literally turn into a half-hour or forty-five-minute delay as each course progresses."

I glanced to the dining room again. No one appeared to be upset by any perceived delay. Well, that wasn't entirely true. Cami sat with a scowl on her face and her phone in her hand, but I had to guess that she would have looked equally dissatisfied even if dinner had been delivered on time. "I don't think you should stress. Everyone looks happy. Listen." I cupped my hand to my ear. "The only thing I hear is caroling and laughter."

"Maybe for now, but as our schedule continues to unravel guests are going to start getting frustrated."

"Are you sure there's nothing I can do to help? Like Mom said, we know our way around a kitchen. I can throw on an apron and help plate dessert or bus tables. Whatever you need."

Emma shook her head. "No. I would never ask you to help. I appreciate it, but it's much worse than that. Someone has destroyed the seating chart and ornaments in the wine cellar. Jon is down there now trying to piece it together again, but he's not going to have time. Usually he makes an appearance at the beginning of service. He goes through each dining room and tells some corny jokes, but then he disappears into the wine cellar and spends the rest of the night learning something special about each guest so that he can pair them with the perfect ornament. He reappears as Santa during dessert and gives everyone a personalized gift. There's no way he's going to have time to organize the ornaments, let alone memorize the seating chart even with dinner being delayed. I don't know what to do."

"Take a long, slow breath." I modeled inhaling through my nose. "I will go help Jon. You focus on the kitchen. We'll figure it out. Don't worry."

"That's very kind of you, but I can't ask you to leave your party to help us."

"You didn't ask. I offered."

Her eyes welled with tears. "I know, but I can't have you

do this. I would feel terrible to put you to work at your own dinner. You're a paying guest."

I squeezed her hand. It was clammy and damp. "Listen, Emma, I know what a friend you've been to Mom. Not only at the beginning when Torte was getting up and running but after my dad died. Please, let me help. Consider it a gift. It's the season of giving and I would feel so grateful to be able to return a favor."

She burst into tears. "Okay, thank you. Thank you so much." Between sobs she wiped her eyes on the sleeve of her sweater. "But I'm going to comp your dinner and figure out another way to repay you."

"Don't worry about it. Go get your chef moving and I'll see if I can play elf to Jon's Santa."

She gave me a giant hug before heading to the kitchen. My sentiment was sincere. I didn't need anything from Emma. This was Christmas in Ashland, the most wonderfully caring community I had ever had the pleasure of calling home. If Emma needed help, I was glad to be able to step in.

Chapter Eight

I headed toward the back stairwell. Unlike the rest of the Winchester Inn, this area was used exclusively by staff. The basement was accessed by a door opposite the kitchen. I ignored the posted sign that read STAFF ONLY and descended the dimly lit stairs. When I got to the bottom of the stairwell, I paused and tried to get my bearings. I had never been in the basement before. I took a guess and headed to the right. The first door I tried ended up being a closet with cleaning supplies.

Nope.

The next door was wrong too. It took me into the hotel's laundry facilities where stacks of pristine white towels and plush bathrobes had been stacked. Otherwise the large space was empty. I figured the cleaning staff would arrive at dawn to restock towels and turn over guest rooms.

I decided that the cellar must be in the other direction. I started to pull the door shut when a loud bang made me jump.

What was that?

The noise had come from the far end of the laundry

area. Without thinking, I headed in the direction of the sound. Maybe a shutter had slammed shut with the gusty wind and snow outside. I inched past large industrial dryers and tripped over something on the floor. I looked down to see part of Scrooge's costume crumpled on the floor. Emma had said that Nate stormed out, but maybe he was just composing himself down here. We were lucky at Torte to predominantly have friendly and easygoing customers, but there had been a handful of customers over the years who were demanding and had even gone so far as to berate my team. On the few occasions that things had gotten heated at the pastry counter, I had advised my staff to take a break in my office or talk a walk outside to regroup.

I picked up Scrooge's nightcap. The laundry room seemed like an odd choice for a hideout, but then again, I hadn't had to deal with Cami. Just watching her interact with the Winchester staff had been painful enough without having to take the brunt of her harassment. Nate had the added stress of knowing that Cami was going to be his new boss.

"Nate?" I called. "Are you down here?"

My voice echoed in the empty space.

"It's Jules. I'm a bit lost. Your mom sent me down. I'm looking for the wine cellar."

Maybe that would draw him from his hiding spot.

I moved on past the row of industrial dryers and quickly realized why Nate wasn't answering. Behind a wardrobe was another door. It read EXIT ONLY. The latch was open, causing the door to bang against the frame in the wind.

This door led outside?

I caught the handle to try and secure it, but a gust of wind yanked it open. The force pulled me out. I was shocked to see snow piled up in the Winchester's back parking lot. It had to be over an inch deep. With the drama in the dining room, I hadn't paid attention to the weather outside. The tops of the cars were dusted with fresh white powder, and fat flakes swirled sideways.

There's an entrance on this level? I thought as I looked up to see the warm glow of the kitchen above me. Since the Winchester Inn sat on a hillside, the bar, kitchen, and main dining room were a level higher than the ground I was standing on. Another set of wooden stairs twisted around the back of the parking lot and property. I couldn't see from this vantage point, but it looked as if they connected to the bar.

Had Nate gone that way?

There was a set of prints in the snow. I considered following them but reconsidered. It was freezing, especially in my party dress, and I had made a promise to Emma. Whatever was going on between them and Nate wasn't something I needed to get involved in. Owning a family business came with inherent issues. Mom and I had been lucky, mainly due to her. She didn't let small problems boil over and become major explosions. When I had returned to Ashland, we had both been a bit timid about sharing some of our personal challenges. Once we came clean with each other we made a pact to stay open and honest in our communication even if it was hard. Thus far our strategy had worked. We shared the burden of ownership, ultimately making both of our loads lighter.

I hoped that whatever had happened between Nate and his parents tonight wouldn't leave lasting damage. Then I closed the heavy door and went in search of the wine cellar. I retraced my steps and ended up at the bottom of the stairwell. This time I turned in the opposite direction and bumped into a solid oak door.

"Nate, Jon, are you down here?" I knocked and tried the handle. It was unlocked so I went inside. The cellar was a sommelier's dream. Walls of wine stored by vintage, style, and make stretched from the floor to the ceiling. The windowless room was frigid. Good for the wine, but not for my hands. I rubbed them together as I stepped farther inside.

"Emma sent me to help," I said, walking past the rows and rows of wine and turning into a small alcove at the back of the cellar.

To my horror, Santa sat slumped in a chair. A bottle of whiskey and an empty shot glass rested on an antique desk. His Santa hat and bag were crumpled on the floor. One look at the pegboard above the desk told me why. An elaborate seating chart had been tacked to the pegboard with names of each dinner guest and small hooks for hanging carefully selected ornaments. The seating chart had been ripped and torn in three places. Ornaments were strewn all over the floor. Some had broken on the desk and others smashed by someone stomping on them.

"This is terrible. Jon, are you okay?" I stepped closer. Jon had his back to me and his head hung down as if he were passed out.

He didn't respond.

Please don't let him be dead. Please don't let him be dead. The tiny hairs on my arms sprung to attention, and not just because the cellar was like a freezer.

"Jon?" My voice sounded shaky.

Had he had one too many shots of whiskey and passed out?

Glass cracked under my feet. I tapped Jon on the shoulder.

No response.

I held my breath and tapped his shoulder again. "Jon, Jon, are you okay?"

"Jon." I shook his shoulder harder this time. He didn't move. What should I do?

I hesitated for a minute.

Then I tried again, forcefully shaking his shoulder and calling his name. "Jon, it's Juliet Capshaw. I'm here to be your helper elf."

Nothing.

This couldn't be happening. Jon couldn't be dead.

My heart thudded as I came around to the front of the chair to get a better look at Jon's face. His cheeks were bright with color. If anything they appeared red and blotchy. That had to be a good sign, right? If Jon were dead, he shouldn't have any color. Unless that was just what I'd seen in movies.

I leaned closer. "Jon, Jon." I squeezed his knee.

His head flopped to one side with the motion.

Maybe you should go get help, Jules.

I watched his chest to see if he was breathing. It was hard to tell under all the Santa padding. My kitchen first-aid training kicked in. I reached for his arm and placed two fingers on his wrist to check for a pulse. Just as I made contact with his skin the lights went out and the cellar was plunged into complete darkness.

Chapter Nine

I dropped Jon's arm and screamed. The darkness was unsettling. It hadn't exactly been bright and cheery before the lights went out, but now it was so dark I literally couldn't see my hand in front of my face. I fumbled toward where I thought the desk should be. Ornaments snapped under my feet.

My hip hit something hard, sending a wave of pain up my side.

Ouch.

I kept my hands in front of me to try and block any obstacles. When I made it to the desk I felt around the top for a book of matches, phone, flashlight, anything that might illuminate the dungeonlike cellar. No luck. The only thing I managed to do was knock more ornaments off the desk. Each time one rolled off and shattered on the floor it made me startle.

I tried the drawers next. Nothing. I felt file folders, stacks of receipts, and a calculator. The calculator seemed like it could be an option, but it was either solar powered or its batteries were dead because when I pressed on the buttons nothing happened.

Now what?

You're going to have to find your way back upstairs, Jules. I tossed the calculator on the desk and gave myself a pep talk.

Before I left Jon, I had to finish assessing whether he had a pulse. I shuffled over to him and found his arm again.

Please, please, please have a pulse.

His wrist was clammy to the touch. I pressed two fingers against his skin and said a silent prayer to the universe. It took a minute, but I found a weak yet steady pulse.

Thank goodness.

I dropped Jon's wrist and inhaled through my nose.

Okay, Jules. Focus.

Jon had most likely passed out. Maybe when he saw the destruction in the cellar, he had reached his breaking point and turned to the bottle of whiskey.

Keep breathing, Jules, I told myself. I had to go get help.

I ran my hand along the wall and tried to retrace my steps. Each movement I made was deliberate. My ballet flats didn't have thick soles. The last thing I needed was to step on a broken ornament and have it cut my foot.

I tiptoed out of the cellar. The rest of the basement was pitch-black. Fortunately I could hear the frenzy of the kitchen staff upstairs and make out little flashes of light. Someone had set a lantern at the top of the staircase, I assumed to mark the top of the stairs so that none of the staff accidentally took a tumble. Happily, it provided me with much-needed light.

The kitchen was in even more disarray than when I'd left. "Behind!"

"On your left!"

"No, on your right!"

The kitchen staff shouted out orders as they tried to plate the next course by candlelight. Meanwhile waitstaff raced between the kitchen and the dining areas wielding flashlights and candles. It was a dizzying display of chaos.

"What happened?" I asked a waiter standing at the ready with a handheld flashlight and tray.

"Power's out. Must be the storm."

"I'm surprised the generator didn't kick on." Hotels the size of the Winchester had backup generators for emergency situations like this. Ashland was prone to winter storms. No one wanted guests to be left in the dark should a weather system linger over the Siskiyou Mountains.

"Yeah. Everyone is surprised. Emma's outside with maintenance looking at it now."

At that moment, Emma burst through the door that led to the parking lot, holding one of the walkway lanterns. Her hair was disheveled, and her sweater was flocked with wet snowflakes. She was followed by a man in coveralls and a parka.

"What are we going to do?" She addressed the maintenance worker.

"Nothing we can do, Mrs. McBeth. Someone intentionally cut the line. Hoses break but they don't get sliced in half."

"Why would anyone want to cut the power?"

"No idea, but you should call the police. I looked, and

the storm hasn't brought down any lines. I'd put my money on the fact that someone tampered with the power lines."

Emma ran her fingers through her hair, making it stand on end. She reminded me of a character from *The Nightmare Before Christmas* rather than the demure Mrs. Claus who had greeted us at the start of the evening.

"Someone cut power to the Winchester?" I didn't realize I'd spoken out loud until Emma turned in my direction. Her eyes were crazed. Maybe it was due to the fact that she was holding the lantern near her chin, which made her entire face glow an eerie red.

"Oh, Juliet, I didn't see you there." She lowered her lantern.

"Someone cut the power?" I repeated, as if repeating it would make more sense of what had happened.

"It looks that way. I can't understand why, and this night can't get any worse." Emma brushed snow from her slacks. "It's like someone is trying and succeeding at sabotaging the Dickens feast. In all my years of hosting this dinner I've never had anything like this happen."

I hated to be the one to break it to her that her husband was passed out in the wine cellar.

She stood paralyzed. "I don't know what to do. I guess I should call the police. Or the power company?"

"Probably both, but you don't need to call the police. The Professor is here. I can go get him to have a quick look and then he can call in reinforcements if necessary."

"Right. That would be good." Her tone was flat. "I'm so frazzled that I had forgotten that Doug was here."

"I'm assuming that cell service is fine. If you want to

call the power company, I'll discreetly ask the Professor to come outside. He might want to secure the crime scene."

"Crime scene?" Emma's voice turned shrill.

"If someone intentionally severed power to the Winchester, then, yes, that's a crime."

She massaged her temple with her free hand. "I don't understand what's happening tonight. Literally everything that could go wrong has."

That reminded me of the other "issue" in the cellar.

I pulled her to an alcove near the kitchen as the wait-staff balanced lanterns and trays. "Hey, at least it looks like dinner is being served to the other dining room."

"I guess I should be grateful for small miracles." Emma didn't sound convinced.

"Before you go, there's something important I need to tell you."

She shielded her face with her hand. The light in her other hand made a perfect circle on the hardwood floor. "That doesn't sound good, and I'm not sure I can handle any more bad news, Juliet."

"I wouldn't tell you if it wasn't important." I reached for Emma's arm. "I went downstairs to help Jon with the ornaments."

"Oh, God! Jon. I forgot all about Jon." Her face blanched. "What's wrong? Did something happen to Jon?"

"He's fine," I assured her. "He's just had too much to drink. I found him passed out in the wine cellar with a bottle of whiskey."

"What? That can't be right. Jon never drinks before he's done playing Santa. We'll often have a nightcap once the last guest is out the door and the dishes are all cleaned, but he never drinks while in character. He has to keep his memory sharp to get the seating chart right. And then of course he's always said you can't play Santa and have the smell of whiskey on your breath. Imagine what that would do to the kids? It would shatter their image of Santa."

"Maybe the stress got to him?" I suggested.

"No. It's not possible. Jon loves being Santa and he was determined to find a way to have the show go on tonight. He wouldn't have been drinking." Emma was adamant.

"I don't know. He was out cold."

"There must be some other explanation," Emma insisted. "There is absolutely no way he was drinking. Are you sure it was him? Maybe someone else was in the costume. I just can't believe that Jon would be drunk and passed out? No, you have to be wrong."

"Emma, I'm sorry, I know this is a lot, but it's definitely Jon. I tried to wake him up but he wouldn't budge. I even checked his pulse because I was worried when he wasn't responding."

Emma frowned. "No. No way. I refuse to believe that Jon is drunk. It's completely out of character. I'll go down and check on him, but what about the power? I wish Nate were here. He would know what to do. He can fix anything. He's our in-house handyman. If he were here, I bet he'd have the power back on already."

"Try to stay calm, if you can. I know there's a lot going on, but the calmer you stay the better it will be for everyone."

"Yeah." Emma sighed. "You're right. I'll call the power company. Can you go ask Doug for his help?"

"Of course." I watched Emma head downstairs. I couldn't blame her for being distraught. Having one or two mishaps in the kitchen or with service were par for the course, but she was right that this evening had been one disaster after another.

I made my way into the dimly lit dining room. The candlelight gave off a romantic vibe. I noticed that both Sterling and Andy had their arms around their dates.

Mom caught my eye right away. "Is everything okay?"

I smiled and knelt next to her and the Professor. Lance was wrapped in a debate with Bethany over the most quintessential Christmas movie. "Clearly, young one, you need to expand your viewing repertoire. *The Holiday* is cute fluff. I mean I won't turn my nose up at anything with Jude Law and Kate Winslet, but if you want a classic find a copy of *Christmas in Connecticut*. They don't make them like Barbara Stanwyck."

"Juliet." Mom brought my attention back. "Is Emma okay?"

"Not exactly." I gave her and the Professor a brief rundown of everything that had transpired, including finding Jon passed out in the basement. When I finished, the Professor folded his napkin into a neat square and set it on the table. He stood and gave Mom a half bow. "If you'll excuse me, my dear, I believe duty calls."

We got our coats from the rack near the reception desk and I took the Professor through the kitchen. Emma was nowhere to be found. I asked the head chef, but he grunted a reply as he whipped mounds of cream by hand.

"She must still be downstairs," I said to the Professor. "Should we check on Jon first?"

"I think it's a wise idea."

The lantern was still placed at the top of the stairs to mark the way, so the Professor and I carefully navigated the steep steps down into the cellar. When we stepped inside the dungeonlike room a single strand of light greeted us. Emma stood next to Jon holding a cup in her hand. It didn't take long to realize that she must have doused Jon with a cup of water.

He coughed. "What's going on?"

"You're drunk! You're drunk! Tonight. Everything is falling apart upstairs, and you're drunk. I can't believe this, Jon."

Jon cleared his throat and tried to sit up straighter. He wobbled so far to one side that he nearly fell off his chair. The Professor hurried over to help steady him.

"What?" Jon was clearly disoriented.

I thought Emma might slap him. "You're wasted! How could you do that to me? To our guests? I thought you came down here to try and fix the seating chart and salvage the rest of the night, but instead you come down and polish off a bottle of whiskey?"

Jon rubbed his head. "Huh?"

Emma pointed to the bottle of whiskey and shot glass on the desk. "Proof. You desert me and sneak down here to drown your troubles. Nice, Jon. Nice."

"Huh?" Jon brushed water from his face. "Why is it dark?" His speech was slurred.

"Because the power is out!" Emma screamed. "While I've been trying to wake you from your drunken slumber, I've been on the phone with the power company and running around upstairs to find every candle, tea light, flashlight, and lantern. We're three-quarters of the way through service and have no power. We're supposed to be a team, remember? This is our last feast after all of these years and tonight is the night that you decide to go on a binge?"

I felt uncomfortable being in the middle of their argument.

Jon blinked as if he were trying to figure out where he was. "I'm not drunk. I found the bottle of whiskey and shot glass on the desk when I came down here. I figured Nate must have had a drink earlier, and yeah, I guess I was stressed so I poured myself a shot to take the edge off, but that's it. I don't remember anything after that." He sounded concerned.

"One shot and you're out cold. Yeah, right." Emma picked up a fur-lined ornament shaped like a boot and squeezed it in her hand.

The Professor, who had been quiet up to this point, left Jon and went to the desk. He picked up the whiskey bottle and held it near the beam of light. "Emma, take a look at this."

Emma glared at Jon then turned her attention to the Professor. "What is it, Doug? Do you want to arrest my husband for drunk and disorderly conduct? Go right ahead."

"This bottle is nearly full." The Professor pointed to the fill line. "Not more than one, perhaps two shots."

I stepped closer for a better look. The Professor was right. The bottle was full.

"What are you saying?" Emma asked.

The Professor returned the bottle to the desk and then went over to Jon. He studied his eyes and asked Jon to track his finger as he moved it from the left to the right, then up and down. "I don't know, but if the bottle is any indication, I would say that your husband is telling the truth. One—even two—shots would not be nearly enough to make Jon incoherent and unresponsive. Unless he has some sort of reaction to alcohol?"

Emma shook her head. "No." She tugged off a piece of fur from the ornament she still held.

Jon twisted his neck from side to side. "I don't know what was in that whiskey, but my head is pounding."

"Mmm-hmm." The Professor nodded. "I suspect that there was indeed something in the shot you drank, and I think it's quite likely you were drugged."

"Drugged?" Emma let out another wail.

How much more could the poor woman take?

"Indeed, something nefarious is at play. I think you should call an ambulance just to be on the safe side, and I am going to call for extra help."

Chapter Ten

Emma called the paramedics while the Professor went to call Thomas and Detective Kerry. I checked in with Jon.

"Can I get you anything? Maybe a glass of water." I glanced at the empty cup that Emma had used to splash water on Jon's face.

"No. I think I need to sit here for a minute. If I drink anything I might throw up." He was probably smart to decline my offer. Sweat poured from his forehead and pooled on the trim of his Santa suit.

"Did anything happen before you drank the whiskey? Did you let anyone in here? Like whoever did this?" I motioned to the mess of broken ornaments.

Jon shook his head. "I didn't see anything. Emma was the one who told me that the cellar had been broken into."

"Is the cellar door normally locked?"

He mopped his brow with his already damp sleeve. "No. We don't lock the wine cellar. We trust our employees. Many of them have been with us for years and years. Like Tim, who manages the wine. Everyone is family here.

You know that. It's the same at Torte, right? It's the Ashland way."

I nodded.

Jon continued. "I suppose we should have thought about locking the cellar, but our waitstaff constantly have to come down here to get bottles of wine for our customers. Cami told me we were idiots not to keep our most valuable asset under lock and key, but that's not the way Emma and I want to run our business."

The mention of Cami brought a question to mind. "About that, do you think someone could be trying to sabotage the sale? Maybe this is related to Cami being here. I mean it's quite a coincidence that you've never had any problems with the Dickens feast and yet everything that could go wrong has, on the one night your new buyer is in town."

"I guess. But why?" Jon swayed in his chair again. "The deal is done. What good would that do? The only person I know who is upset with the sale is Nate, but he's family and he'll get over it. None of the other staff know about the sale yet. We didn't want to upset the balance during the holidays. Emma and I intend to tell everyone about the sale after the new year."

"Right." I nodded. "What about Nate? Could he have done this?"

"Nate? No. You know what it's like to work with family. We argue, sure, but he wouldn't do anything to hurt us. He was angry tonight, so I told him to leave and go cool off. I'm sure he's at home sharing a bottle of wine with his wife Melissa and my two beautiful granddaughters."

I wasn't so sure, but I dropped it. The paramedics ar-

rived and assessed Jon's vital signs. I made way for the first
responders. Detective Kerry, Thomas, and the Professor
had all come into the small cellar. It was quickly becoming cozy with so many bodies.

"I'll go back upstairs," I said to the Professor. "Is everyone wondering what's going on?"

He had removed a small Moleskine notebook and pen
from his jacket. "Not as of yet. Although Lance and your
mother are both in the know. The rest of the dining room
was being entertained in candlelight by the carolers. I don't
think anyone is the wiser. Thank you for your help, Juliet.
With any luck, we'll be up shortly for the dessert course."

As I went upstairs I bumped into Tim. He was hover-
ing outside of the cellar.

"Sorry. I didn't see you there," I said. That was true. He
blended into the dark wall.

He flinched. "Yeah. It's hard to see down here. What's
going on in there?"

I hesitated.

"I saw the ambulance lights in the parking lot. Everyone upstairs is starting to freak out. We haven't seen either
of the McBeths for at least a half hour."

"They're both okay. Jon wasn't feeling well, so Emma
called the paramedics as a precaution."

"Is he having a heart attack?" Tim sounded concerned.

"No. It sounds like it was stress." Technically that
wasn't a lie, but I didn't want to go into detail about what
had happened, especially if the Professor was in the
middle of investigating. For all I knew, Tim had been the
person who had laced Jon's whiskey with something—if
the Professor's theory was correct. He had access to the

wine cellar, after all. No one would have thought anything about seeing him go in and out of the basement room; it was his job.

"Good. That's a relief." Tim dabbed his brow with a dish towel hanging over his arm. "I should return to the bar. The kitchen is plating dessert and that's my cue to pop open bottles of chilling champagne."

"I'll follow you upstairs."

We parted ways at the top. I noticed not only the flashing lights from the ambulance through the reflections of the kitchen windows but also yellow construction lights from a city work truck. The power company was already on the scene. Maybe the cursed evening was about to improve. If the lights came on in time for dessert, we could end the evening on a good note.

Mom and Lance had scooted their chairs next to one another when I returned.

"Juliet, you must dish this minute." Lance patted the empty chair to his left. "You've been gone for ages, darling. We were about to send out a search party."

I glanced at the carolers who were at the opposite end of the table taking song requests from my staff. Then I recapped everything that had happened, from finding Jon passed out, to the power being cut, and the Professor's theory that someone may have spiked Jon's drink.

"How terrible." Mom's forehead crinkled with worry.

"A poisoning." Lance clutched his throat. "I'm beginning to think that you've orchestrated this entire evening, tragedy after tragedy, just to lure me into the holiday spirit."

"Ha. I wish."

"Jon's going to be okay though?" Mom asked.

"Yeah. He's being treated by the paramedics now and didn't appear to be in any danger."

"My, my. That does give new meaning to spiked eggnog, doesn't it?" Lance tapped his index finger on his chin. "I mean, of course that's most comforting news to hear that he's out of the woods, but this evening is so much more than I expected. Any other tidbits you have to offer?"

I told them about hearing someone slam the exit door down in the laundry room and the footprints in the snow. "The Professor is checking on that too. It has to be connected."

The carolers clapped to get everyone's attention. Francine shook a string of silver bells. "Let's do a round robin of 'Jingle Bells,' Frank Sinatra-style. We'll start at this end of the table. When I ring these bells, that end of the table will chime in, and then we'll move around the room."

When she nodded to Cami's table I realized Cami was gone. At least I didn't have to worry about her and Francine getting into it again.

We joined in the singing. I almost momentarily forgot about the behind-the-scenes chaos of the Winchester while watching my happy staff bellow out the melody of the holiday favorite.

"What wonderful voices. You're absolutely angelic." Francine applauded our efforts when the song ended. "We'll take a short break and return for one last set after you've finished the decadent pear trifle that's coming your way."

The quartet bowed and made their exit as Tim swept in balancing a tray of beautifully layered pear trifle, with fluffy clouds of cinnamon whipped cream, almond custard, and rum-soaked sponge cake.

Bethany jumped up and snapped at least a dozen pictures. "This is like the best possible night ever. I mean it's like they scripted a power outage. Do they do that every year? Our social followers are going to go bonkers over the lighting." She held out her phone so that I could scroll through the photos. "Look at how amazing everything looks with that natural glow."

She couldn't seriously think that the Winchester intentionally cut the power? "These are great," I said, handing her the phone. I guess it wasn't impossible to imagine why Bethany might think that the power outage was orchestrated. Tiny orange flames flickered off the crystal bowls. Wax melted and pooled on ceramic holders. Condensation formed on the windows as snow continued to fall outside.

It could have been the 1840s. I half expected to see the Cratchit family gathered around the stone fireplace.

In a flash, the moment was lost.

The power came back on with a whoosh and hum. Three loud beeps sounded nearby. Everyone reacted with surprise and shielded their eyes from the light. A few people cheered and clapped.

I blinked rapidly. The glare from the overhead lights caused bright yellow halos to blur my vision. It took a minute to adjust to the light.

Mom massaged the corners of her eyes. "Well, there's one piece of good news for Emma and Jon. At least they can finish dinner service with power. That will be a relief."

"True." I reached for my water glass as a piercing scream shattered our newfound relief.

Lance, Mom, and I jumped from our chairs and raced toward the sound. It was coming from the foyer where a young waitress stood at the bottom of the staircase. Her finger shook violently as she pointed to the bottom of the stairs.

She moved to the side to allow us a better view as diners from the other dining room started to cram in as well. Cami's body was sprawled across five steps. I didn't have to check to see if she was dead. A steak knife had been plunged into her chest.

Chapter Eleven

"She's dead. She's dead." The waitress quivered and stepped backward into the forming crowd.

More and more people crushed closer. Cami's lifeless body reminded me of the ghosts of Christmas past with her ashen skin.

"What do we do?" the waitress asked in a timid whisper.

Mom took charge. She turned toward the group gathered in the foyer. "Everyone, please return to your seats and stay calm."

Lance consoled the waitress as people began to disperse.

"Juliet, go downstairs and get Doug." Mom hovered near the base of the stairwell, protecting Cami's body.

I sprinted down the hallway, past the kitchen, and down the back stairs. The EMS workers were still attending to Jon. They had him hooked up to an IV and portable EKG.

Thomas stood with one arm propped against an empty wine rack but there was no sign of the Professor, Detective Kerry, and Emma.

"Thomas, where's the Professor?" I asked, trying to catch my breath.

"Outside. Why?"

"Cami, one of the dinner guests, she's dead. She's been stabbed."

"Dead?" Thomas's voice boomed in the cavelike room. The paramedics turned in our direction.

"Yes! She's dead. There's a steak knife in her chest."

"Let's go." Thomas motioned for the paramedics to follow him.

Jon tried to stand but fell back into the chair. "You stay, Jon. I'll be right back."

I showed them to the body. Thomas cleared out the few remaining stragglers gawking at Cami's body to make way for the paramedics. "Back to your tables, everyone. I need to secure the scene. No one is to leave the inn. Sit tight and we'll have further instructions for you soon."

People shuffled back to their seats. The emergency responder gave Thomas a thumbs-down, confirming what I already knew—Cami had been murdered.

Thomas took off his thick blue police jacket. "Jules, can you go find the Professor?"

"Sure." I left without a second of hesitation. I had to get the Professor, but I didn't want to leave Jon alone downstairs either. Odds were good that whoever had killed Cami had tried to kill Jon too. If they learned that Jon was alive, would they try again?

I ran outside to find the Professor, Emma, and a team of police officers scouring the parking lot. Trails of footprints ran in a zigzag pattern.

The Professor was placing small yellow markers near

the footprints that were rapidly disappearing under new falling snow. "Juliet." He looked up with surprise. "You look distressed."

"There's been a murder," I blurted out. "Cami's dead. She was stabbed. It must have happened when the lights were out." I shuddered.

Emma's face dropped. "Cami's dead?"

I nodded. "When the lights came on, your waitress found her in the foyer."

The Professor handed the stack of yellow markers to a nearby officer. "Kerry, can you come inside with me?"

Detective Kerry was interviewing the two members of the power line crew. She finished taking a note and then came toward us. "What's going on, Doug?" Her red curls were hidden underneath a fuzzy ski hat. She had wisely worn boots and a long wool coat.

I noticed that she used the Professor's first name.

"Come with me." The Professor pulled her away.

"Cami's dead?" Emma repeated in disbelief, staring off behind me.

"Yes." I could tell that she was in shock. "Let's go inside. It's freezing out here and I don't think that Jon should be alone."

A dazed look crossed her face. "Okay." She stood frozen in the snow.

"Emma, everything is going to be fine." I wrapped my arm around her shoulder. "Let's check in on Jon and we'll take it step by step from there."

She moved like a zombie. I practically had to drag her inside. Had she hit her breaking point? Jon had likely been drugged, Nate had deserted them, someone had intentionally cut the power, and now Cami was dead. Emma was so limp in my arms as we returned inside that I was worried she might collapse.

"Do you want to stay here?" I pointed to the kitchen. "I can go check on Jon."

"No, I'll come with you." Her voice wavered. "How can this be happening? I feel like I'm living some kind of terrible nightmare. I want to pinch myself and wake up."

"Don't worry. The Professor will get everything sorted out. Thomas has already given the guests instructions, and I'll do whatever I can to help."

"You've been too kind." She wrung her hands together. They were nearly blue from the cold. "How can I repay you?"

"Let's get through the night without any other disasters, how does that sound?"

She attempted a smile.

We found Jon in the same spot we'd left him. The paramedics had unhooked him from the machines. A juice box and package of candies sat untouched on the desk.

"Have you heard?" Emma asked, giving him a knowing look.

"Cami's dead," Jon said. They spoke in code with their eyes. I guessed after a lifetime together they didn't need words, but I wished I could interpret their thoughts. Emma appeared dazed but neither of them seemed broken up about Cami's death.

I was about to suggest that we start by cleaning up the ornaments, when the door to the wine cellar swung open.

"Mom, Dad, I heard the news, are you okay?" Nate stopped in mid-stride at the sight of the ornament carnage on the cellar floor. "It looks like an earthquake hit down here."

"Nate, what are you doing here? I thought you went home." Emma ran over to embrace her son.

"I couldn't leave you guys stranded. That wasn't fair. I let Cami get the best of me and I should have been more professional."

What did he mean by that?

Emma released him. "I got halfway to Nevada Street and turned around. I felt terrible about leaving you guys in the lurch and ran back."

Traces of white makeup from his Scrooge costume was smeared on his cheek. His face was blotchy and red. I didn't doubt that he had run back to the inn, but the timing didn't add up. At most it would have taken Nate twenty minutes to get halfway to Nevada Street. Aside from hills, Ashland is an extremely walkable town. Most housing is located within a few miles of the plaza. Nate had been gone for at least an hour.

"I'm sorry, Mom." He bent over and picked up a shattered glass star. "What happened?"

Emma began explaining the evening's mishaps to her son. Was it just my imagination or was he looking for something? As Emma spoke, Nate scanned the wall of wine bottles and sifted through the broken ornaments.

"Cami's dead, huh?" He carefully extracted a bottle of merlot from the wooden shelves and blew dust from it before returning it to its spot. "I can't say I'm terribly shaken up about that. She was a total witch, and like I tried to warn you guys, she was going to demolish this place."

"Don't start, Nate," Jon cautioned.

"I don't know why you refuse to believe me. She had no interest in the Dickens feast or maintaining the small-town charm and hospitality you guys have spent the last three decades building. I guarantee you the minute she took possession of the inn the bulldozers would be here."

Emma stood on her tiptoes to kiss him on the cheek. "None of that matters now. Thanks for coming back. Having you here is a huge relief. Tonight has been an absolute disaster and the thought of you being angry made it all the worse."

"Sorry, Mom. I know I shouldn't have stormed off. That was stupid." They shared a long, sweet embrace. I was glad that the McBeth family had reconciled, but I still wasn't sure I believed Nate.

"What are we going to do about this?" he asked, picking up an ornament in the shape of a latte. I wondered if the ceramic ornament had been originally intended for Andy. In my notes, I had mentioned that Andy loved any and all things coffee.

"Maybe we can salvage the ornaments and at least try to match up as many people as we can. I can help with our party," I offered.

"But will the police even let us?" Emma frowned. "I don't know how we can orchestrate that. The police have sent everyone to the bar to keep guests contained in one space. If everyone's in the bar, how will we deliver the ornaments?"

"Let's start by sorting through the mess," I suggested. "One thing that I've learned from the Professor is that having something to focus on during times of crisis can be helpful. Once we see if there are even enough ornaments to pass out, I can go check in with the Professor and see if it's okay to share them with everyone. It's not like anyone is going anywhere until the police are finished with their initial investigation so I'm guessing the Professor will agree that a distraction will be good for morale."

We spent the next twenty minutes sorting through the broken ornaments and making piles of ones that could be salvaged. It felt cathartic to have a task to do, and yet strange to see such bright and cheery ornaments while knowing that there was a body upstairs. Nate kept close watch on Jon while we stacked glittery snowflakes, fur-lined red ski boots, and a vintage typewriter on the desk. I was impressed by the vast assortment of ornaments the McBeths had acquired. These weren't your average big-box store decorations. They had clearly spent time find-ing unique, beautiful ornaments to match their guests' personal taste.

Since the seating chart had been completely thrown off we went through the guest list and assigned a gift to each person. My staff was easy. Andy would get the latte, Ster-ling a vibrant teal and orange hummingbird much like the tattoo on his forearm. Bethany would receive a pink and white layer-cake ornament, Marty a rolling pin, Steph a purple pastry bag, Sequoia a peace sign, and Rosa a mossy green pair of gardening shears. The McBeths had a special surprise for Mom and the Professor—bride and groom ornaments.

"Oh, don't let Juliet see that one," Emma exclaimed, scooping up an ornament before I saw it.

"Don't worry about me. I don't need an ornament."

"Everyone needs an ornament." Emma's voice sounded

almost normal for the first time all evening. The project seemed to have helped calm her nerves somewhat.

After we had paired guests with their ornaments, we cut up sticky notes and tagged each one with a name. It wouldn't have the same effect as Jon's magical Santa delivery, but hopefully sharing the thoughtful tokens would end the night on a more positive note.

I went to check in with the Professor. As I came upstairs, they were wheeling Cami's body out the back door next to the kitchen. I paused, closed my eyes, and allowed her a moment of silence. The ambulance lights cut through the snow. The Professor, Thomas, Detective Kerry, and the two uniformed officers stood at attention until the ambulance was out of sight. While they might see death up close in their line of work, it didn't mean that it ever left them untouched.

"Juliet." The Professor turned away from the parking lot and met my eye. "I didn't hear you come outside."

"I saw them taking Cami's body away. I didn't want to disturb the moment."

He gave me a grateful, "Silence is a source of great strength."

"Is that yours?"

"No, that is a quote from the Chinese philosopher Lao Tzu. It's fitting for the moment, don't you agree?"

"Absolutely." The realization that a woman had been murdered made my head start to feel dizzy.

The Professor took my arm. "The other wise philosopher who comes to mind in a moment like this is Buddha, who said, 'It is a man's own mind, not his enemy or foe, that lures him to evil ways.'"

"You think Cami is partly responsible for her own death?"

"No. Murder is never the answer. Nor is it the victim's fault, but given the brutal nature of this killing, I do suspect that Cami's behavior this evening, and in the days leading up to her death, likely triggered the killer to extract their rage upon her. I don't condone it. Not in the slightest. It does offer us guidance and direction as we begin the task of gathering evidence for a conviction."

Detective Kerry and Thomas joined us. "Should we start taking statements?" Thomas asked.

"Yes. I'd like you to start with the guests so that we may release them first. Then we'll move on to the staff."

"Are you feeling all right, Juliet?" Detective Kerry asked. She reached into her police jacket and handed me a box of mints. "Want one? They help perk me up."

I let go of the Professor's arm and took a mint. "Thanks." She was right, the spicy mint made my tongue tingle, but it took away the bitter taste in my mouth.

Kerry gave me an encouraging smile. "Want another one?"

"No, thanks, this is good."

Thomas gave the Professor a salute and nodded to me, then he and Kerry went inside. "Speaking of the guests, I was wondering what you think about delivering the ornaments tonight? The McBeths have them all sorted and tagged. We thought it might be a good distraction to send people home with a little gift, but we don't want to interfere with your investigation."

"Excellent idea, Juliet. In fact I welcome it. One of the most difficult things about interrogating a large group of witnesses like we have tonight is to keep them from tainting one another's recollections. The less guests talk to each other right now, the better. Plus, I'd like to observe the McBeths interacting with the guests, and ornament delivery sounds like an ideal way to make that happen without raising any suspicions."

"Do you think one of the McBeths could have killed Cami?"

The Professor walked inside with me. I was grateful because the tips of my fingers had begun to go numb. "It's too soon to know, Juliet. We are in the very early stages of the investigation and things can change rapidly. I will say that whoever killed Cami tonight was here at the inn with us. This is not an outside job or the work of a madman. I'm afraid I have to say that the killer is one of us."

Chapter Twelve

The Professor's words left me with a chill. It made sense, but I hated the thought that Cami's killer was most likely someone I knew, or at least someone who was among us now. I thought about the McBeth family. They were Mom's oldest friends in Ashland. I couldn't fathom any of them killing Cami, even if she had intended to bulldoze the Winchester. But I also knew I had to stay open to every possibility.

Jon could probably be ruled out as a suspect. He'd been incapacitated in the cellar, and it sounded like he might have had a narrow miss with death himself. That made it more unlikely that either Nate or Emma could have killed Cami. The McBeths might have bickered but clearly they loved each other deeply. The other possibility was that Jon's attempted poisoning and Cami's murder were unconnected.

If that was the case, Emma and Nate were definitely suspects. Nate had disappeared for at least an hour. He knew every nook and cranny in the Winchester. He easily could have hidden in a closet or waited outside. Maybe he was the person I'd heard leaving through the laundry room exit. His motive was clear—he didn't want the inn sold. He'd grown up at the historic mansion. The inn was more than a job, it was his childhood home and family legacy. It was plausible that he had done something drastic in order to preserve the Winchester. But at the same time, I couldn't reconcile the quiet, studious classmate I'd grown up with turning to murder.

Then there was Emma. Mom's dear friend and closest confidante couldn't be a murderess, could she? She'd been high-strung tonight, but that was understandable given the many unfortunate circumstances. I couldn't figure out what her motive might be. She and Jon had seemed excited about selling the Winchester and retiring to a tropical beach. I'd heard her joking with Mom about taking off for a long stay at a sunny island or using some of the proceeds of the sale to buy a motor home and tour the United States. If Cami was dead that meant the sale of the Winchester was too. Unless Emma had had second thoughts. Maybe, like Nate, she had realized too late that Cami wasn't going to preserve the Winchester's rich history. Could the realization that everything she and Jon had built over the last thirty years was about to be demolished have led her to murder?

No way, I answered my own question as I returned to the basement. Yet a tiny voice nagged in my head. Emma had the same access that Nate would have. She had been outside earlier. What if she cut the power? What if she intentionally slipped something into Jon's whiskey to shift suspicion? She could have added just enough to knock him out, but not harm him. She had had plenty of time to slip into the cellar unnoticed to spike Jon's drink, and then kill Cami. The chef had mentioned that he couldn't find her during the height of the power outage.

Stop it, Jules. I shook my shoulders. Jumping to wild conclusions wasn't going to do me or the McBeths any good. There must be a reason that the Professor wanted to observe them interacting with the guests. He had known them longer than me. I was confident that there was a logical explanation for wanting to watch the McBeth family tonight. The Professor was one of the wisest and most astute detectives in the region—most likely in the country. I knew that he would be professional, but also fair.

In the wine cellar the McBeth family was deep in conversation. "I'm back." I tried to keep my tone light.

"What did Doug say, Juliet?" Emma asked. She had twisted a piece of dainty red ribbon from a broken ornament around her pinkie.

"He likes the idea. He thinks it will help lighten the mood a bit, and he said that his team is going to have to personally interview each guest, so we're going to be here for a while."

"Great." Nate sighed. "I promised the kids I would read them a bedtime story. I guess that's off."

"Yeah, I wouldn't count on it," I said. "The Professor and his team are going to start conducting interviews in the dining room and then with everyone waiting in the bar. After they finish that, then they'll start questioning staff."

"Questioning?" Emma sounded nervous. "They're going to question us?" She stared at Jon.

I nodded. "It's standard procedure. They want to talk to everyone while details are fresh. The Professor once told me that it is vital to interview witnesses immediately as memories quickly change or get cloudy. He and Thomas and Detective Kerry want to keep guests from talking with one another. They're worried that people might unintentionally taint each other's memories."

"Oh." Emma twisted the ribbon tighter around her pinkie. "I see."

"They'll also have to take down and verify contact information for each guest in attendance tonight and interview your staff."

"So what you're saying is that we could be here long into the night." Nate rubbed his cheek with the palm of his hand, causing a bigger streak in his makeup. "I guess I better call home and let my wife know that a bedtime story is out."

"Let's hope we're not here all night." I wondered what time it was. The last time I had checked it had been going on nine, but that was before we had discovered Cami's body. Time had blurred in the aftermath of her murder. "Thomas, Detective Kerry, and the Professor are extremely efficient. They don't want to detain anyone longer than need be, but with over eighty guests and then your staff, it will probably take a while." The fact that Nate was married with young children made me wonder why I was even considering him as a possible suspect. He wouldn't risk his family's well-being by killing Cami, would he?

"This is so lame." Nate tossed a broken ornament in the trash. "This literally goes down as the worst Dickens feast in the history of Dickens feasts."

I wanted to point out to Nate that the night was probably worse for Cami and for her family.

"Maybe we should take everything upstairs now," Emma suggested, picking up a cardboard box of ornaments.

"Sure. It sounded like the Professor thought you could deliver ornaments while they are conducting their interviews." I was eager to leave the cold cellar.

"What about Santa?" She pointed to Jon's Santa hat on the floor. "Do you think we should try to play up the event? Nate, you could do it, right?"

Nate held up a finger as he made a call. I assumed it was to let his wife know that it might be a while before he was home.

"Or is it in poor taste?" Emma asked me.

"I think it's probably better to just hand out ornaments." Providing a small distraction felt like a good idea, but having Nate play a jolly Santa in the middle of a murder investigation seemed like poor taste. I looked at Jon. "Are you feeling up to walking around?"

He shook his head. "Nope. I'm still feeling like I'm on a roller-coaster ride."

"You can't stay down here in this freezing cellar by yourself," Emma scolded.

I was glad that she had voiced her concern. Otherwise it would have been difficult to come up with an excuse why Jon should join us upstairs.

Nate hung up the phone. "Yeah, Dad, you should come with us and at least sit by the fire and warm up." He helped Jon to his feet. Emma and I gathered the remaining tagged ornaments and followed them upstairs. It was slow going. Jon was barely able to navigate the stairs, even with Nate's help. If there was any validity to my theory that he or

Emma might have slipped a drug into Jon's drink to shift suspicion away from them, then they had come dangerously close to harming him.

"What did the paramedics say?" I asked Emma as we waited at the bottom of the stairs just in case Jon were to topple over backwards. "He doesn't look good."

"I know," Emma whispered. "They said it could take hours for the full effect to wear off, but they didn't seem very concerned. Although they did tell me to keep a close eye on him, not to let him sleep for more than an hour at a time tonight, and to call immediately if he gets worse.

"Who would do such a thing, Juliet? I don't understand what's happening tonight. It feels like someone is out to get us, and frankly I'm scared. Why would anyone target us, especially Jon? Everyone loves Jon."

I rubbed her shoulder. "It's normal to feel scared, Emma. Anyone would in your position. I know that Jon is beloved in Ashland, but do you think there's a chance that this could be tied to Cami and selling her the inn?"

Emma shifted the box of ornaments in her arms. Jon had only made it three steps thus far. "It's possible, but why? First, there are only a handful of people who know about the sale—Jon, Nate, myself, and our accountant. We've been very tight-lipped about it. No one on staff has been told. Of course, I shared the news with your mom because she's a dear friend and I wanted her input. And, everyone in Ashland knows that Helen is a vault when it comes to keeping secrets."

"True."

"Aside from the family and a couple of other good friends, we wanted to keep the news quiet until after the holidays. The deal wasn't going to be final until the beginning of January anyway and it's so crazy around here through the new year that we didn't want our staff or our guests to be distracted."

"What about the staff? Do you think someone could have learned about the sale? Cami was pretty vocal tonight. She fired Tim. Maybe your staff does know. It's possible that one of them could have killed her if they thought their job was in jeopardy."

"No. None of our staff would do something so terrible. Most of them have been with us for years. They're like family." Emma brushed off the idea. "And Cami pledged to keep the staff intact. We talked that through with her. She promised that she didn't want to make any big moves in terms of staffing. In fact she said that in her experience with other takeovers it's imperative to keep things normal in the transition process. Nothing was going to change with the sale, other than Jon and I not being here anymore. We offered to stay on for three to six months to help with the transition, but Cami wanted to hit the ground running. She told us that the Winchester ran so smoothly that she wouldn't even need our help. Of course, now I realize that was a lie."

"Exactly," I said. "If someone on your staff learned that Cami intended to tear down the inn and let everyone go, that could be motive for murder."

"But why attack Jon?" Emma stared above us. Jon was halfway up the stairwell. "Something doesn't add up. That's why it feels like whoever killed Cami is targeting us. What if I'm next? Or they come back to finish up their botched job with Jon? I don't know how I'm going to sleep tonight."

"Don't worry. The Professor will make sure that you're safe and that the inn has been secured before they leave tonight."

"I hope so."

My brief conversation with Emma made me more confident that she was innocent. She wasn't acting like a cold-blooded killer. She was clearly terrified.

Upstairs the choir was singing "It Came Upon a Midnight Clear" in the dining room. Nothing felt clear to me at the moment. This wasn't how I had imagined our holiday staff party would end, but there was no point in dwelling on it.

I watched Nate help Jon navigate three steps that led down to the sunken bar. He got Jon situated in front of the stone fireplace that burned low. The long walnut bar with glass shelves had become the Professor's temporary headquarters. The mood in the bar was solemn. Thomas, Detective Kerry, and the Professor had staked a claim in separate corners. They were interviewing guests one-on-one.

The Professor looked up from his Moleskine notebook. "One moment," he said to the woman he was questioning. "Yes, Juliet?"

I pointed to the box of ornaments. "Is it okay to share these in the dining rooms?"

He gave a nod of agreement and returned his gaze to the notebook.

We left Jon and went into the first dining room. Francine and the quartet had just finished the song.

"That will be all for now," Emma said to Francine. She tugged Nate forward. "Can you say something to the guests?"

"What do you want me to say?" Nate hesitated.

"Just thank everyone for coming and apologize."

Nate reluctantly agreed. He stood in front of the windows where snow continued to fall outside. "Everyone—we want to thank you for your patronage tonight. As many of you know, the highlight of the Dickens feast is usually a visit by jolly old St. Nick. Unfortunately that won't be happening this evening, but he did ask us to deliver these gifts that he and his elves made by hand just for you."

A few people chuckled.

"My mom, Emma, the owner of the Winchester, and I will be coming around and handing out ornaments. We apologize for the strange turn of events tonight and hope that the rest of your holiday season is bright and merry."

I wondered if we should take a moment to acknowledge Cami's death, but Nate was already moving to the table nearest him.

Lance snuck up behind me. "Penny for your thoughts, darling."

"It's going to cost you more than that. I can't seem to make my brain work right now, so there's little chance I could be able to tell you the crazy scenarios it's running right now."

"I can tell." Lance tapped the side of my cheek. "Those beautiful cheekbones start to slouch whenever you're deep in thought."

"Thanks."

"I call them like I see them, but not to worry, darling. Chin up. There is one bit of good news tonight."

"What's that?"

With a look of glee, he rubbed his hands together.

"You've been wanting me to embrace the holidays and join in the revelry, yes?"

"Yes . . ." I was worried about the Cheshire-cat grin on his face.

"Well, darling. You've succeeded. We have a *murder* on our hands. A holiday murder."

Chapter Thirteen

I waited, like everyone else, for my turn to be interviewed. Thomas came to get me and directed me to a table in front of the bar. "Well, Jules, what do you think? Crazy way to end an otherwise perfect dinner."

"The worst."

Thomas tapped on his iPad. "Anything you can add that you haven't already shared?"

He probably regretted asking me that question because I launched into every theory I'd come up with, from one of the McBeths being involved to a disgruntled employee.

"Wow, Jules, how long have we been here?" He glanced at his watch. "You've formulated enough theories for an entire police squad."

"Sorry. You know how my mind starts to spin."

"Hey, I'm not complaining." He pointed to the screen. "I wrote them all down. The Professor will be happy, especially to have such a reliable witness. Oh, that reminds me, do you remember what time it was when you heard the laundry room door slam and saw the footprints in the snow? That's going to be really important in determining the window of time our killer had to operate."

I wished I had paid closer attention. "It had to be around eight, give or take five to ten minutes."

"Okay, I can work with that." Thomas made a note. "You are free to go. I'm sure the Professor will follow up tomorrow."

I said good night to my staff as they departed and then to Mom. "Are you sticking around?"

She nodded to the Professor who was sitting next to Emma. "He's my ride."

"Do you want me to wait with you?"

"No, you go, honey. I'll be fine." She wrapped her hands around a steamy mug of tea. "Doug shouldn't be too much longer, and I know you have to open the bakeshop in the morning. Go get some sleep."

"Like that will happen."

She gave me a knowing smile. "True. Go try to rest."

"I'll see to that," Lance replied, joining us with my wrap and coat. He kissed Mom on each cheek and escorted me to the door. I would have loved to hear the Professor's theory, but to be honest I was tired and if I didn't get some sleep, I would be worthless tomorrow.

We exited the Victorian inn in silence. The newly fallen snow cast an angelic glow on the grounds. Twinkle lights reflected against the brilliant white layer of icy snow. Ashland slept in peaceful slumber, unaware of the darkness that had descended on the Winchester.

I buttoned my coat and stuffed my hands in my pockets.

"Out with it," Lance demanded as we crunched through two inches of fresh snow.

"With what?"

"Don't toy with me, darling. You snuck off sleuthing without me. I put on a pretty face for your team, but we're alone now and I want all of the gory details. Do not leave out one single thing."

It felt freeing to replay the night for Lance. He hung on my every word. I was barely aware of the fact that we were halfway down Main Street by the time I finished.

He clapped his gloved hands together. "As I suspected."

"What did you suspect?"

"Nefarious doings at the Winchester. Something is amiss with the McBeth family, and I'm putting my money on the kid."

"The kid?"

Lance huffed. "Scrooge. The son. It's obvious, isn't?"

I nearly slipped on an icy patch. Lance caught my arm. "Obvious how?"

"Why does anyone work in a family business as long as Nate has?"

"Because he enjoys it?"

He scoffed and addressed me as if I were a schoolgirl. "No, darling. Not at all."

"I happen to love working for my family business."

"That's because Torte is the exception to the rule. Who wouldn't want to work with your charming mother and be surrounded by gorgeous pastries all day?"

I didn't bother with a response. We passed Ashland Springs Hotel where a twenty-foot Christmas tree draped entirely in gold decorated the lobby.

"Exactly." Lance gave me a triumphant nod. "Not so for poor, blithering Nate. I'd bet my last dollar that he has been hanging on all of these years for his inheritance. Like an understudy waiting in the wings, he has toiled away at the inn, patiently waiting for his chance to take over. It's textbook really. He thinks that he's due ownership with his parents' retirement. When he learned that they had sold the inn right out from under his feet, he formulated a plan. A deadly plan."

"Maybe."

Lance snapped, "Not finished, darling. One moment, please."

I rolled my eyes.

"Think about it. You learned that Cami had no intention of keeping the Winchester as the quaint, quintessential Ashland landmark that it's become. No, no, she wanted to bring in the sledgehammers. You know what that means?"

I shook my head.

"Guess who else would have gotten the hammer?"

"Nate."

"Yes, Nate, the entire staff—everyone. You said it yourself. Cami declined the McBeths' offer to stay on during the transition. Why? Because her master plan included giving Nate and their staff the boot. Nate must be the killer. He lost his chance at finally playing a grown-up role at the inn and he was about to lose his job."

"It's possible." I sighed. "But he and his parents genuinely care about one another. I can't imagine him poisoning Jon."

"Desperate times." Lance scooted around a small branch on the sidewalk. It must have snapped from the weight of the snow. "Absolute desperation. He fits the bill perfectly. Motive. Check. Means. Check and Check." He made a check in the air with his index finger. "Yes, yes, darling. We're on the right trail. I can feel it. Who else knows the Winchester as well as Nate? And he 'left in a huff.' Ha! I doubt he left at all. He could have snuck out the laundry exit, cut the power to the building and the generator, and then slipped into the dining room unannounced through the employee entrance to kill Cami. It's no coincidence that he suddenly had a change of heart and showed up shortly after the murder."

"I agree. I do, but I still can't picture him doing anything that would risk harm to his father. There was a real tenderness between them."

"Right. Because he's probably heavy with guilt at the moment."

We had made it back to the center of the plaza. Diners and shoppers had gone home for the evening, but the dazzling lights glinted in the fluffy snow. A plow rumbled up Main Street leaving a wake of powder in its path.

"I suspect that Nate did some reading up on things he could safely slip into his father's drink that would put him in a nice winter's sleep, but not do any lasting damage. He needed a diversion. The ornaments, the seating chart, Santa slumped in the cellar. It all adds up. Don't deny it. In some ways we should give him credit. It was a well-thought-out plan. I almost hope that I'm wrong. Otherwise our sleuthing will be over before it's even had a chance to start."

"I hope you're wrong because I think it would destroy Emma and Jon if Nate ends up being a killer."

"On the bright side it would likely give the Winchester

some killer press. Can't you see the headline now? 'Scrooge Behind Bars. Dickens Dinner Turns Deadly.'"

"Lance, you're the worst." I punched him in the shoulder.

He massaged his arm. "And you, darling, are much too serious." We stopped in front of the massive tree in the center of the plaza that was twinkling with hundreds of red, yellow, blue, green, and purple lights. "It's off with you. You need your beauty sleep tonight, but I do have an idea."

"What's that?"

"Now that you've turned me into a regular Christmas-crazed maniac, I'm going to have to deck my own halls. What do you say about a diversion tomorrow?"

"Sure. What are you thinking?"

"This." He pointed to the towering evergreen tree. "Let's go tromp through the mountains and cut down a tree. Are you with me?"

I kissed his cheek. "I thought you would never ask. I'll pack a thermos of hot chocolate and some snacks."

"It's a date, darling." He blew air kisses as we parted ways. "Don't worry your pretty little head about the murder. We'll trek through the forest tomorrow and devise a game plan for snagging the killer too."

I wasn't sure about snagging a killer, but there was nothing I loved more than heading out into nature in search of the perfect Christmas tree. The idea of pulling on my favorite pair of boots, a wool sweater and hat, and crunching through the snow sounded like an ideal way to silence the barrage of questions and concerns about the deadly turn of events that were assaulting my head.

Chapter Fourteen

The next morning, as usual, I was the first person to arrive at Torte. I made a strong pot of coffee, warmed up the ovens, and cranked some holiday tunes. The meditative act of baking alone was just what I needed. And I knew exactly what I wanted to bake this morning—Mom's famous Antoinettes. They were a holiday classic—a simple butter cookie with chocolate and raspberry.

I started by creaming butter and sugar together. Next, I added a splash of almond extract and a touch of salt. The Antoinette base was a basic spritz cookie that didn't require a leavening agent or eggs. I finished the batter by slowly incorporating flour and a dash of salt. Now came the fun part—rolling the dough into small balls.

I rolled up the sleeves of my red fleece and dug my hands into the soft dough. The Antoinettes were best when bite-sized, so I rolled tiny balls not much bigger than the size of a dime and placed them on baking sheets lined with parchment paper. Once all of the cookie sheets were filled, I used my thumb to press down each dough ball. The uniform flattened circles were now the size of quarters.

They wouldn't take long to bake. I slid the baking trays into the oven and set a timer for five minutes.

Usually I could tell the cookies were done by their buttery, aromatic scent. They might need longer than five minutes, but I didn't want to risk overbaking them and having them turn crisp. I wanted cookies with a golden exterior and a soft interior.

While the cookies baked I gathered jars of our raspberry jam from the pantry. Each summer during the height of berry season we canned jars and jars of raspberry, blackberry, and marionberry jams. We used our signature jams in just about everything in the bakeshop, from slathering it on thick slices of our brioche to drizzling it over our creamy vanilla concretes in the summer. I always made sure to stock away reserves for the winter. There's nothing like the intense flavor of sun-ripened raspberry preserves served with a stack of our cornmeal hotcakes and hand-whipped cream on a cold winter morning.

My timer dinged. I pulled on a pair of oven gloves and checked on the cookies by gently pressing their centers with my index finger. If my finger left an indent they weren't quite done. I wanted the top to spring back when touched. They needed another two minutes, so I set to work on gathering ingredients for my chocolate buttercream.

The kitchen began to warm. The scent of the almond cookies and the evergreen boughs hanging from the exposed beams brought a smile to my face. Cami's murder felt like a fuzzy memory. Had that only been last night?

I wondered if the Professor had uncovered any new clues as I loaded my arms with confectioners' sugar, vanilla, baking chocolate, salt, and cream for the frosting.

The timer dinged again. I set the frosting ingredients near the mixer and removed the first round of trays from the oven. I set them to cool on racks while I repeated the process with the waiting trays. Since the cookies were dainty they would cool quickly. That meant I could assemble and frost them in plenty of time to serve for the morning rush.

I poured myself a cup of the bright holiday roast we were featuring for the month of December. It had notes of cinnamon and allspice. I added a healthy glug of the cream I would use in the frosting and then savored a long, slow sip. Coffee is my cure for anything.

Before I began whipping the butter for the frosting, I inserted the whisk attachment for the mixer. One way for home bakers to elevate their skills is simply to use the right attachments. Paddle attachments (also known as flat beaters) are excellent for cakes and cookies, while a dough hook is necessary for making bread. Frosting requires a whisk attachment to whip air into the butter. I love watching the process of a stick of butter transforming into airy, fluffy silk.

I whipped the butter and carefully added the confectioners' sugar one cup at a time. Then I added vanilla, salt, and alternated splashes of cream and baking chocolate. Once everything had been incorporated, I set the mixer to high speed and let it whip for eight to ten minutes, checking it every once in a while, to scrape down the sides. Whipping is a step that many novice bakers skip, leaving them with a thick and often grainy frosting. Nothing produces a finer buttercream than time. Stephanie once asked Mom how long to beat the buttercream, and Mom hadn't missed a beat with her quick and clever response, "Until it's dead."

That wasn't so far off. I've left buttercream whipping for fifteen minutes and ended up with a luscious smooth frosting. Some pastry chefs argue that beating for too long can cause air bubbles to form, but that's never been a problem for me and can easily be remedied by giving the frosting a good stir with a spatula.

When the cookies cooled, I began assembling them. I started by matching pairs. Then I flipped them over with the flat side up. I spread a generous layer of raspberry jam on one cookie, then I sandwiched it together with its partner. The final step was slathering chocolate buttercream on the top. Soon I had rows of the bite-sized Christmas cookies lining the countertop.

I couldn't resist popping one into my mouth. Memories of childhood flooded me as I bit into the soft, buttery almond cookie with layers of the bright and tangy jam, finished off with the rich chocolate buttercream. It was a good thing that Andy and Steph arrived for the early shift because I might have eaten the entire tray of Antoinettes, without anyone to stop me.

"You made another batch, boss?" Andy snatched two cookies. "We sold out of these in like ten minutes the other day. You could probably bake around the clock and we'd still not be able to keep the case filled."

Stephanie shuffled to the sink to wash her hands. "They are good."

That was high praise at such an early hour.

"Great party last night," Andy said through a mouthful of cookie. He tugged off a heavy ski parka.

"Minus the murder." Stephanie scowled.

"Well, yeah. There was that, but otherwise it was a cool night." Andy pointed to the coffeepot. "You couldn't even wait for me to fire up the espresso machine upstairs?"

"No. I got an early start."

"Story of your life, boss." Andy brushed snowflakes from his hair.

"Is it snowing again?" I asked.

Steph wrapped an apron around her waist. "Yeah. It's coming down hard."

Andy did a little dance. "You know what that means? Mount A, baby! I'm heading up to the slopes as soon as we close. They said there's enough new snow for night skiing all week."

Mount Ashland was less than twenty minutes from the plaza. During the winter months the ski bus picked up snow lovers across the street in front of the Lithia Fountains and carted them up to the mountain for the day. It was always fun to see kids of all ages waiting with boots, poles, and skis. Torte did good business with the ski bus too. We offered our winter version of picnic lunches with premade sandwiches, bags of chips, and cookies.

"I didn't realize it was snowing again." I finished my coffee and started to pour myself another cup.

"Hey, boss, save room. I have a snow-day special in store that you're going to want to try."

"Not to worry, Andy. I always have room for coffee."

He went upstairs to prep the coffee bar for the morning. Stephanie started in on our bread orders with barely a word. I liked to test new lunch specials with my staff, and last night's decadent dinner had given me inspiration for a chicken cordon bleu crescent-roll sandwich. I went to the walk-in and found bacon, chicken breasts, Swiss cheese, sliced ham, and cream cheese.

I started by frying the bacon.

"Sterling's going to be mad he's not here yet," Steph said, kneading bread dough with her elbows. "Bacon is his weakness."

"Don't worry. I'm making this for everyone. If you guys like it, then I'll have Sterling make more for lunch."

Using tongs, I removed the bacon from the frying pan and lined it on cooling racks. I cut the chicken into small cubes and drained the bacon fat, reserving a tablespoon to cook the chicken. Then I rolled and arranged crescent-roll dough in a cross shape on a pizza stone. I layered more dough to form a complete circle without any gaps. I set that aside and mixed cream cheese, garlic powder, onion powder, and black pepper together. I added the cooked chicken to the mixture and spooned it into the center of the dough.

Hopefully this will work, I thought as I pressed slices of ham around the sides of the mixture. Part of being a professional chef is experimenting in the kitchen. Sometimes experiments turn out to be masterpieces and sometimes they turn out to be disasters, but I had tried to impart the message to my staff that it was the process that mattered. Even when a dish didn't come together as I imagined, I learned something in the process.

I diced the cooled bacon and sprinkled it on top. Then I covered the mixture with Swiss cheese. I folded the edges inward to form a round pie.

"What is that?" Stephanie asked, passing by me with a large bowl of dough ready for proofing.

"I think it's going to be a chicken cordon bleu crescent pie, but we'll see how it turns out." I brushed the top of the dough with melted butter and Italian seasoning. "Fingers crossed," I said as placed it in the oven to bake for thirty minutes.

Soon Marty, Sterling, and Bethany arrived. Rosa and Sequoia's shifts began shortly after opening. Everyone was excited about the snow and eager to rehash details from the Winchester last night.

"Do you have the inside scoop for us, Jules?" Sterling asked as he reviewed a recipe for split pea soup with ham. "Also, what smells so good?"

"I'm baking a lunch special." I stacked the finished Antoinettes on a tray to take upstairs. "I'm as in the dark as anyone, and still trying to convince myself that it wasn't a bad dream."

Marty dusted a cutting board with flour. "What a way to end the night. Everyone was in such good spirits."

Bethany organized a stack of custom cake orders. "It's true. I have so many great pictures that I would love to post, but then it feels kind of gross, you know? Are you supposed to share our happy pictures when a woman died?"

"Maybe hang on to them for a little while and we'll figure out how best to use—or not use—them." I was impressed by the flawless precision of my team. Everyone knew what they were supposed to do and were on task without asking for any guidance.

"No problem. It's so pretty outside with the snow that I thought today I would do a whole day in the life at Torte with a variety of inside and outside pics." Bethany's curls bounced as she spoke.

"Good plan." The chicken cordon bleu pie was ready. When I removed it from the oven everyone let out a collective moan. The crust had puffed up nicely and turned a golden brown. When I cut into the pie the melted Swiss oozed out the sides. "Everyone want a taste?" I cut slices for my staff and served them.

"Jules, this can't go on the special board," Sterling said after eating his slice.

"You don't like it? What else does it need?"

"Nothing. You can't serve this because I'm going to eat all of it now." He pretended to try and swipe Andy's plate.

"No way, man," Andy said through a mouthful of the savory pie. "It's all mine."

"What about your date from last night?" Sterling teased. "Aren't you going to save a slice for her?"

Bethany stabbed her fork into her pie.

"We're not at that stage yet. I have to be serious about a girl before I share this with her." Andy huddled his plate next to his chest.

"It's really good," Marty agreed. "A holiday lunch classic, I would say."

We had a quick review of the morning while everyone finished their slices of my latest creation. Sterling would make two more chicken cordon bleu crescent pies and the split pea soup for our lunch special. We would serve two types of grilled cheese with the soup, a traditional cheddar on our white bread and a panini with Havarti and thinly sliced red peppers and green olives. Marty would oversee holiday breads and rolls. Bethany and Steph would tag-team our custom cake orders as well as our pastry case offerings.

"I have a feeling it's going to be a mob scene today with the snow, so be sure to speak up if you get bogged down or need help. I'll try to float and have Rosa do the same."

I almost wanted to have us all put our hands together and cheer, "Go team Torte!" as we broke off, but instead, I scooted upstairs.

Andy stood ready behind the espresso machine. The scent from the kitchen had wafted upstairs. I was engulfed in the wonderful smell of bread and Andy's freshly ground coffee beans. "It already smells divine up here and we're not even open yet."

"That's how to draw them in, boss." Andy waved his hands over a shot of espresso in an attempt to waft the scent toward me.

"I like it, but I don't think that drawing people in today is going to be a problem. The first snow day of the season and at Christmastime—it's a bit of divine intervention." I noticed a bundle of pine needles next to the shiny espresso machine. "Does your latest experiment involve pine?"

He grinned. "It does." In a flourish of quick movements Andy reached for a bottle of house-made ginger syrup, pulled a shot of espresso, steamed whole milk, and snipped tiny sprigs of pine needles on the top of the latte. He finished the drink with a dusting of gold sugar. "Here, tell me what you think, and be honest. I'm calling it Ode to the Bard. It's a spicy latte infused with old-world flavors and a hint of pine. Be honest, boss. I won't freak out if you hate it."

"As if I could ever hate anything you create, Andy." I took the drink. Andy had designed an outline of a star from the foam. "It's too pretty to drink."

His cheeks warmed from the praise.

The scent of the pine opened my sinuses as I took a taste of Andy's Ode to the Bard latte. It was beautifully balanced between the creamy milk, punch of sweet ginger, and the herbaceous pine needles. "This is incredible."

Andy's smile widened. "You think so? It's not too out there?"

"We had a cheese tea latte special on the board for a month. This is tame in comparison," I teased. The cheese tea latte had been a sore subject initially because it was Sequoia's suggestion. Andy came around quickly when customers raved about the unique offering. I loved encouraging our guests to stretch their palates and try something they might not find at a chain coffee shop. "I think you should add it to the holiday special board."

"Will do, but I'll make sure Sequoia likes it first. We made a pact to have each other's back when it comes to the specials board. It's better if we both really love a drink. That way we're more likely to talk it up to customers."

"And to think you didn't want us to hire her."

Andy hung his head. "I know. Stupid. She's great. I don't know what I'd do without her. We make a great team."

I smiled internally. Knowing that our staff was operating as smoothly as a freshly whipped batch of buttercream brought me tremendous relief.

We finished morning prep, and as expected the minute we flipped the sign on the front door to OPEN a large crowd burst inside. Torte's front windows soon steamed with the heat of bodies and hot-from-the-oven pastries. The atmosphere was light and happy. It reminded me of my school days when classes were canceled early, and I would walk to Torte through the snow to help my parents feed the hungry crowds.

I didn't have a minute to spare during the first few hours we were open. Between chatting with customers and running up and down the stairs with fresh trays of sweets, I had worked up a sweat by mid-morning. There was a brief lull in the rush, so I took the opportunity to grab one of Sterling's egg-and-sausage croissants and a caramel apple cider. I was about to go take a seat at one of the window booths when I saw Tim, the Winchester's wine steward, sitting alone at a two-person table.

"Good morning, mind if I join you?" I asked.

He glanced up from the book in front of him, which was upside down. "Oh, uh—sure."

"You're studying the wine business?" I asked, pointing to the cover of the book. It was titled *An Industry Insider's Guide to Distributing the Grape.*

"Part of the job." He took the book and stuffed it in a duffel bag resting on the floor. "I have to stay up-to-date on the industry, you know. Jon and Emma are great, but they only want to buy regional southern Oregon wines. I keep telling them that we have to expand. Our customers demand it. Many of them are coming from California and expect to be able to drink a label from one of the award-winning Napa vineyards that they're already familiar with."

"But isn't part of the draw to experience the local region's wine?" I asked. The Rogue Valley boasted over one hundred and fifty wineries from bigger producers distributing throughout the States to small, family-owned vineyards like Uva. Wine tourism was booming in the valey. We might not have the same name recognition as some of the more established wineries in Napa, but our Mediterranean-like growing season produced some of the finest grapes in the world.

Tim fiddled with his black tie. He looked like he hadn't changed since last night. "You would think, but what customers say they want and what they actually want are two different things."

I disagreed. At Torte we saw it as our mission to introduce tourists to southern Oregon's bountiful flavors whether that was marionberries in the summer or locally grown Royal Riviera pears in the fall. It was too early in the morning to debate the merits of promoting our region, so I changed the subject. "I'm surprised to see you here this early. I figured that with the police investigation they might have kept staff late."

Tim dunked a chocolate chip molasses cookie into his black coffee. "They did. It was almost one o'clock when I got home to my apartment." He didn't elaborate.

"That really was a shocking turn of events." I hoped that if I kept our conversation light at first, he might be willing to divulge more. "I still can't believe Cami was killed."

"Doesn't surprise me. The woman was a witch."

Maybe I wasn't going to have to tiptoe around the topic after all.

"Did you know her well?" I asked.

Tim snapped off a piece of cookie. "No. I had the unfortunate job of waiting on her for the past few days. She's been at the Winchester for a week. Emma and Jon told everyone on staff that she was here to do some comparison of mid-sized inns of our caliber." He grunted. "Like anyone on staff believed that. We're not idiots. I can see the writing on the wall. The McBeths have talked about retiring for years. It was obvious that Cami was here to inspect the inn as part of a sale agreement." He twisted his narrow black tie again. "That's why I'm up early. I have a meeting this morning. I'm not waiting around for everything to go south at the Winchester. I'm taking my future in my own hands."

I wasn't sure how to respond. I didn't want to betray Jon and Emma's confidence, but it appeared that they had underestimated their staff.

"Not that I blame them," Tim continued. "The McBeths have been good to me over the years. They've been good to the entire staff, but they should have been straight with us. They should have been more up-front about the sale instead of pushing a lame story about Cami being some kind of hotel consultant. I don't buy it and neither does anyone else."

"Was Cami acting like she did at dinner all week?" I decided not to mention anything about the McBeths' retirement plans.

"It's been the worst week of my life." Tim ripped another bite of cookie off with his teeth. "She is the vilest person I've ever met. Her demands were ridiculous, and she was parading around like she already owned the place."

"What kind of demands?" The news that she had been at the Winchester for a week meant that she had had ample time to make plenty of enemies and for rumors of the buyout to spread among the staff. I sipped my apple cider.

"Stupid stuff. She wanted her wineglasses chilled and then complained that I hadn't aerated her wine long enough.

She was furious that we didn't have a specific bottle of Burgundy and wanted me to overnight a case to her at no cost."

I took a bite of the flaky croissant sandwich. Sterling had fried the egg with expert finesse. The yolk was tender with a soft center that oozed as I bit into it. "What did Jon and Emma say?"

"Nothing. They told us to try and meet as many of her demands as we could. The staff was ready to revolt. Everyone hated her. I mean everyone—from the dishwashers to the head chef."

My suspect pool had just widened.

"Whatever." Tim gulped his coffee. "I can find a new job. In fact, I'll probably already have one by the end of the morning. The person I feel bad for is Nate. He thought he was going to have a chance to take over. We talked this summer and he told me that he and his wife had applied for a small-business loan. They were serious about keeping the Winchester in the family. He asked me if I would stay on and help manage the bar. Nate is a master at maintenance. He can fix anything, but said he was going to need help without his parents around. He wanted me to fully take over bar management."

"I wonder what happened," I thought out loud. "It seems like Jon and Emma would want Nate to take over."

Tim shrugged. "I don't know. Nate hasn't said anything. It's a good thing that Cami is dead though because the Winchester was about to have a massive walkout."

"Walkout?" I asked.

Tim dunked his cookie and drank more coffee. "Everyone was going to quit."

"Surely not *everyone*."

"No, everyone." He looked around us for a second. "Don't repeat this because I do feel bad for Jon and Emma—like I said, they've always been great bosses—but I'm the one who was organizing the walkout. They might have wanted to keep us in the dark about Cami taking over, but I overheard a conversation between them the second night of her stay. They were down in the wine cellar. I wasn't trying to eavesdrop. I was just doing my job—the end-of-service inventory. I wasn't expecting anyone to be downstairs, but I heard arguing." He didn't sound particularly remorseful about listening in to the McBeths' private conversation, but then again if he thought his job was in jeopardy I couldn't exactly blame him. "Jon was really upset. He kept saying that Cami was violating the terms of the contract. Cami was condescending. She said something about them being small-time and that they should have a lawyer review the paperwork before they signed off."

"Did they go into any specifics?" I dabbed my sandwich into the runny egg yolk on my plate.

"No. I didn't stick around to hear any more. I didn't want to get caught, and I finally knew that I wasn't imagining things. I had proof that the McBeths were selling. That was all I needed. They were so busy running around after Cami, trying to kiss up to her, that they didn't show up to our preservice meeting. We have a brief staff update every night before dinner service. I had just gotten a new shipment of wine in from the Applegate and I wanted everyone to taste it, so they could help suggest it to the dinner guests. Since the McBeths weren't around, I used the opportunity to fill the staff in on the sale. We decided as a group to stage a walkout. It was supposed to happen today. We wanted to protest the sale and make it clear that none of us were going to work for that beast. I would rather work five jobs around town than work one minute for that woman."

I took another sip of my cider and tried to gather my thoughts. Tim seemed forthcoming and didn't appear to be hiding his disdain for Cami, and yet at the same time he could easily be lying. He and the entire Winchester staff had motive to kill her.

"The problem is I don't know what I should do now. I feel like I need to tell the McBeths that we knew and that we don't blame them for the sale, but it's weird with Cami turning up dead last night." He took a swig of coffee and pushed back his chair. "I should go. I've got an interview across the street. Then I told Nate I would meet him at the inn. You should have seen him last night. He was like a different guy."

"What do you mean?"

"After he learned that Cami was dead, he was practically dancing around the bar. Last night things came to a head. Cami went off on him. They got in a huge fight about the sale of the inn before dinner service started last night."

"What?" I stood and gathered my dishes.

"Yeah. It was nasty. She flipped out in the kitchen right before the guests arrived. She fired Nate, who laughed in her face and told her that he would like to see her try to fire him. It was bad—like a scene from one of those day-time talk shows."

"Then what happened?" I asked as we walked to the front together.

"I don't know. The next time I saw Nate he was in costume and ready to go as Scrooge. I guess Emma or Jon must have talked to her. I stayed out of it, but it was all the more fuel for our staff walkout. She fired me too, remember? I told Emma I was going to quit on the spot when that happened, but Emma begged me to stay. She said she would make sure I didn't have to have any more interactions with Cami as long as I would agree to at least finish service."

"Right."

"No one liked that woman." He shifted his duffel bag. "You should have seen her and Francine La Roux, you know the singer? They had a physical fight."

"What?" I moved closer to the Christmas tree to make room for a group of teens coming inside for snow day treats.

"Yeah. I had to break them up. Francine was getting ready upstairs. She likes a glass of whiskey before her performance, so I brought one up to her room. Cami was there. Francine had her in a chokehold. I thought she was going to kill her. If I hadn't been there, I think she might have." Tim glanced at the clock next to the chalkboard. "I have to go. See you around."

He left, letting a gust of wind in through the front door. I watched as he crossed the street and walked past the snow-capped fountain. His path led him straight to the steps of the Merry Windsor. Was he meeting with Richard Lord? He must be desperate for a job if he was willing to work for Richard.

I shut the door and returned inside. My conversation with Tim had been very enlightening. The Winchester staff had planned a walkout, they knew about the sale, and Cami had fired Nate. I wasn't sure what any of it meant yet. But I did know one thing—everyone at the Winchester had motive to kill Cami.

Chapter Fifteen

The morning wore into early afternoon. More and more people appeared on the plaza as the skies cleared and the cold winter sun shone down on the glittery newly fallen snow. The view from Torte's front windows made me want to pull on a pair of snow boots and drag my old sled out of the attic.

The chicken cordon bleu crescent pie was such a hit that we sold out of it in an hour. One customer begged Rosa to make it a daily feature. Since our primary focus at the bakeshop was our artisan coffee and pastries, we rotated our lunch specials. It was a way to keep the menu fresh and give my team a chance to try new recipes. I overheard Rosa promise that we would feature it again soon.

I went downstairs to check in on the kitchen. Marty was on lunch break. Stephanie was out delivering two custom cakes, Sterling was scrubbing the stove, and Bethany was dipping shortbread cookies into melted dark chocolate. The kitchen was divided into sections to make workflow as smooth as possible. On the far wall the built-in wood-fired oven smoldered with red coals. Long, stainless steel pizza paddles hung next to it. The brick oven was the jewel of the kitchen. When we had started renovations on the basement, we had no idea our contractors would unearth the oven under decades of old Sheetrock. Everything that we baked in the pizza oven tasted better infused with the scent of hickory or applewood.

The center of the rectangular kitchen housed our baking stations with rows of powerful mixers and ample countertops for rolling dough. We had installed extra overhead lighting above the decorating station where Bethany was dipping shortbread. The meticulous task of design work required specialized tools like frosting tips, paintbrushes, edible-icing pens, and silicone molds. The opposite end of the kitchen was Sterling's domain with the gas range and space for chopping and dicing veggies.

"Are those the winter solstice cookies?" I asked Bethany after washing my hands with lavender soap and tying on a clean apron.

"Yeah." Bethany plunged half of a cookie in bowl of melted chocolate. "They're looking cute, aren't they?"

"For sure." I was impressed with her perfectly tempered chocolate and even lines on the cookies. Each had been dipped to the midpoint in the shiny dark chocolate.

"When the chocolate cools, I'll dip the other side in white chocolate." Bethany looked over her shoulder to the sink where Sterling washed dishes to the beat of whatever was playing on his headphones. "Can I talk to you for a minute?"

"Sure. Here or do you want to go sit down?" I glanced to the seating area. The couch was empty, but there was a group of teens hanging in the lounge chairs.

"No. Here is fine. I'll keep working and Sterling isn't listening anyway." She made sure to allow any excess chocolate to drip before placing a cookie on parchment paper. "I have a confession to make."

"What's that?" I was glad that Bethany felt comfortable confiding in me. Mom had always lent a listening ear to customers and staff. Her ability to actively listen without placing any judgment on outcome was a rare gift.

"It's about last night." Bethany whisked the warm chocolate. "I have a confession to make. I didn't bring a date. That was my cousin."

"Oh." I wasn't surprised by this news given the family resemblance and Bethany's awkward introduction of her "date" last night.

"I wasn't going to lie, but I got flustered when I saw Andy's date. She's gorgeous. Did you see how skinny she was? I have to lay off the brownies."

"Bethany, you're beautiful. Don't compare yourself to Andy's date, or anyone else for that matter." I met her eyes.

She stuck her pinkie in the chocolate and licked it. "Who am I kidding anyway? I'll never give up chocolate."

"Never give up anything for a guy."

"Good advice, Jules." She dipped the next cookie. "It was mortifying. I'm pretty sure everyone at the table figured out I didn't have a real date. It's so embarrassing. Andy was obviously totally into his date and I brought my cousin. He must think that I can't even get a date."

"I highly doubt that." I handed her a new stack of cookies.

"No, you missed it. You were gone but Andy asked

my cousin how we met. I pinched him under the table so hard to shut him up and then blabbered some stupid story about meeting him at the costume shop where we were both searching for Christmas costumes. Why would I even need a Christmas costume? That's so pathetic." Bethany flicked the spatula. "My cousin texted me this morning to tell me I left a mark on his leg. I was sure he was going to say he was my cousin. Can you even imagine? Apparently, Andy met his date skiing."

"Bethany, I don't think you should dwell on it. I know it's hard to have perspective, but I'm sure that no one else had any clue."

"Oh no, they did. I could feel my neck burning as I just kept embellishing my story with more unbelievable details. It was like my mouth was being controlled by a puppeteer or something. I ran out of the dining room to go splash my face with water. You know how red I turn."

Even in the retelling, her face had started to blotch.

"What am I going to do? Every time I've seen Andy today my neck does this." She pointed to the patchy red spots.

"Here's the thing, I think you should try to let it go. Your secret is safe with me and I'm betting it is with Steph too, right?"

Bethany nodded.

"Good. Then just try to distract yourself and give it a little time. In a few weeks, you'll look back on this and laugh."

"I wish." Bethany poured a splash of cream into the chocolate and gave it a stir. "It's totally obvious that I have a crush on him, isn't it?"

"Maybe to you, but not to Andy."

"I hope you're right."

Sterling pulled an earbud from one ear. "We're down to the last two bowls of soup. I'm going to run upstairs and let them know. Anything need to go up?"

Bethany grabbed a tray of Neapolitan cookies. The layered red, green, and white cookies were sandwiched with apricot jam and raspberry jam and topped with chocolate. They were a popular seller. "This is the last of these for the day too."

Today was Sunday which meant that we closed early. Whatever was left in the pastry case was it for any customers who came in after lunch. Sterling took the tray of Neapolitans.

Bethany waited until he was out of earshot. "I appreciate you listening, Jules. Sorry to be so needy. Love sucks."

"You don't have to tell me. I've always blamed Mom for naming me Juliet. Do you know how much pressure there is in a name like that?"

The redness in her cheeks subsided. "True. That's much worse than my crush. I bow down to you." She bowed her head. "There was another reason I wanted to fill you in on my disastrous night—it has to do with the murder."

"Really?" I walked to the pizza oven to separate the wood embers.

"I already told the police this last night, but I know that you've helped the Professor in the past, so I thought you might be interested in hearing what I saw."

"What's that?"

"Well, after I fibbed my way through a fake story of meeting my date, aka cousin, I ran to the bathroom to splash water on my face. The main hallway bathroom was occupied so I went downstairs. I know I shouldn't have, but I was so flustered that I just needed a few minutes to hide and to try and pull myself together."

I walked back to the decorating station.

"I thought maybe there would be a bathroom down there, but I ended up in the wine cellar. Well, at least I started to go in the wine cellar." She finished dipping the last cookie in chocolate.

What had Bethany seen? My pulse sped up.

"When I opened the door, I saw Santa and a woman toasting with shot glasses."

"You did?" I interrupted. Why hadn't Jon mentioned that last night?

"Yeah. They didn't see me though, so I got out of there pretty fast. I could tell that they were deep in conversation, and the woman wasn't his wife."

"Who was she?"

Bethany placed the final cookie on the parchment and took the empty bowl of chocolate to the sink. "I don't know. Santa was blocking most of my view, so I couldn't see her. I know it was a woman from her voice. I saw her hand, if that helps. She had red nail polish. That's what I told the police last night. They asked if I would recognize the hand. Isn't that crazy?"

"How do you know it wasn't Emma—Mrs. Claus?"

"Because I saw Emma on my way downstairs. She was in the kitchen talking to our waiter when I ran by."

The mystery woman with red nail polish had to be the person who had spiked Jon's drink. But again, why didn't he mention that to me or to the police? Was he trying to keep something from Emma? Had I misread their relationship? From the outside they appeared to be a strong couple, but could there be cracks in their marriage?

"I'm glad you shared that information with the police. I'm sure it will be helpful." I grabbed a sponge to wash down the counter.

"Except now I'm going to be staring at women's hands." Bethany unwrapped bars of white chocolate. "The Professor asked me to keep my eyes and ears open. He said you never know when a voice might trigger a memory."

"That's good advice."

"I hope it's helpful and they find the killer. At least then something good would come out of my embarrassing night." She broke the bars into small pieces and placed them in a saucepan along with heavy cream.

Sterling returned to ladle the last of the soup and Marty came back from lunch break. Bethany began dipping the other half of the cookies in white chocolate while I reviewed orders for the next day. I wasn't sure what she had seen, but I was sure of one thing: Jon had lied. He had made the sale of the Winchester sound like a breezy process and insisted that nothing would change when Cami took over management. Nothing could be further from the truth. Had he been trying to save face, or was there another reason he had been less than honest about the Winchester's future?

Chapter Sixteen

Lance called as I gathered dishes from a few straggling lunch tables to say he would be down in five to steal me away for a tree-hunting excursion before it got too dark. I checked in with Andy and the team in the kitchen to make sure everything was under control before I left.

"Are you good with closing up?" I asked Andy, who had already started wiping down the espresso bar and inventorying product.

"You bet. Sequoia and Rosa are boxing up the few remaining pastries to drop off at the shelter, and then as soon as this baby is shiny, I'm hopping on the shuttle and heading up to Mount A." He massaged the espresso machine with a soft cloth rag.

"Have fun, but don't break any bones. I need you intact for the rest of the holiday season."

"Not to worry, I know how to fall." Andy winked. "And I know how to shred."

"Are you meeting anyone on the mountain?" I set the dishes in a tub to take downstairs.

"My snowboarding bros are already up on the summit.

They'll probably be hanging at the lodge, if they've been doing runs all day. I'll find them."

I considered asking about his date, but it wasn't my place to get in the middle of staff relationships.

The bell jingled on the front door and I turned to see Lance standing in the doorway. It was all I could do to stifle a laugh at the sight of his sheepskin hat with ear flaps, thick buffalo plaid coat, and steel-toed boots.

"Lance, what are you wearing?"

"My casual clothes, darling. I didn't want to ruin a suit."

"Those are your casual clothes? You look like a lumberjack."

He did a spin. "We are cutting down a tree, aren't we? As they say, 'if the shoe fits.'"

Fair enough. I said good-bye to everyone and grabbed my wool hat and mittens, along with a thermos of hot chocolate and box of Antoinettes that I had packed earlier. Then I followed him to his car.

"Where to?" Lance asked as he slid behind the wheel. "You must know the best spot for tree hunting, no?"

"Usually we would go to Mount Ashland," I replied, buckling my seat belt. "But we'll need to stop and get a permit first." The Forest Service offered five-dollar permits to harvest a tree in the Rogue River–Siskiyou National Forest. With an abundance of trees in the wilderness surrounding Ashland, it was always a favorite holiday tradition to venture into the forest for a hand-cut tree. Not to mention that five dollars was a steal in comparison with prices at Christmas-tree lots, some of which charged upward of eighty to one hundred dollars for a twelve-foot tree.

We stopped at the outdoor store to pick up a permit and then drove south to Mount Ashland, passing organic vineyards and horse farms. The golden hills to the east were layered with snow. We gained elevation, climbing higher into the tree line where sturdy evergreens bent under the recent snowfall.

"What's the gossip so far?" Lance shifted into four-wheel drive as we turned off the highway and onto the winding road that led to the summit. Red lava rock had been scattered over the packed snow and ice to help cars gain traction on their ascent. The old highway was not for the faint of heart. It was a series of twists and turns with sheer drop-offs on the five-mile climb to the summit. The cloudless blue sky and brilliant winter sun made the snow look like glitter. We passed a herd of deer nibbling on low-hanging moss. As we rounded the next bend the sweeping view of Mount Shasta and the peaks of the Siskiyou range nearly took my breath away.

"I don't know what to think. I'm more confused than ever. It seems like everyone connected to the Winchester has a motive." I told him about my conversation with Tim and what I had just learned from Bethany.

Lance kept both hands on the wheel as he navigated the narrow road. Snow was piled on both sides, making it feel as if we were driving through an ice cave. "It sounds like the Winchester staff was staging a coup. Perhaps one of them opted to take it a step *further*—with *murder*." He threw his head back and laughed. "Sorry, sometimes I can't help myself from rhyming. It's a blessing and a curse to be this clever."

"And humble."

"But of course. Humility is one of my most endearing assets."

"Lance, you're incorrigible."

He tapped the brakes as a ski van headed down the highway skimmed our side of the narrow road. "Darling, if you toss such easy bait into the water, I'm simply going to have to cast away and snag it."

We reached a spot about halfway up the mountain that was popular with cross-country skiers and snowshoers. Lance pulled into the parking area. There was only enough space for five or six cars and less than an inch to spare where Lance squeezed us in between an SUV and a car with ski racks attached to the top. "Good thing we're both svelte."

Lance sucked in his breath as he got out of the car. I stood as tall as possible to keep from bumping into the SUV. He went around to the trunk and proceeded to pull out item after item—a glistening silver saw that had obviously never been used, a balaclava, a scarf, a wool buffalo plaid blanket that matched his jacket, and a retro sled.

"Are you Mary Poppins?" I asked, peering into the trunk. "What else do you have hiding in there?"

"You jest, but I come prepared and ready for battle."

"Battle, as in, with a Christmas tree?" I craned my neck toward the sun. "You hardly need a balaclava. It's a beautiful sunny afternoon."

Lance tossed the scarf around his neck. "You never can be too careful. Frostbite on the cheeks. Shudder." He took my advice and left the balaclava behind. Instead he tugged on a pair of leather gloves. "Imagine if this delicate skin had to touch actual dirt." He threw a gloved hand in the air. "Wait, wait, banish the thought. It will never happen."

We loaded the sled with the supplies, including my thermos of hot chocolate and the cookies. I didn't bring up the fact that we were also going to somehow have to fit the tree on the sled.

The smell of pine and the cool air brought a quickness to my step. Winter crows circled above. Southern Oregon's conifer forests were some of the most dense in the world. We trekked past Douglas firs, ponderosa pines, white fir, sugar pines, and cedars. The contrast of the evergreen trees against the white snow reminded me of a picture postcard. In the distance I could hear the happy sound of children's laughter echoing from the sledding hill.

We followed the main trail that was used by cross-country skiers until we hit a fork. "Which way?" Lance asked.

"Either." I pointed to the left. "That trail will take us to the sledding hill." Then I pointed the other way. "That trail goes for miles and miles. We're inside the boundary now. Basically any tree you see from here on can be yours as long it's under twelve feet."

Lance tried to clap but the sound was muffled by his gloves. "Excellent, on with the hunt!"

I had figured that Lance might tire of snow in his boots or complain about frostbite, but I was mistaken. He chattered on about his earliest Christmas memories before his mother died as we traipsed through the snow. "I must admit that I had forgotten how much fun this could be. Of course back in my day we didn't need a Forest Service permit. We simply went out onto our family land

and I watched in awe as my father hacked down not one but three or four trees. My mother liked one for the dining room, another for the foyer, and of course a grand fir in the living room."

I hadn't expected our outing to trigger happy memories for Lance. Although the mountain air and exercise had lifted some of my anxiety over Cami's murder.

"You should have seen the family chateau back in those days, Juliet. My mother had quite the eye for design thanks to her Parisian roots. She mastered the art of simplicity and elegance. In fact, you remind me of her in many ways." Lance's eyes misted.

"Thank you, Lance. I wish I could have met her." I patted his arm with my glove.

"As do I. She would have absolutely adored you and Helen." He froze in his tracks and flicked the saw as if he were choreographing a sword fight on stage. "There it is! Look no further. We have found the *arbre de Noël* as my mother would have said."

I looked in the direction of his saw. The ponderosa pine that Lance had lasered his eyes on must have stood nearly twenty feet tall and ten feet around. The late afternoon sun hit the top of the tree like a spotlight. I half expected to hear the sound of a swelling orchestra as I squinted to block the sun.

There was no way we could cut it, let alone get it back on top of his car. "Lance, that's a giant. It has to be close to if not over twenty feet tall."

He marched up to the tree's base, kicking up snow as he went. "This? It's barely over my head." He attempted to prove me wrong by raising his hand over his head and touching the top of the tree.

"You're not even close." I dragged the sled behind me.

"How far away is the top from the tip of my fingers? Five, six inches?"

"Try feet."

"No! Don't say such a thing." He skirted away from the tree, yanked my arm, spun me around, and pushed me against it. "Raise your arm in the air, darling."

I acquiesced.

Lance scowled. "Fine. Maybe it's a tad too tall."

"Right, just a tad." I laughed. "What about that one over there?" I directed his attention to a ten-foot tree that was nicely shaped with a branch at the top that would be the perfect spot for a Christmas star.

"Humph. It's not very tall." Lance slunk over to the tree. He walked around it three times before he finally retrieved the blanket from the sled and placed it at the bottom of the tree. "I suppose it will do."

Lance was full of surprises. He made quick work of the trunk, sawing with gusto and felling the tree in a matter of minutes. The log slice was as clean as a surgeon's incision.

"Wow. That was impressive."

"Darling, I never said that I didn't *know* the family business. I just said I didn't enjoy the family business."

"I stand corrected." I unpacked the thermos and poured us steaming cups of cocoa. I handed him a mug and an Antoinette. "Cheers to a successful Christmas tree adventure."

We drank the hot chocolate and polished off the entire box of Antoinettes.

"Any word from your Latin lover?" he asked as we repacked the sled to make room for the tree.

"No. We've been playing phone tag. The holidays are always busy on the ship and then there's the time difference, and my schedule."

"Long-distance love." Lance looped the sled rope over his glove. "What's that saying? 'Distance is temporary, but love is permanent.' True?"

"True." I marinated on that thought in silence. My love for Carlos had endured our time apart. That had to mean something.

The return trek left us both breathing heavily and damp with sweat. "Nothing like some high mountain exertion to get the blood pumping," Lance said when we made it back to the car.

Tying the tree to the top of the car was another challenge. Lance's lumber skills didn't extend to tying trees. I had to convince him to use more than one rope. "If we don't tie it down in more than one spot it's going to slide off the top on our way back down the mountain."

Lance tossed me two bungee cords. "Fine, have it your way."

As soon as the tree was tightly bound to the car, I was happy to be inside with the heat blasting.

"Fancy a hot drink at the lodge?" Lance asked.

The lodge, Callahan's, was at the base of the mountain. It was a three-story A-frame with a green slate roof and massive timber beams constructed to weather the elements. In the summer months the lodge's decks were a favorite spot for bird and flower lovers. Hummingbirds flocked to the lodge's many hanging flower baskets and window boxes. Guests would lounge outside on the deck and the expansive green lawns sipping summer cocktails on red Adirondack chairs.

In the winter people gathered in front of the lodge's massive stone fireplace for Sunday evening jazz and for their famous roasted garlic and baked Brie.

"I would not refuse a warm drink," I said to Lance as he steered the car down the mountain.

When we arrived at the lodge I wasn't surprised to see the parking lot full. Many skiers and snowboarders finished a day on the slopes with dinner at the lodge. The Nordic lodge always reminded me of my travels in the Swiss Alps.

"Looks like we might have company." Lance stomped snow from his boots.

"I think I read that they have Christmas music on Saturday and Sunday nights for the rest of the month."

We walked to the entrance where firewood had been stacked four feet high. Snow shovels, skis, and boots rested on both sides of the hand-carved wood doors. Sure enough, the minute we stepped inside we were greeted with the sound of holiday carolers.

I stopped to take in the rustic beauty of the lodge. Vintage wooden skis hung on the walls. A four-tiered chandelier with cutouts of bucks glowed in the center of the reception area where leather couches and bearskin rugs were arranged in front of a rock fireplace. There were bookshelves with board games, books, and puzzles. A knotty pine staircase led to guest rooms on the second and third floors. For the holidays it had been wrapped in garlands, lights, and bows.

Lance walked with purpose to the dining room and immediately started flirting with the hostess. I doubted there was any chance of us getting a table, but Lance turned and waved me over.

"This way, darling, we have a table near the fire, how does that sound?"

"Perfect." I followed after him as the hostess led us to a round pine table in front of the massive twelve-foot-wide stone fireplace in the dining room, where a fragrant fire was crackling. The warmth and the woody scent made me want to plant a kiss on Lance's cheek. I don't know what he had said to the hostess to score this table, but I didn't care.

I sat next to him and stared at the crackling fireplace. Along the stone mantel there was a collection of wooden beer steins and antique irons. Sprigs of holly berries and tapered candles gave the mantel a festive glow. In front of us was a small stage with a piano and two large speakers. "That's Francine." I almost didn't recognize her and her quartet without their Dickens costumes.

"What a happy twist of fate, yes." Lance studied the menu. "I don't know about you, but I'm famished. I worked up an appetite with all of that sawing. What do you say? Shall we stay for dinner?"

"I could eat."

"One of the many reasons that I adore you. I love a woman who's not afraid to rip into a steak in a man's company." He winked. "And, if we linger for a while we can pepper the singers with questions. Surely they'll have to take a break at some point."

I wasn't going to admit it to Lance, but the same thought had crossed my mind. Maybe one of the singers had seen something. Francine La Roux and Cami had gotten into not one but two fights last night. One that I had witnessed in the dining room and one that Tim had told me about. I wondered if Francine would be willing to divulge any details about their argument.

"Your drink, madame." Lance gave me a half bow as the bartender placed a steaming mug in front of me.

"What is it?"

"A hot buttered rum of course." Lance pointed to his matching coffee cup. "It's their signature drink." He picked up the creamy mug and toasted. "To a day of adventure and an evening of misadventure."

I warmed my hands on the drink. The aroma of brown sugar, butter, nutmeg, vanilla, and cinnamon wafted toward me. I swirled the fragrant drink with a cinnamon stick the bartender had added for garnish.

"This smells amazing."

"Don't dally, drink up." Lance took a sip of his. "Your taste buds will thank me."

The drink wasn't too heavy on the rum, which was a good thing in my opinion. I tasted spicy notes, followed by the creaminess of the butter.

Lance took another sip and then tugged off his plaid jacket. "You're not angry that I took the liberty of ordering a round, are you?"

I couldn't complain. Heat radiated from the earthy fireplace. Between that and the hot buttered rum I would be warm again in no time. Plus, we were just a few feet away from Nothing but Treble. We listened while they performed a few selections from last night along with some newer material.

"Francine really is a talent, isn't she?" Lance commented as he looked over the menu.

"Her range is incredible," I agreed.

"The question is, how's her temper?"

"Does she have a temper?" I whispered.

Lance shot me a sideways nod. "Oh yes, I've heard rumors of a nasty temper that doesn't come out on stage. Only in the dressing room and with the 'underlings' as she calls them."

"Really? Why didn't you say anything about that before?"

"You didn't ask." He clapped as Francine and the carolers finished their set. Francine caught Lance's eye. He motioned for her to join us. Then he stood to greet her with a kiss on both cheeks. "Sit, sit. Let me order you a drink. What's your poison?"

Francine gave a longing glance at Lance's hot buttered rum. "Oh, I don't drink. I'll have tea with lemon, dearest. The vocal folds are being taxed. It's a nonstop tour for the holidays which means I'm putting the chops to work every day. You know how it goes in the biz—first and foremost one must protect her instrument."

"Do you have to worry about overuse?" I asked. Was Francine lying about drinking? Tim had clearly said that she drank whiskey prior to every performance.

Francine looked my way. She wore a long black dress with a sprig of red roses pinned to the chest. It was a completely different style than last night's Victorian caroler

costume. "I don't believe we've been formally introduced." She extended a hand.

I almost let out an audible gasp when I stared at her fingers that were painted with a bloodred polish. Could she
be the woman Bethany had seen in the cellar with Jon?

"Many apologies. Allow me." Lance cleared his throat.
"Francine, this is Ashland's resident pastry muse, Juliet
Montague Capshaw. And, Juliet, I know you're already fa-
miliar with the work of the legendary Ms. Francine La
Roux—singer extraordinaire of stage and screen."

She dismissed him with a flick of her wrist, but I could
tell from the smile tugging at her lips that she relished the
praise. "Enchanted." She held her hand out again, waiting
for me to respond. I wasn't sure if she wanted me to shake
it or kiss it. After a minute of hesitation, I went with the
shake.

"Lovely nail polish," I noted.

Francine stared at her fingers. "Thank you. It's Christmas red. Fitting for the season, wouldn't you say?"

I nodded. I wanted to kick Lance under the table but
didn't trust his response. "We heard you at the Winchester
last night. Your performance was amazing."

"Thank you, dearest. You are too kind." Francine fluffed
her dark hair that I was fairly sure was a wig. Up close
it was obvious that Francine used a heavy hand when it
came to stage makeup.

"It's such a shame that things ended the way they did
though. If it weren't for Cami's death it would have been
a perfect night."

Francine coughed, then she massaged her neck.

Lance waved our waiter over. "A cup of hot lemon tea for the lady, please."

Francine gave him a look of gratitude. She tried to swallow but couldn't.

"Are you all right?" Lance jumped from his seat.

She pressed the sides of her neck and forced a swallow. It looked painful. "Sit. I'm fine. My vocal cords are seizing up on me, that's all."

The waiter came with the tea. Francine timidly took a sip. I wondered if she was in a lot of pain because she grimaced each time she swallowed.

"Dearest," Lance addressed her with her preferred greeting. "I think you should sit the next set out, you don't want to do any permanent damage."

Francine started to protest but winced when she tried to speak.

"Do I need to call the company physician?" Lance asked with concern.

"No." Francine held up a finger. The deep red nail polish was impossible to miss. She swallowed another sip of tea. "There's no need for a doctor." Her voice was husky. "You know as well as I do that the show must go on. The people have come tonight to hear Francine La Roux, and I will give them Francine La Roux."

I've always been suspicious of anyone who refers to themselves in the third person.

Lance placed his menu on the table. "Yes, I of all people understand the draw to give our audiences what they want, but not at the expense of your instrument."

Francine squeezed lemon into the tea. "This will do the trick. I can't leave those three to their own devices.

They'll end up entirely off-key." She looked off toward the bar where the rest of the quartet was drinking a round of hot toddies.

Our waiter returned to take our order. Lance opted for the fettuccine with grilled prawns and I went for a stuffed Tuscan-style chicken. Francine declined dinner.

"Can't you call an understudy?" Lance suggested. "I have the names of some wonderful singers who would gladly step in." He was careful to frame the idea with lavish praise for Francine's abilities. "Certainly, they aren't anywhere near your caliber but in a pinch they'll do."

"No. I will perform tonight as intended. I must." She was insistent to the point that I wondered if there was more to the story.

Lance shrugged. "If you change your mind, let me know. I can make a call and have someone here in five."

That I didn't doubt.

Since it was obvious that Francine wasn't budging, I decided to try and shift the conversation back to Cami's murder. "I take it you're not performing at the Winchester tonight because of the murder?"

Francine scowled. "That's right. My manager had to scramble to find us something for tonight. The holidays are the busiest season, so we can't allow any opportunity to go to waste."

Lance kicked me under the table. I had no idea why.

"Did they have to cancel tonight's feast?" I asked Francine.

"Yes, and it's ridiculous if you ask me." Francine's voice cracked as she spoke. "That foul woman ruined everything."

Chapter Seventeen

What was Francine talking about? Cami ruined every-thing?

Lance beat me to the questioning. "Dearest, did you know her?"

"Know who?" Francine asked.

"Cami—the deceased."

"No." She recoiled at the thought.

"But you just said that she ruined everything."

A look of horror flashed across Francine's face. She tried to speak but nothing came out.

Lance kicked me again.

I shot him a look to knock it off.

Francine coughed twice. "I don't know the dreadful woman. I only had one interaction with her and that was plenty for my taste."

"What did she ruin?" Lance pressed.

"This." Francine swept her hand across the dining room. About half the room was made up of skiers and snowboarders back down from the mountain, drinking beers and refueling with loaded plates of fries smothered with gorgonzola, green onions, and chilis. The other half were diners who had come for a festive evening out. They were dressed for the occasion and sampling stuffed mushrooms, prime rib crostini, and crab cakes. "I'm stuck playing the lodge instead of the Winchester—which attracts more of my crowd, if you know what I mean."

She pushed a lemon wedge into her tea with a spoon and stared at the table next to us where a group of snowboarders in their twenties were drinking pints of frothy beer. "Who knows how long it will be until the police give the McBeths the green light to continue. We could be out of work for the remainder of the season. Do you know that I have been the lead singer at the Dickens feast for the last fifteen years? The McBeths have always given me free rein in putting together my quartet, song choices, everything. The Dickens feast is the best gig in town. Highly revered food, exquisite atmosphere, top-notch customer service, a paying job every night of the week for thirty days, and guests who always leave us lovely tips."

The waiter arrived with our food. Francine slugged more of her tea and then excused herself to go prepare for the next set.

When she was out of earshot I leaned across the table. "Why did you keep kicking me?"

"Because she's lying, darling. She doesn't have a manager."

"She doesn't?"

He scoffed. "No. Don't get me wrong. Ms. La Roux has graced many a stage and even performed in a few movies back in the day. But let me emphasize 'back in the day.' No manager is getting her gigs here at the lodge, or even at the Winchester for that matter."

"Fair enough, but why does that matter? She seems like she likes the attention and flattery. Maybe she's just trying to make herself sound more important."

"Maybe. Or maybe she's the killer." Lance stabbed a prawn.

"I know. Did you see her nails? They were just like Bethany described. Why would she have tried to poison Jon though? Maybe she was trying to stage a distraction? She could have been the one who broke all of the ornaments too."

Lance twisted his fork. "It's possible."

"I still don't understand why Jon wouldn't have admitted that he had shared a drink with someone. Do you think he knows who drugged him and is scared?"

"Perhaps, but that doesn't feel quite right, does it?" Lance swallowed the shrimp. "Let's consider what we do know. Reading between the lines it sounds to me like Francine needed the consistent cash. If she caught wind of the fact that Cami had plans to bludgeon the Dickens dinner to death, that gives her a solid motive for murder."

"That's true." I cut into my juicy chicken breast that had been stuffed with olives, tomatoes, artichoke hearts, and feta cheese. My toes and hands had finally warmed, thanks to the heat from the fire. Snow was piled so high on the deck outside that the wall of windows behind the stage were completely white.

"She was in the dining room when the lights went out," Lance added.

"Was she?" I tried to replay the details of the evening, but some of it was a blur. "She definitely would have known her way around the hotel. Emma told me that they reserve a suite for her for the entire month. That way the quartet can change upstairs and have a quiet space to rest between sets."

Lance was in the zone now. He snapped both fingers. "Spot on, darling! Francine has been performing at the Winchester for decades. She must know the ins and outs of the inn—see what I did there?"

I rolled my eyes.

"She easily could have done the deed and then snuck back upstairs to her suite with no one the wiser." He dug his fork into another prawn. "Juliet, I do believe we have another suspect."

We finished our dinner before Francine and her merry band of singers returned. On our way out, Lance stopped at the hostess station. "Now, remember, use my name when you call for tickets. I want to be sure that you get the best seats in the house."

"So that's how you scored a fireside table," I said on our way to the car. "You offered her OSF tickets?"

"Of course, darling. That's how business is done. I should have sweetened the deal with breakfast at Torte. Then she really would have rolled out the red carpet."

I was lost in thought on the drive home. Could Francine be the killer? She had made no attempt to mask her hatred of Cami, but was the Dickens performance motive for murder?

"What do you say to a nightcap?" Lance asked when we pulled into the plaza. "It looks like there's a crowd at Pucks."

"That hot buttered rum did the trick for me. I think I'll take a rain check."

Lance pointed to the roof of his car. "Not so fast, darling. You're forgetting an important detail. My tree. What am I supposed to do with the wild weed on top of my car? You promised to help. There's no sloughing off your best-friend holiday duties."

"I would never think of it. I just meant that I don't need a nightcap."

"Fine. To my place then?"

Lance's house was up Scenic Drive with sweeping views of downtown Ashland and the east hills. The opulent stone mansion was gated, with a private drive that led to terraced decks that reminded me of the homes I'd seen in the Italian lake district.

The interior was equally posh with marble floors, a grand staircase, and ornate chandeliers. We brought the tree inside. "Where do you want it?" I asked.

Lance pointed to the formal living room with picture windows that reflected the city lights. "It has to go there, don't you think?"

"Absolutely. It's like it was made for a Christmas tree."

We maneuvered the tree into position. Lance's stylish furniture and impressive collection of art were styled in such a way that they could have been a set on OSF's stage. It hardly gave off a warm vibe.

"Do you have decorations?" I asked.

Lance lifted a pitch-stained finger. "Yes, let me wash my hands, pour us some hot tea, and I'll bring out the decorations from the garage."

If Lance's garage was as pristine as his house, it could probably serve as a clean room in a lab.

While I waited, I wandered through the living room, parlor, dining room, and study. Every room was painted a monochrome gray with white trim. None of the mid-century-style teal and gray couches looked as if they'd ever been sat in. I knew that Lance, like me, spent most of his time at work—in his case OSF—but his place reminded me of a set for the stage, not somewhere anyone actually lived.

A few framed photos of Lance with his parents and brother were on display in the study with its floor-to-ceiling bookcases, but otherwise the entire first floor was devoid of anything personal. A wave of sadness washed over me. One lonely tree, regardless of how beautifully we decorated it, wasn't going to fill the void. I decided on the spot to invite Lance to Christmas Eve dinner and Christmas brunch at Mom and the Professor's new house.

He returned with a neatly packed box of gold, silver, and opaque white ornaments. "What are the rest of your holiday plans?" I asked as we strung tiny golden lights around the tree.

"You're looking at it, darling. It's going to be me and a martini in front of the fireplace." He paused and with a hit of a button on a remote control sitting on the coffee table his gas fireplace burst on.

"That sounds great." I formulated my approach to convince him to come spend the holidays with us.

"There's nothing like a reprieve for the soul. I have a stack of new plays to read and headshots to look through.

I plan to spend the next two weeks on my couch before the madness of the new season begins."

"Fair enough." I clipped a silver partridge to the tree. "I have to ask you a favor though."

"Anything, darling. You know that—anything."

"Will you come to Christmas at my mom's place?"

Lance's lips turned down. I knew that he couldn't stomach the thought of pity. "Why?"

"I don't think I can do it alone. Mom and the Professor are so over the moon, which—don't get me wrong—is wonderful, but I've been missing Carlos and Ramiro, and I could really use some moral support and a friend."

I wasn't sure, but I guessed that Lance could see through my excuse.

"What, and leave all of this?" He swept his hand over the tree. The décor felt almost Parisian.

"Please, for me?" I bit my bottom lip and begged.

Lance sighed. "Oh fine. I suppose I can muster up the strength to spend the holiday with you. Only because I find Helen most delightful and the Professor excellent company. What do I bring? What should I wear?"

"Just bring yourself or a favorite bottle of wine." I knew that Mom and the Professor would both be fine with me inviting Lance. "And, it's strictly casual. Come in your pajamas on Christmas morning. It's tradition. Mom will make brunch and we'll lounge around all day, gorging ourselves on food, playing games, watching old Christmas movies."

"How positively charming. It sounds like a scene from a Frank Capra movie."

I could tell that he was secretly pleased with the invitation. We finished decorating the tree and called it a night. I might not have had any answers as to why and how Cami was killed, but at least I could sleep well knowing that my friend wasn't going to spend Christmas alone.

Chapter Eighteen

We were in the mad dash to the finish at Torte for the next few days. Personal orders ramped up in the days leading up to Christmas. It happened every year. People would have grandiose plans of baking pies, cakes, and cookies themselves, but once the calendar approached December 25 they placed frantic calls to the bakeshop asking if there was any chance of getting a dozen sugar cookie cutouts or a Christmas butter stollen. We did our best to say yes to as many people as we could. It meant some late nights and early mornings, but it was worth it.

The closer we came to December 24 the busier we became. There were only three days left until Christmas Eve and I found myself giving the team a daily pep talk.

"We're in the home stretch," I said, kicking off our morning meeting. "I know we're all running on fumes and caffeine." I held up one of Andy's pine-infused lattes. "We're almost there though, so try to keep your spirits up."

"It's hard to do when Richard Lord is your first customer of the morning." Andy stuck out his tongue. "I don't know what that guy is up to, but he's been at the door every morning this week. I'm tired of starting my day with his angry face."

"Let me handle Richard this morning." We reviewed the day's orders and set off to our individual tasks. I wanted to bake some specialty tarts that we could sell as both individual slices and whole versions. The local chocolatier who supplied us with all of our chocolates had dropped off red and white striped peppermint chocolate buttons that would be a perfect decoration for the tart I had in mind.

I started by making a chocolate shortbread crust. In a food processor I combined butter, flour, sugar, cocoa powder, and vanilla to create a crumbly, sandlike dough. After greasing a tart pan, I firmly pressed the dough along the bottom and up the edges and then I set it in the oven to bake for twenty minutes.

Meanwhile I whisked eggs, heavy cream, sugar, cornstarch, and peppermint extract over low heat to form a bubbling pudding. Once the pudding had thickened, I added a few drops of red food coloring to give it a festive candy color.

"Your shortbread is ready, Jules," Marty said, as he delivered the wonderfully crisped and aromatic crust. "The smell of this makes me want to shove it in my mouth." He contorted his face. "I need to walk away now."

I had to agree with him. The entire kitchen smelled like butter and chocolate. I allowed the crust and pudding to cool, and turned my attention to adding whipping cream, sugar, and a splash more of the peppermint extract until it formed stiff peaks.

Now my chocolate shortbread tart was ready to assemble. I carefully removed the crust from the tin. Its fluted edges gave it an elegant appearance. Next, I spread the red peppermint pudding with a flat spatula. Then I layered on the whipped cream and finished it with a circle of the striped red and white peppermint chocolate buttons and a dusting of red sugar.

"That is so pretty," Rosa said when I brought the tart upstairs to be displayed in the pastry case.

"Thank you." I set the tart on the top shelf. "Go ahead and serve this in slices. Bethany is making more in ten and six inches for customers to purchase whole."

Sequoia and Andy had already brewed pots of signature Torte roast and our special holiday blend. "Are we ready to open the doors?" I asked.

"Go for it, boss. Your favorite person is first in line." Andy pointed to the window where Richard Lord's rotund head peered above the wreath.

"Morning, Richard." I unlocked the door. "Things must be slow at the Merry Windsor. My staff tells me you've been here every day."

"Only to keep my eye on you." He pushed past me. This morning he wore a pair of red and green plaid pants and a green sweater that was at least one size too small. I would never understand why Richard insisted on wearing clothes that didn't fit him. "I warned you, Juliet. You're not getting your grubby hands on the Winchester. It's mine. I've already had a number of meetings that have solidified my position."

"You mean by hiring Tim?" I decided to toss Tim's name out there and see how Richard responded.

He huffed. "What do you know about Tim? Have you

been spying on me? I'll go to the authorities. Don't you doubt it."

"I don't." With that I turned and walked away. Richard Lord was never going to divulge anything to me and there was no point in ruining the morning.

Cami's murder took a backseat to baking. We cranked out more chocolate shortbread tarts, cinnamon rolls, rum raisin bread puddings, and last-minute shopping fuel in the form of eggnog lattes.

I took a much-needed break with a cranberry-ginger scone and vanilla spice latte midway through the afternoon, only to find Emma and Jon seated at a booth by the window.

"How are you two?" I asked as I walked by. "Do you have a minute to catch up?"

Emma looked up and offered a wan smile. "We're hanging in. Can you sit for a minute?"

"Sure." I slid onto the bench next to her.

Jon stared at his coffee mug. His face looked as black as his drink.

"Is everything okay?"

"It's all a mess, Juliet," Emma replied. She had broken an angel cookie in half. I noticed her fingernails were also painted red.

"I like your nails. They're so festive."

She studied her hand. "Part of the Mrs. Claus costume. I can never wait for January to switch out the polish. My nails are red for the entire season."

Had they been painted the night of the murder? I kicked myself for not paying attention.

"Are they still investigating Cami's murder?" I asked.

Emma nodded. "Yes. They did give us permission to start the Dickens feast again. It's been back on for the last four nights, but our hearts aren't in it, are they, Jon?"

Jon kept his head down. "No."

"Have the police said any more about Cami's murder? Do they have a suspect?"

Emma cracked the cookie into fourths. "I thought maybe you would know. They haven't told us much, although the news this morning is terrible."

"Why? What's the latest?"

She broke down. Tears streamed from her eyes. Her shoulders heaved.

Jon reached out to console her. He handed her a crisp red handkerchief from his breast pocket. Not many men my age carried handkerchiefs. The Professor and Jon harkened from a different era.

"They think that Nate killed Cami," Emma said between sobs, dabbing her eyes with the red handkerchief.

"Nate?" I wasn't shocked by the news, but I hated to hear that Thomas and the Professor considered him a serious suspect.

"They've questioned him multiple times," Jon said. "Nate was angry with us for selling to Cami. He didn't trust her, and now I wish we could rewind time. He was right. I should have listened to him, but we were eager to sell. We were ready to be done and go spend some time on a sunny beach for a while."

"Do they have evidence linking Nate to the crime?"

Emma wiped her eyes with a napkin. "They're not saying. The only thing Doug could tell me is that the evidence they have on him is connected to the power outage. I wanted to call your mom, but then again, I feel terrible putting her in the middle. I thought maybe she would be here today and could offer some input and advice. I know Doug can't tell us details about the case. I do understand that, but Nate is our only son. He's not a killer. He never would have harmed Cami. You know that, Juliet. You went all the way through school with him."

"I know, I can't imagine Nate hurting anyone," I said. That was true, but I also couldn't refute the fact that Nate had disappeared right before the power went out and Cami was killed. He had a motive and he knew everything about the Winchester. The McBeths themselves had said that he was the inn's resident handyman.

"That's because he's not a killer. He's not!" Emma buried her face in Jon's handkerchief. "What can we do? I don't know how to help him or make this right."

"Did the police arrest him?"

Jon pressed his hands together. "Earlier this afternoon. His wife called us to let us know that he had been taken into custody. We've called our lawyer who is going to recommend someone who specializes in criminal defense."

"Nate isn't a criminal," Emma interrupted him. "He's cooperated with the police and now they've arrested him. I can't believe it and it's only days before Christmas. What are we going to do?"

I couldn't imagine what they must be going through. Having your child (even if Nate was an adult) arrested would be awful. "Emma, you've known the Professor for as long as Mom has. You know how thoughtful and intelligent he is. He must have a reason for arresting Nate. Maybe he's doing it to protect Nate."

"Protect him, how?"

"I don't know." I thought for a minute. Christmas songs played overhead, and the bakeshop was vibrant with customer conversations. The atmosphere felt at odds with our conversation. "I'm as in the dark as you are, but I trust the Professor completely. I'm sure that he's going to be fair in his treatment and I'm also sure that he and his team are following up on every possible lead. Maybe it's just a formality."

Jon shook his head. "They don't make arrests on formality. That's why we're hiring a lawyer."

"Is there anything else that either of you remember about the night that Cami was killed? Or what about the days leading up to her death? I heard that she had been staying at the inn for a few nights before the Dickens feast."

Emma choked on a piece of cookie. "How did you hear that?"

I didn't want to betray Tim's trust, so I made up a little white lie. "I don't think I heard it from anyone specifically. Apparently, she made her presence known around town."

Jon pounded his fist on the table. "Awful woman. Our staff wanted us to ask her to leave; thank God they don't know the truth. If they found out she was about to take ownership of the Winchester, we probably would have had mutiny on our hands."

If he only knew how close he was to the truth.

"We made the biggest mistake of our lives selling to that horrible woman."

Now it was Emma's turn to try and console her husband. "Jon, we didn't know."

"We did though. Nate tried to warn us and now he's locked in a jail cell."

I tried to steer the conversation back to the days leading up to Cami's murder. Rehashing their choices wasn't going to help Nate. "Did you notice anything out of the ordinary during Cami's stay?"

"You mean other than her ludicrous requests?" Emma asked.

"Yes, for example did you see her interacting with any of your staff? What about the group of people she brought with her? Could any of them be suspects?"

Emma rubbed her temples as if trying to stimulate her memory. "It's hard to say because like Jon said she was antagonistic with everyone she interacted with on staff, Francine and the carolers, other guests."

"But there was that incident with Tim," Jon interjected.

My interest was piqued. "What incident?"

"Cami had been going over our books and tax returns for the past five years. It was frustrating because she'd already laid out her offer and we had signed the paperwork. Her lawyers reviewed all of our financials for weeks before the offer came." He took a sip of coffee. "She claimed that there was fat to trim in the budget and our staff. Emma and I tried to explain to her that we've always run lean on staff. You know what it's like during the off-season. We've never hired more than the minimum amount of staff to maintain us because we never wanted to have to worry about laying people off."

Emma nodded. She folded the handkerchief into a

square. "We saw too many of our fellow business owners going through the gut-wrenching process of having to lay people off, right after the holidays, which is just the worst. So sad for everyone involved. Jon and I made a commitment to ourselves from the start to stay lean and try our very best to get by with a small but efficient staff."

"I hear you," I agreed. "Mom and I have had many conversations about how to manage our growth without hiring dozens of people."

Jon waited when Andy came by with a fresh pot of coffee for refills. "We tried to impart that to Cami, but she wouldn't listen."

"What does this have to do with Tim?" I asked.

"Cami came to us the night before she was killed and said she'd found a number of discrepancies in the books. It was like she wanted to add insult to injury. She was already planning to level the inn, but wanted to highlight how terrible we were at managing a staff."

"Discrepancies?"

Emma smoothed the handkerchief with one hand. "Yes. She claimed that someone on staff was stealing from us."

"Who? Tim?"

Jon cracked his knuckles. "Tim's been with us for years. I don't believe it. I think she was trying to stir up more trouble, but yes, she was convinced that our wine inventory counts were off and that someone has been stealing from the cellar for years."

"Do you think that could have anything to do with why the wine cellar was ransacked the night of the murder?"

Emma tapped her index finger on her chin. "I don't know. I guess I never thought of that. We were sure that had to do with the Dickens feast because of the ornaments being broken."

"What if that was a smoke screen of sorts?" I suggested. "Maybe whoever ripped down the seating chart and broke the ornaments wanted to distract you from their real crime—stealing valuable bottles of wine."

Jon and Emma shared a look.

"Did you do a count of your inventory after the break-in?"

Emma shook her head. "The police had us do a brief walk-through. Nothing seemed out of place with our stock of wine, but to be honest that's been a project that we handed off to Tim and Nate. They've been working to digitize our inventory. We've always done it the old way—with paper and pencil. I know that sounds silly, but we had a system that worked. Nate has been begging us to modernize. It's been a slow process. We started with our reservation system."

Jon chuckled. "When we were first open we had all the calls sent to our home phone. Nate was a baby then. Emma would have him propped on one arm and take reservations in our old book with the other."

"That's another thing that Nate was right about. Once we implemented online booking and a payment system it's made our lives so much easier," Emma said. "Now that that side of the business is up and running Nate had started working on a digital system for our employee schedules, dinner reservations, and inventory."

"How did Tim get involved?" I asked.

"Nate recruited him," Emma said. "Tim knows our wine cellar better than anyone. He's done the ordering for us for years now and knows every vintner and winemaker in the Applegate Valley by name."

"And Tim is the only person outside of your family who has those inventory numbers?"

"Yes." Emma's eyes darted from side to side. "Wait, what are you thinking?"

"Nothing. This is just speculation, but if there was a chance that Tim was stealing from you and he learned that Cami was about to make that public knowledge, it would give him a motive for killing her."

They both looked dumbfounded.

Jon finally spoke up. "I did see them fighting outside the wine cellar."

"You did?" Emma sounded surprised. "When?"

"Not long before I blacked out. I caught them by surprise when I came downstairs to start working on pairing ornaments with guests. They both scattered when I showed up."

"Did you tell the Professor any of this?" I asked.

"Maybe. I think I did." Jon took a long drink of his coffee. "I was pretty out of it that night, so to tell you the truth I can't remember. All the details from that night are blurry. I remember bits and pieces, but I don't know if that's from what Emma and the police have told me or if my memories are real." He sounded sincere, but I couldn't help wondering if his fuzzy memory was a convenient excuse for not wanting to reveal that he had shared a drink with whoever had tried to poison him.

"I just can't imagine Tim stealing from us," Emma said. "He's like family."

"There might not be any truth to Cami's accusations," I said. "But I definitely think you should fill the Professor in on all of this. It could be important to the investigation, and it could help clear Nate."

Emma rested her unused napkin on her plate of broken cookie pieces. She handed Jon his handkerchief. "Let's go find Doug now, Jon. That will give us a chance to find out what he has to say about Nate too."

Jon agreed.

"One more thing before you go. Richard Lord was here this morning and said that he is trying to buy the Winchester."

Emma threw her head back and laughed. "Over my dead body."

"We're ready to retire," Jon agreed. "If Richard is our only buyer then I'll work until I drop dead too."

That was a relief.

"It's too bad Nate can't take over." I wanted to see how they would respond.

They shared a look. "We agree. We had hoped he would. In fact, he and Melissa went through the process of getting a loan and we had offered to stretch payments out and do whatever we could to make sure they didn't have a huge financial burden." Emma's eyes misted. "That was always our dream, to pass it on to Nate."

Jon patted her shoulder.

"What happened?" I asked.

"He and Melissa ultimately decided the responsibility was too great. They have young children and Nate had seen how many hours Jon and I put in when he was young. It's one of my greatest regrets. We shouldn't have worked so hard. We should have taken a few more breaks and more family vacations." Her tone was wistful.

"I always thought Nate loved growing up at the inn."

"He did. There were many perks of having full run of the property when he was a kid." Jon looked to Emma for confirmation.

"Jon's right. Nate loves the Winchester, maybe more than we do, but when he and Melissa had a heart-to-heart about the reality of owning a small business, they decided their priority was with their children and we couldn't argue with that. Once we knew that Nate wasn't going to continue the family legacy, we found a broker and started the process of looking for a buyer."

"So Nate wasn't upset with Cami because he wanted the inn?"

"No. He was upset because he didn't think she had the Winchester's best interest in mind, and it turns out he was right." She scooted out of the bench. "We shouldn't keep you, especially when talking about how much work a small business is."

She hugged me, and they left to go find the Professor. As I watched them go, I wondered if the McBeths had been too trusting. Maybe Cami's inspection of their financial records had uncovered a crime. If Tim had been stealing from them, could he also be a killer? The fact that Nate had been the one to opt out of buying the inn changed everything. I had assumed Cami had stolen what he saw as his rightful inheritance, but I had been completely wrong.

Chapter Nineteen

After the McBeths left, I found Mom downstairs in the kitchen with her elbows deep in sweet bread dough. "Hey, I didn't know you were coming in today," I said, kissing her on the top of her head.

"What? And miss the final frenzy of the Christmas rush? Never." She had a spot of white flour on her nose.

"Did you sneak in the back?" I asked as I walked to the sink to wash my hands.

"Guilty as charged." She reached for a rolling pin.

Steph and Bethany both had headphones in at their piping station. Dozens of two- and four-layer chocolate peppermint and white chocolate and cranberry cakes had been iced with a thin layer of buttercream and awaited the decorator's artistic final touches. The chocolate cakes would be finished with decadent chocolate buttercream and hand piped with bright red and white polka dots. The white chocolate and cranberry cakes were frosted with cream cheese frosting and deep red poinsettia buttercream flowers. This level of design work required focused attention, so I wasn't surprised to see both of my young artists listening to their own music while spinning cakes on the wheel.

Marty stood near the pizza oven watching over flatbreads toasting with bubbly layers of mozzarella cheese and basil. Sterling ladled bowls of hearty sausage and potato soup for Rosa who was waiting to take the tray upstairs.

"Things are running better than I expected," Mom said. "Do you remember last year when we had half the staff? I felt like I was seeing bread and pastry dough in my sleep."

"It's true. I was just talking about that with the McBeths upstairs."

Mom frowned. "Were they here? I wish I had known. I would have come said hello. Did they tell you the news?"

"About Nate?" I picked up an order sheet for eight pies.

"Yes. Doug is so upset, but he has to follow the letter of the law."

I gathered butter, flour, salt, and my secret ingredient for pie crust—vodka. "Does he think that Nate did it?"

Mom twisted the sweet bread dough into two long ropes. Then she brushed butter on both ropes. She sprinkled cinnamon and sugar on one side and slathered our apricot preserves on the other. "He doesn't want to believe it. Nate, like his parents, has always been an active member of the community. He even served as president of the chamber a few years ago. It's hard to imagine that he could have done it, but the evidence doesn't look good. The only thing I know is that he had a long chat with a representative from the power company and after that they made the arrest."

Mom twisted the ropes together and placed the sweet bread on a parchment-lined baking sheet.

"Is there any specific evidence linking him to the crime?"

"Doug hasn't said, but there must be. If they only had circumstantial evidence on Nate, I can't imagine Doug making an arrest."

I grated sticks of frozen butter. The key to a flaky pie crust is lots of chunks of butter and I've learned the best way to achieve that is by grating the butter. I simply freeze sticks of butter for thirty minutes in the walk-in freezer. Once the butter is frozen solid, grating is a breeze.

Another pie tip that I learned in culinary school years ago was to always bake a pie in a tin plate. Sure, ceramic and glass plates are prettier for displaying pies, but they don't allow the crust to bake evenly. Pies tend to end up with a soggy bottom if baked in glass or ceramic. At Torte we bake all of our pies in tin plates and then transfer them into beautiful red, teal, and white ceramic plates for display. These pies would be delivered to a nearby business for their holiday staff lunch. We would keep them in the tins and package them in our Christmas boxes tied with red and green twine for delivery.

"Oh, I almost forgot. I invited Lance to Christmas." I used my fingers to fluff up the flaky shreds of butter.

Mom brushed flour on her hands before starting on another batch of the sweet bread. "That's wonderful, honey. We'd love to have him. The more the merrier. In fact, Doug invited Thomas, his parents, and Detective Kerry. We are so excited to host Christmas in our new house that I wouldn't put it past him to start extending invitations to strangers on the street."

"That is in the holiday spirit."

Mom chuckled. "Fair enough. I'm thrilled to have Lance join us." She wrinkled her brow. "How did you convince him?"

"It took some nudging and a plea not to leave me as the only single person at your house." I tried to wink.

"Smart move, Juliet." Mom mixed cocoa powder and spices with chunks of semisweet dark chocolate for the next batch of sweet bread.

I kneaded my pie dough, rolled it out, and pressed it into tins.

"Could there be a sliver of truth in your pitch to Lance?" she asked as she brushed the bread with melted butter.

"What?"

Her eyes held a knowingness that I had never been able to escape. "I mean, is there part of you that is lonely? It's okay to admit that you're missing Carlos and Ramiro."

"Mom, how is that you can still see through me even as an adult? I thought I had outgrown that phase years ago." I poked holes into the bottom of the crust with a fork. In professional pastry kitchens the process is called docking. Poking holes allows air to escape and ensures that the crust won't bubble.

"Oh honey, you'll never outgrow that phase. Our connection is too deep. Do you remember when you were on the ship how one of us would pick up the phone to call the other just as the phone would ring?"

"True." Mom and I had had a standing Sunday check-in call during my years on *The Amour of the Seas,* but inevitably whenever I was thinking about her or missing her the phone would ring and she would be on the other end of the line.

"I'm not trying to pry, but I want to remind you that I'm always here to listen, and that Carlos and Ramiro are welcome too."

A lump caught in my throat. "Thanks, Mom. I know, and I appreciate that, but Carlos and Ramiro won't be coming for the holidays. Carlos is on the ship until Christmas Eve and then he's flying to Spain. They already have plans with Ramiro's mom."

"I understand, but I wanted to remind you that they are always welcome here at Torte, at our new home—wherever."

When Carlos and Ramiro had been in town for the wedding, they had hit it off with Mom and everyone on the team. Ramiro was a natural. He had inherited Carlos's love for food and people. Andy had taken Ramiro under his wing, teaching Ramiro how to use the espresso machine and showing his technique for latte art. It was one of the reasons I had been surprised that Andy had reacted so strongly to hiring Sequoia. With Ramiro he had been patient and welcoming. Granted, Ramiro was much younger and my stepson, but nonetheless I was very glad that Andy had mended things with Sequoia.

There's no need to dwell on the past, I thought as I fluted the edges of the pie crusts and slid them into the oven to blind bake the crust. I wasn't sure if I was talking about Andy and Sequoia's rough start or Carlos, but either way I tried to shake off the topic and focus on finishing the pre-baked pie tins with our signature mincemeat, pumpkin, and apple cranberry fillings.

"Those look divine," Mom commented as I slid the trays of pies into the oven.

"We're in the home stretch. A handful of holiday party orders to finish for tomorrow and then it will be the last of the individual cakes and breakfast pastries for Christmas Eve and Christmas morning."

We always closed early on Christmas Eve and then gave our staff Christmas Day off as well. It would be back to business the day after, but everyone was excited for a little minibreak, myself included.

Once the pies had baked and cooled, I offered to box them up and take them out for delivery. I could use a bit of fresh air and the police station was right across the street. If time allowed, I could pop in and see if Thomas or the Professor were around.

The pies were being delivered to the Cabaret theater that was located off Main Street. The theater kept a full winter schedule, unlike OSF. Currently they were offering matinee and dinner performances of a holiday classic— *How the Grinch Stole Christmas.* The Cabaret was known for its zany productions and incredible acting talent, especially when it came to musicals. It was housed in an old converted church. The venue was intimate. Stage directors had to get creative with set designs and often choreographed actors running between rows of dinner tables and up and down stairs between the stage and the balcony.

I delivered the pies for their staff party and returned down Main Street. There was a change in the air. Ashland's typical laid-back vibe had shifted into a last-minute dash. Shoppers hurried between stores and skirted around piles of shoveled snow with stacks of boxes and packages. Christmas was three days away. If today was already this busy, I couldn't imagine what tomorrow would be like, let alone Christmas Eve.

Working the morning of Christmas Eve had always been my favorite during my late teen years. Typically the shoppers who came into Torte (predominantly men) were eager to get their hands on any of our products. Mom had learned early on that the last-minute shopping rush was a boon for business, and for years we had packaged pretty boxes of our truffles and assortments of petits fours and cookies for grown-up stockings. It was fun to banter with the last-minute shoppers and offer them a steaming cup of coffee to go as they made their rounds to every store on the plaza.

I stopped at the police station, wishing I had thought to bring a box of pastries as a friendly bribe. Thomas stood behind the reception desk wearing his standard blue uniform and a scowl. He was on the phone, so I waited for him to finish.

"Hey Jules, what brings you by?" he asked, hanging up the landline's receiver.

"I was out doing deliveries and thought I would see if there's any news on Cami's murder."

Thomas glanced behind him. The plaza station was small. It served as headquarters for police cadets who patrolled Lithia Park and for the few staff who worked downtown. I wondered if Thomas was double-checking to make sure we were alone.

He picked up a pencil and tapped it on a notepad. "Funny timing. That was the electric company again." He pointed to the phone. "I know more about power than I think I'll ever need. Maybe I should offer my services and teach a class at SOU."

"What did they say?"

"They confirmed what we already knew—someone cut the main power and power to the backup generator."

"That's not a surprise though, is it?"

He shook his head. "No, the Professor's been following this lead for a while and it's one of the key reasons we have a suspect in custody."

"You mean Nate?"

"So you heard?"

I nodded. "It's Ashland. News travels fast. Can you picture Nate killing Cami though? Thomas, we grew up with him. He's not a killer, and I just learned that the McBeths offered the inn to him. He turned them down. Not the other way around. What would his motive be for killing Cami?"

Thomas scribbled on the notepad. "Yeah, I know. I agree with you, Jules. The problem is that cutting the power could have been dangerous—even deadly—to the culprit. The Professor had been waiting for confirmation because it might change our next steps in the investigation."

"How so?"

"We're going to sit down with Nate and go over what the power company has informed us. We know for sure that whoever cut the power had to have a lot of knowledge and expertise."

"And that means Nate is the most likely suspect."

Thomas frowned. "I don't know. Maybe he wasn't

working alone. Maybe he had a partner. Or maybe he knows more than he's letting on. Either way it means the case is still wide open and at this point I doubt we'll have it closed before Christmas."

Chapter Twenty

Thomas looked so dejected that I wanted to give him a hug and offer to bake him a batch of his favorite holiday cookies to try and cheer him up.

"You never know," I said, reaching for his arm. "Maybe you'll get a break in the case soon."

"I hope so, Jules. It's going to be such a bummer to work a case over the holidays, and I can't help imagining what Cami's family must be going through. Losing a loved one during this time of year. We'd like to be able to give them some closure."

"That has to be the worst part of your job—breaking news that a family member has died." I didn't envy Thomas.

"The Professor said it never gets easier." Thomas straightened his badge. "He said if it ever does get easy, that's the time to turn in the badge."

Thomas's words exemplified his and the Professor's approach to community policing. The job wasn't about wielding power for either of them. It was about making Ashland a safe and thriving place to work and live.

"Is there anything I can do to help?"

He started to refuse, but then he changed his mind. "Actually, there is something you might be able to do."

"Sure. Anything."

"Would it be totally out of left field for you to get a meeting with Tim?"

"No, I don't think so. He was at Torte the other day and we had a long talk." I gave him the condensed version of my conversation with Tim. "Why? What are you thinking?"

"I'm wondering if you can ask him about Uva and how to go about distributing Uva's wines to a wider customer base. If the McBeths are right about Cami's accusation that Tim was stealing wine, maybe there's a way you could get some information out of him."

"Yeah." I nodded. Uva was a small vineyard that I co-owned with Carlos, Lance, and the ghastly Richard Lord. We only produced grapes for our estate blends. Thus far we had yet to come to a consensus on how we wanted to run the vineyard and tasting room or a vision for Uva's future.

"What if you ask him for some input? You could mention your conversation about him looking for other work and see if he is interested in some side work."

"You bet. I'm game."

"Play it cool, though, Jules. Don't do anything too rash, okay?"

"Me, never." I pointed to myself and gave him a goofy grin.

"I'm serious. At this point everyone who was at the dinner is still on our suspect list. I don't want Tim to get wind that you're fishing for information, understood?"

"Juliet Montague Capshaw reporting for duty." I saluted him.

"Funny, Juliet. But, in all seriousness, be careful. This could be a good opportunity to see if Tim might accidentally let something slip if he's not being interrogated by us. But he could be a killer so keep the conversation to wine and only wine."

"Don't worry about me. I won't do anything stupid."

"Seriously though. The McBeths are going to get started right away on doing a full inventory of their wine cellar. It's too soon to know if there's any truth to the theory that Tim has been stealing from them, but if there is, he could be dangerous. Keep it super casual, okay?"

"Okay." I gave him a sincere nod.

"Yeah, on that note, don't rope Lance into this either. This is between you and me. I know how off script Lance can get."

"Deal."

I returned to Torte with a sense of purpose. If I could help Thomas and the Professor with any detail (however small) that might shed light on who killed Cami, my holiday season would feel complete.

At the bakeshop I placed a call to the Winchester and asked for Tim. The reception desk informed me that he was in the middle of a staff tasting and wouldn't be available until after the Dickens feast.

"Is the bar open late?" I asked. I hadn't paid attention the night of Cami's murder. I knew that the bar was open for regular business with a limited menu during the feast, but I wasn't sure if it stayed open late.

"The bar is open from four until eleven every night and midnight on Fridays and Saturdays."

"Great. Do you know if Tim will be around later?"

She asked me to wait for a moment and then returned to the phone to let me know she had checked with Tim and he would be in the bar from nine until closing. I thanked her for her time and hung up.

A plan formed in my mind. I could do some solitary baking after we closed for the evening and wait for Tim to finish dinner service. Maybe he'd be more inclined to open up on his home turf over a glass of wine.

I said good night to my staff and Mom and locked the front door. After doing a final sweep of the upstairs, I headed for the basement and heated up a bowl of Sterling's leftover soup. Since I had the space to myself I knew what I wanted to bake—a special holiday surprise for Christmas Eve dinner.

I had sketched out a design for a two-tiered ginger and cranberry cake that I could drape with white fondant. I would adorn the top tier with green holly leaves and red berries cut from colored fondant and hang three matching antique red ornaments piped with a white filigree from strands of green fondant. The ornaments would dangle on the bottom layer and I would finish the cake with dainty balls of white fondant and a cluster of holly berries.

Mom and the Professor had been so generous in offering me my childhood home that I wanted to create something special for their first holiday as husband and wife. I had already been wrapping presents that I had collected for both of them over the past few months. For the

Professor I had found five new ties with varying theater and Shakespeare themes. My favorite was a royal-blue tie with Shakespeare's manuscripts printed in Old World script. I knew the Professor would love it. For Mom, I had a more nostalgic gift in mind. I had taken all of her and my father's original recipes from Torte and had them scanned. Then I found a company that bound the recipes together and made them into a cookbook. I had added photos of Torte in its early days along with pictures from my childhood and new pictures of her and the Professor. Each page in the cookbook had a quote from our rotating chalkboard.

I had a feeling that when Mom opened the cookbook on Christmas morning she would turn into a blubbery mess. I couldn't wait to give them their gifts. Holidays on the ship had been focused on providing our guests with an unforgettable experience. Inevitably Carlos and I would work through Christmas, preparing elaborate buffets and decadent sweets. We would find time to sneak away to the top deck to toast with a glass of champagne and exchange small gifts, but that was the extent of our holiday celebrations. Thus far I had experienced more holiday magic in Ashland in a few short weeks than all my time on the ship.

The thought triggered memories of Carlos. I heard his accent in my head. "Julieta, the holidays are a time to be together, no?"

One year we had gotten leave together on Christmas Day. When the ship docked at port in Cozumel, Mexico, we had rented a convertible Jeep and driven around the island. I remember the warm tropical breeze blowing my hair and palm trees wrapped in Christmas lights. We explored ancient ruins, swam in azure waters, and joined the locals in a children's parade complete with Mexican carols.

Stop, Jules.

I forced myself into the moment, polishing off my soup, and tying a fresh apron around my waist. For the cake, I creamed butter, sugar, and vanilla together in a mixer. Then I incorporated eggs and sifted in the dry ingredients—flour, baking powder, salt, ginger, nutmeg, and cinnamon. I wanted a moist cake, so I added cranberry sauce and buttermilk, along with chopped cranberries and walnuts.

Once the oven had come to temperature, I slid the cake pans in to bake for thirty minutes and shifted my attention to making a batch of cream cheese frosting. My design for this cake involved using fondant to cover each tier, but fondant on its own isn't particularly full of flavor. I would smother each layer with generous amounts of cream cheese frosting along with diced cranberries. Then I would frost the entire cake and use the fondant as a finishing tool.

I whipped butter, cream cheese, confectioners' sugar, vanilla, and pieces of candied ginger until it was as smooth as silk. Next I started on my fondant designs. Working with fondant was a bit like working with modeling clay. I wanted to cut out the leaves, holly berries, and ornaments tonight. I would keep them, along with the cakes, in the walk-in and assemble everything tomorrow.

Rolling out the fondant required arm strength. I coated the countertop in powdered sugar and began kneading the fondant until it was pliable and easier to roll. Once it was stretchy, I divided it into three large balls. I tinted the first ball with green food gel and massaged the color into the fondant. I repeated the same step with red food gel, and then rolled out three sheets of red, white, and green until they were about an eighth of an inch thick.

I felt like a kid again as I pressed holly leaf models into the green fondant. The leaves were so perfect that if I didn't know better, I might have thought they were real. Once I had cut dozens of holly leaves, I turned my attention to the berries and ornaments. The berries didn't take long, but I cut each of the ornaments by hand into balls and then piped an antique Victorian design with royal icing.

My timer dinged for my cakes after thirty minutes. Somehow over two hours had passed while the cakes cooled and I worked on trimming perfect edges on my ornaments. I arranged each of my fondant pieces on a cookie sheet to allow them to harden. Once the cakes had completely cooled, I cut them into eight layers, stacked them with cream cheese frosting and cranberry bits, and gave the tiers a crumb coat. Crumb coating is the process of applying a thin layer of frosting in order to seal any crumbs into the cake. Many bakers only use a crumb coat before covering a cake with fondant, but I added one last layer of cream cheese frosting. There's no reason to skimp on frosting. Plus, I wanted my cake to have as much flavor as possible.

On the off-chance that Mom decided to go snooping in the walk-in, where I would store the cake until Christmas Eve, I hid it in a pastry box and marked it with a fake customer name.

I checked the clock. It was after nine. Tim should be done with the Dickens feast by now, so I grabbed my coat, hat, scarf, and gloves and headed out the basement door. The temp had plummeted. A bitter breeze hit my cheeks as I climbed the slippery basement steps up to the plaza. Most shops had closed for the night, but restaurants and pubs were packed with late-evening diners.

"Evening, Juliet!" the owner of Pucks Pub called as I passed by.

A band of tuba players dressed in Santa suits had taken over Pucks' small stage.

"Whoa! Sounds like you have quite the party going tonight," I noted.

He stuffed a finger in one ear. "Tell me about it. These guys have played for the past three years and it's always a sellout, but my ears are ringing."

"Tuba-playing Santas. That's pretty unique."

"They're really good too. Do you want to come in and listen? I can squeeze you in behind the bar?"

"Thanks, but I'm off to the Winchester."

"Next year. Mark your calendar. I mean, come on, Jules, tuba-playing Santas; if that doesn't say holidays in Ashland, nothing does." He waved as I crossed the street toward the Lithia bubblers. The fountains had been turned off for the season. I missed the comforting sound of the gurgling water but knew that the city had to shut them off for winter as otherwise they would freeze solid.

I stuffed my hands into my pockets. Frosty air poured from my mouth as I trudged up Main Street. Hopefully the receptionist had been correct, and Tim would still be at the Winchester.

I turned off Second Street and puffed my way up the steep hill. I hadn't been back to the inn since Cami's murder and the memory of the night sent a tingle up my arms.

Was this a good idea?

Thomas had said to be discreet, but maybe I was making a mistake.

I hesitated for a moment. Maybe I should turn around and sleep on it.

What could possibly happen? I gave myself a pep talk as I headed up the brick walkway. I was meeting Tim at a public place. It was hardly likely that he would attack me at the Winchester bar. And, as I had promised Thomas, I intended to be very subtle in my approach.

The grounds looked just as idyllic as they had the night of Cami's murder. Had the McBeths added more lawn décor? In addition to the grapevine deer there were now two matching snowmen lighting the pathway to the bar. A dazzling display of miniature star-show lights rained down on the Victorian mansion.

I'd never seen anything quite like it before and stopped to take in the show.

Suddenly the sound of a woman screaming pierced through the quiet night sky. I looked up to the top floor of the historic inn to see the silhouette of a woman and someone in a dark mask holding what appeared to be a baseball bat above his head. Was he going to hit her? Without thinking I sprinted for the front entrance. If I couldn't get there fast enough there was about to be a second murder.

Chapter Twenty-one

"Stop!" I screamed as I took the steps two at a time and tried the handle on the front door. It was locked.

"Help!" I yelled at the top of my lungs, pounding on the doorway. "Someone help!"

I wasn't sure what to do. If I waited for someone to come open the front door, the woman's assailant might have already knocked her out, but my other option was retracing my steps on the slippery path and then weaving through the icy garden to the bar entrance.

"Is anyone in there? Emma? Jon?" I banged on the door so hard that my knuckles ached.

"Help!"

I was about to turn around and head for the bar when the door clicked open. Nate stared at me like he was seeing a ghost.

"Juliet, what's going on?" He looked behind me.

My expression must have matched his. "Nate? What are you doing here? I thought you had been arrested?"

"They let me go."

There was no time to waste. "We have to get upstairs."

I didn't wait for him to respond. I grabbed his arm and dragged him to the stairway.

"What's wrong?"

"I don't know. I saw something in the window. A woman. She was about to get her head smashed."

"What?" Nate stopped halfway up the stairs.

"I'm serious, Nate. There's no time. We have to get up there."

He finally seemed to pick up on my urgency and took the rest of the stairs in four long strides. When we crested the stairwell, Nate looked to the left then the right. "Which room?"

"That one." I pointed to the first door on the left.

Nate motioned for me to stay back. I watched as he knocked on the door. "Hello, Francine? It's Nate."

This was Francine's room?

No one answered.

Nate cupped his hand over his ear and placed it on the door. He listened for a moment. Then he turned to me.

"Can you hear anything?"

He shrugged and shook his head.

"Maybe you should knock again."

He followed my advice and knocked on the door, announcing himself as management and that he was doing a well-guest check.

Again, no one answered.

"What should we do? You have a key, right?"

Nate nodded. "Yes, but I can't enter a guest room without cause."

"We have cause. I swear, Nate. I saw a woman, probably Francine, in the window. A man, or I guess it could have been a tall woman, was standing behind her with a baseball bat. It looked like they were about to smack her head."

Nate sighed. "Francine, are you in there? Are you okay? We have a report that you might be in danger. If you don't answer, I'm going to enter the room, understood?"

He waited.

I could feel my heart pounding in my chest.

"Let's go," I said with urgency. "She could be hurt."

Nate fumbled with a large key ring clipped to his belt. He sorted through keys for what felt like an eternity. When he finally found the right key, he knocked one final time. "Francine, I have reason to believe that you could be in danger. I'm coming in." With that, he turned the key and stepped inside.

The room was pitch-black. Nate flipped on the lights.

I almost didn't want to look. What if we were too late? What if Francine was dead?

"There's no one here, Juliet." Nate surveyed the room.

"That can't be. I just saw them." I followed Nate's eyes. Sure enough the room looked vacant. Victorian caroling costumes were piled on the bed. The desk had a collection of throat remedies, including honey and essential oils, along with a teapot and fresh lemons.

"What about the bathroom or closet?" I whispered.

Nate nodded. He cleared his throat. "Francine, it's Nate. I'm here to do a well-check. Are you okay?" He walked to the closet first. Another round of fear pulsed through me. He flung the closet door open. The closet was more like a wardrobe. Victorian houses had been built long before the walk-in-closet trend. Nate shook his head. "Nothing. Just a couple coats."

We moved toward the bathroom. Once again, he repeated his statement. This time, I expected him to find Francine with her assailant forcing her to keep quiet, but the bathroom was empty too.

"Are you sure you saw someone in the window?" Nate asked, opening every drawer in the bathroom cabinet.

"I'm positive." I rubbed my eyes. Was I? Maybe the stress of the holiday season was finally making me crack.

"Could your eyes have played a trick on you? We have thousands of lights strung along the roofline. Maybe you saw the lights flickering and accidentally mistook them for a silhouette."

"Maybe." Mom had always teased me about my active imagination, but what I had seen felt so real.

Nate pointed to the door. "Let's go downstairs and check. Francine told me earlier that she was going to ask Tim for something strong to help soothe her throat. It had been giving her trouble during the performance tonight."

"Okay." We started toward the door, but something shiny caught my eye. "Wait, what's that?" I pointed to the floor in front of the window. The four-paneled window was angled to create an alcove with a view of the Winchester's grounds.

This was the exact spot where I had seen Francine in the window.

Nate squinted.

We both inched toward the alcove. Lying on the carpet was a two-foot-tall candelabra. It was made of pewter and looked quite heavy.

Nate started to reach down to pick it up.

I stopped him. "Don't. You shouldn't touch that, just in case it's evidence."

"Evidence?" He frowned.

"Yes. What if that's what I saw? It wasn't a baseball bat. Whoever was about to hit Francine over the head was going to do it with that candelabra."

Nate went white. He crouched down to get a closer look at the candleholder.

"Don't touch it, Nate. I'm serious. If anything happened to Francine, that could be evidence."

"Trust me, Juliet, I'm not going to touch it. I spent hours in police custody. I don't want my fingerprints on anything. I just wanted to see what this is." He pointed to something on the carpet.

I knelt next to him.

"Juliet, is that what I think it is?"

"What?"

He pointed to tiny bright red dots on the cream carpet. "That."

My eyes focused in on the small spots.

Nate looked at me. "Could that be blood?"

Chapter Twenty-two

I blinked. There were tiny blotches of something red staining the carpet near the window. Nate studied the candlestick. "I can't tell if there's blood on it. Can you?"

I shook my head. The pewter was too dark.

"What do we do next?" Nate asked.

At least he believed me now. "I think we should go check the bar and see if Francine is there or if anyone has seen her." I stood up too fast, making little flashing lights go off in my head.

Nate caught my arm. "Are you okay?"

"Just stood too quickly. Blood rush to the head."

"Yeah, that happens to me all the time." Nate ushered me toward the door. I stopped him.

"You know, on second thought, one of us should probably stay here. Do you want to go check and see if Francine is somewhere on the premises and I'll stay here until you get back? That way if this is a crime scene it will be protected until we call the Professor."

"Good idea. I'll be back in a flash." Nate left with a purpose.

I tried to piece together how much time had passed since I had walked up the pathway and seen motion in the window. How long had it taken me to run to the front door and for Nate to answer? A couple of minutes? If someone had injured—or worse, killed—Francine would they have had time to move her, and where? There were no other signs of a struggle in the hotel room. There also weren't any other guests around. Or if there were guests they had already turned in for the night.

How could someone have hit Francine on the head, knocked her out, and hidden the body in five minutes?

My mind briefly looped back to the theory that I had imagined everything. I hadn't been sleeping well. Not that I ever slept much anyway, but with the holiday crush I had been up late and awake early. Maybe this was all in my head.

But that didn't account for the red spots and the candelabra.

I paced back and forth between the desk and closet. Francine had been complaining about her voice. Maybe she had come up here to change and take some medicine. Then she planned to get a drink in the bar. Could the killer have been waiting for her? Could he or she have taken Francine by surprise?

What if they whacked her on the head from behind and then dragged her somewhere else? The question was, where could a killer hide a body in the Winchester?

I studied the room with a better eye. There was a four-poster bed with matching pewter bedposts. The bed frame came within a few inches of the floor. There was no possible way a killer could have forced Francine's body underneath the bed. I returned to the bathroom. It was more of the same. Short of hiding the body in the bathtub, the antique basin sink and Victorian cabinet were much too small. Could the killer have pushed the body out of one of the windows?

I tugged at the bathroom window. It didn't budge. From the thick layer of caulking and paint around the trim, I would guess it hadn't been opened in decades. The same was true for the bigger windows in the bedroom. Plus, everyone in the bar would have seen a body falling from the third floor.

I moved to the closet next. As Nate had mentioned there were two coats hanging from the rack. Otherwise the closet was bare, except for an extra blanket, pillow, and sheet set resting on the top shelf. I was about to shut the closet door, when I noticed a second, half door near the very back.

I had to duck to open it, but unlike the windows, this door wasn't locked.

My heart rate spiked as I pushed it open.

Did it lead to extra storage or maybe the eaves of the antique inn?

It was too dark to see anything, so I went to check the nightstands to see if either of them had a flashlight stashed away. Emma had mentioned that they kept flashlights in the guest rooms.

Jackpot! I found a flashlight in the nightstand and returned to the secret closet door.

A voice in the back of my head cautioned me to wait for Nate's return, but I pushed the warning voice away and ventured deeper into the hidden space.

I scanned the area with the flashlight. No sign of a body. That was good.

The secret door led to a secret passageway. The ceiling opened up about five feet inside so that I didn't have to crouch down too much.

This could be dangerous, Jules, I told myself.

Is this how Francine's killer made his escape?

If I followed the narrow passageway, what if I came face-to-face with the killer? I didn't have a weapon, and no one knew that I was here.

Not smart, Jules.

I sighed.

Should I return and wait for Nate?

But what if the killer was getting away now? I could feel my rational and emotional brains warring. It was like my head was being pulled in two directions.

Finally, I decided to risk it. I had left the closet door open. Nate would figure it out.

That gave me a new thought. Who would have known that this secret chamber existed? Nate and his parents. Anyone else?

Could the killer have used this secret passage the night that Cami was killed?

I continued on, guided by the dim glow of my flashlight. There were dusty cobwebs, a few old cardboard boxes, and some empty bottles of whiskey and wine. I watched my footing.

After about fifty feet the passage stopped at another door.

This is the moment of truth.

I twisted the handle, but the door didn't open. I tried again and put my weight into my hip to try and force it open, but nothing worked.

Voices echoed nearby.

Where was I?

I had no sense of my bearings in the dark tunnel.

If I couldn't get the door open, I might as well go back and wait for Nate. He would know where the passageway went and probably had a key to the other door. I crept back through the corridor, using the flashlight to illuminate the way. From the mass of cobwebs sweeping across my face and the piles of dust on the floor, I assumed that the passageway rarely got used. I knew that the practice of constructing hidden rooms or secret passageways wasn't unheard of in homes built at the turn of the last century. Could the Winchester's history as a hospital have anything to do with its secret passages?

I made it back to Francine's room, but when I went to open the hatch in the back of her closet, it was locked.

Uh-oh.

I banged on the door. "Hello! It's Juliet! I'm in here!"

Had Nate returned and intentionally locked me in the secret passageway? Or had the door shut on its own? I hadn't paid attention. Nor had I thought to make sure to prop the door open.

Smart, Juliet.

I pounded on the door again and again.

My attempts were futile. As were my screams. The chamber was well insulated and unless someone was very nearby I had a sinking feeling that I wouldn't be heard.

The night had gone from bad to worse.

I couldn't stay here forever. No one knew that I had come to the Winchester tonight, except for Nate.

What if the Professor had mistakenly let him go? If Nate

was the killer, had he come back finish the job? Maybe Francine had witnessed him killing Cami. He could keep me locked in the narrow passageway forever.

A chill ran down my spine.

Nate is your childhood friend, Jules. I let out a long, slow breath. Trust your instincts.

I decided to retrace my steps, slower this time, and see if by chance I had missed another hidden door or trap in the floor. I scanned the light from the dusty wooden floor to the ceiling. The narrow chamber felt like it was closing in on me. I'd never been claustrophobic before, but if I didn't find a way out soon I had a feeling that panic would begin to mount.

Focus, Jules.

I took another long breath through my nose and tried to steady my breathing. Where was I in relation to the other guest rooms? Maybe if I made enough noise one of the other guests would hear me.

There were at least two or maybe three guest rooms on this side of the inn. What else was on the third floor? If memory served me from childhood parties where Nate would take us upstairs to play hide-and-seek while the adults lingered over late-night cocktails and coffee, I was fairly confident that there was a supply closet and small library. When we were kids the McBeth family had lived on the third floor, opening only half of the rooms to guests. I had always imagined that living in a hotel would be so luxurious. Nate would swipe plates of cookies from the kitchen and get the housekeeper to unlock the supply closet as an extra hiding spot.

He had to have known about the secret passage. Not

that it was ever part of our childhood game. After I had scanned every square inch of the tunnel, I resorted to banging and screaming again. This time I pounded on the arched walls and yelled as loud as I could for help.

I tried the far door again.

The longer I was locked in the passageway the more convinced I was becoming that Nate had to be the killer. It made the most sense. When I had come up the walkway and seen someone in the window about to hit Francine with the candlestick, my scream had probably startled him. He would have had enough time to drag Francine through the passage and into the locked room I was trying to break into. Then he could have come downstairs and let me in. He played along with the charade of searching for Francine, when he had known where she was the entire time. He was likely trying to wait me out.

I had left the closet door open, I was sure of it.

Maybe I shouldn't be screaming. But what other choice did I have? I was a lame duck.

If Nate was the killer I had to get out of here—now.

I used the flashlight to bang as hard as I could on the handle. It was futile. The old brass doorknob was stuck.

I gave it one final try using the force of my entire body weight to smash the handle. To my shock, it snapped off and landed on the hardwood floor with a heavy thud. With the doorknob free, I was able to squeeze my finger inside of the lock and turn it until it clicked open. With a huge sigh of relief, I pushed open the door and stepped out in the library.

Chapter Twenty-three

My relief was temporary. A man was seated in front of a low-burning fire, smoking a pipe. The dimly lit room shrouded his face from view. I coughed.

He looked up.

"Jon?" I peered out of one corner of my eye, trying to make sure that Francine's body wasn't sprawled near his feet.

"Juliet." He jumped and dropped his pipe. "You startled me. How did you . . . ? Where did you . . . ?" He stuttered as he reached down to pick up his pipe. "Did you just come from the passageway?"

"Yeah." I glanced behind me. Hadn't he heard me banging?

"I didn't even know that was still open. I thought Nate boarded it up years ago."

"I didn't see any boards." I studied his body language. He looked relaxed as he puffed his pipe. "Did you hear me calling for help?"

He pressed a finger in his left ear. "No, don't hear like I used to." Jon stood. "That's not right. I told Nate to seal it up. That old thing is a trap. The doors get stuck all the time and we were worried that a guest might accidentally find their way in there and not be able to get out."

"That's kind of what happened to me just now."

"Nate told me he made sure there was no way for anyone to get in." Jon puffed on his pipe. "Mind if I borrow that flashlight for a second? I want to go take a look myself."

"Please." I handed him the light.

A waft of smoke trailed after him as he entered the passageway mumbling to himself. He returned a minute or two later, shaking his head. "Where's Nate?" His voice was thick with anger.

"He and I were looking for Francine, but then we got separated."

Jon chewed on his pipe. "Francine? She left earlier. Said she wasn't feeling well. Decided she wanted to head home and sleep in her own bed."

"Are you sure?"

He gave me a funny look. "Positive. Why?"

I gave him a brief recap of what I had seen and then told him that Nate was looking for her in the bar.

"No. She left. I watched her go. It was at least an hour ago. If you saw someone in the window, it wasn't Francine."

"But who else could it have been?"

He puffed a perfect ring of smoke. The earthy scent of the pipe reminded me of my youth when my parents were involved with a group of playwrights, musicians, and actors who would convene at the Black Swan Theater for midnight brainstorming sessions and underground productions. My dad would always return home with his coat smelling of pipe tobacco.

"Any of the other singers," Jon suggested. "Or one of our housekeeping staff."

"Maybe."

Nate burst into the room. His face was blotched with color and his breathing was labored. "There you are. I couldn't find you anywhere. When I came back you were gone. Then I totally freaked out. I thought maybe someone came after you."

I told him about how I had found the secret door to the passageway.

Jon shook his pipe at Nate. "You promised me that you boarded that up months ago. I distinctly remember our conversation and seeing you lug sheets of plywood upstairs."

"I did."

"Obviously you didn't." Jon pointed to the open doorway.

"Yes I did. It was completely sealed off. I have no idea what happened. I put up plywood on both doors." Nate sounded sincere. "I don't get how anyone could have gotten it open. They would have needed a drill. And where did the plywood go?"

Jon frowned. "When's the last time you checked this area?"

Nate shrugged. "I don't know. Housekeeping inspects the rooms. None of the staff ever mentioned seeing sheets of plywood in the closet. I think someone would have mentioned it."

"Unless someone on staff did it," I said, not realizing that I was speaking out loud.

"Good point." Jon let the pipe hang from one side of his mouth. "Let's talk through who on staff had access to the guest rooms. You, your mother, and I. And anyone in housekeeping."

"How many cleaners do you have?" I asked.

Nate counted out the staff on two hands. "Seven and then we have some seasonal help that come to help during busy times—like the height of the summer season."

"But then Francine and the singers all had a key to that guest room," Jon said. "We block out the room for the en-tire month. That way they have a place to relax between sets and change."

"That's right. I had heard that. So there are four more people who have been in the room recently." I thought back to Cami's murder. "Could the killer have used the passage-way the night Cami was killed?"

"I guess," Nate responded with a frown. "But why? It leads from that guest room into here. Cami was killed at the base of the stairs. How would going between the room and library have benefited the killer?"

"That's a good question." I cleared my throat. The pipe smoke was making my eyes sting. "It's a new clue and could be a big development or even break the case. I'm going to call Thomas and see if he or the Professor want to come take a look. Plus we still have the unsolved mys-tery of who was in the room tonight and if that's blood spatter on the carpet."

"Blood spatter?" Jon choked. "You didn't mention any-thing about blood."

"Come with us, Dad. You should take a look at what we found." Nate headed for the main door. "Juliet, I looked everywhere and couldn't find Francine, but three staff members claim they saw her getting into her car about an hour ago and that she was just fine."

"That's exactly what your dad said." I followed him out of the cozy library.

Jon set his pipe in an ashtray near the fireplace and then came with us. While he and Nate inspected the spots on the carpet, I called Thomas who agreed to come over right away. "You know the drill, Jules, don't touch anything."

"We won't," I promised, and hung up the phone.

"This could be blood," Jon said, using the flashlight to illuminate the spots. "It could also be red wine or plenty of other things. The singers have been in and out of here for weeks. It could be something from one of their costumes or that they dragged in on a shoe. It's impossible to tell."

"Thomas is on his way. He'll bring equipment to get test samples of the spots, so he can send them into the lab for analysis."

"I sure hope it's not blood." Jon stood. "I don't think we can weather another disaster at the Winchester. We've been through enough for a lifetime these past few days."

Nate placed a hand on his father's arm. "Don't worry, Dad. It will all work out."

Much of the evidence pointed to him, but I couldn't reconcile the idea of him doing anything to put his parents in jeopardy.

Detective Kerry and Thomas arrived shortly. Thomas greeted Nate with what Lance referred to as a man hug—an arm around one shoulder. "Hey man, long time no see."

Nate let out a long whistle. "Glad I'm seeing you here

instead of at the station. I was sweating bullets earlier. Sorry for the bad pun."

"I get it," Thomas said. "Like the Professor said, we can't take any risks, even if it is with an old friend."

Detective Kerry cleared her throat. I knew it was a warning to Thomas to stop talking. He and Nate had gone all the way through school together from elementary to high school. They had played on the same football team and had been junior park rangers. I had a feeling that, like me, Thomas didn't want to believe that our childhood friend could be a killer, but he was a professional. He couldn't let his personal opinions get in the way of official police work.

They went about their work with precision and focus. Kerry twisted her hair into a ponytail. "Show us what you found," Thomas said, slipping a pair of blue latex gloves on his hands.

Nate walked them to the spots on the carpet and then showed them the access to the secret passage in the back of the closet.

"Has anyone made contact with Ms. La Roux?" Detective Kerry asked, stretching a pair of disposable gloves onto her hands too.

We all shook our heads.

"When was she last seen?" Kerry sounded annoyed.

"About an hour and a half ago," Jon offered. "She wasn't feeling well."

Kerry made a note in a spiral-bound notebook. She obviously preferred pen and paper like the Professor. "Did you call her?"

Jon's cheeks reddened. "No. I didn't even think about it."

"Can you do that now?" Detective Kerry waited for Jon to move.

"Oh, you mean right now?"

"Yes."

Jon turned to Nate. "Do you know Francine's number?"

Nate nodded. "It's in her file. I'll go find it and see if I can get a hold of her."

Thomas snipped small pieces from the carpet with a pair of scissors. He tucked them into a bag and sealed it tightly.

"What is it?" Jon asked.

"No idea." Thomas handed the evidence bag to Kerry who labeled it with a Sharpie. "That's for forensics to tell us."

"How long will that take?"

"We'll get it to the lab in Medford tonight. They should have something for us by morning. It could be faster, depending on whether or not anyone is able to locate Francine." Thomas scanned the area with a black light.

Detective Kerry pointed to the closet. "This is the area that had been previously barricaded?"

Jon looked distressed. "Yes. Although to be honest, I never saw it boarded up. I left that project to Nate. Emma and I have been trying to scale back the amount of time we spend at the inn. I probably should have checked that the work had been done."

"But you have no reason to believe it wasn't, right?" Thomas asked.

For the briefest second a look of concern flashed across Jon's face, but he recovered. "No. Not at all. I simply meant that I should have given my son more help."

Detective Kerry shot Thomas a look.

They inspected the passageway next.

"Do you think they'll find anything?" Jon asked me, wringing his hands together.

"Doubtful. I was stuck in there for a half hour and didn't see a single thing other than cobwebs and a lot of dust."

Nate returned as Detective Kerry and Thomas re-emerged from the closet.

"Did you make contact?" Kerry asked.

Nate shook his head. "No. She didn't answer her home number or cell."

"In that case, we should go." Thomas caught Detective Kerry's eye.

She nodded. "We'll check Ms. La Roux's property and then head to the lab."

"Yep." Thomas stuffed his mini iPad in his police jacket. "I need you to secure this room and the passage-way. Make sure no one gets in here tonight, understood?"

Jon gave him a thumbs-up. "We'll lock everything, in-cluding the library. Most of our guests have already gone to bed by now anyway."

"We'll be in touch. If you hear from Francine, call us immediately."

With that he and Detective Kerry left. Jon and Nate discussed getting more boards to secure the passageway. I went to see if Tim still happened to be at the bar. My original plan had gone way off course. I just hoped that it didn't mean that there had been a second murder.

Chapter Twenty-four

Only a few tables were occupied in the candlelit bar. No one was the wiser of the commotion and drama upstairs. I started toward the bar, dazzled by the rows of beautiful liquor bottles stacked almost to the ceiling. A ladder on sliders had to be used to access the top shelf. In my training at culinary school I had learned the phrase "top shelf" was a literal reference to the fact that restaurants housed their best and most expensive bottles of alcohol on the top shelf.

"Darling, where are you off to?" A familiar voice sounded behind me.

I turned to see Lance sitting with none other than Tim at a four-person table. "Lance, what are you doing here?" I joined them.

Lance patted the empty chair next to him. "Sit. Join us. Tim and I were just having a tête-à-tête about hosting a wine experience for some of our most valued donors to kick off the new season."

"I didn't know you were hosting a wine dinner."

Lance's catlike eyes narrowed. "Juliet, don't be daft.

Of course you do. We were just discussing the menu of lovely tasting bites and nibbles that Torte will be producing. The holiday rush must be getting to your head."

I had no idea what Lance was talking about. We hadn't discussed any menus. I was about to say as much when he raised one eyebrow and kicked me under the table.

"Darling, it's the best news ever. Tim has agreed to be the sommelier for the evening. I can't believe what a twist of good luck it is to see you here. You two can put your heads together and come up with something fabulous. Since Tim is one of the most knowledgeable wine experts in the Rogue Valley he will most certainly be able to direct you to reasonably priced wines that taste like they are worth beaucoup bucks."

"Sure." I looked at Tim. His attention was elsewhere. He was staring at the entrance to the kitchen.

"What are you drinking this evening? Let me get us a refresher." Lance stood. Then he mouthed "you're welcome" to me.

I threw my hands up. What was he doing? Had he come to try and exact information from Tim? Was he actually hosting a wine-tasting event? I was confused.

"Your drink, darling?"

"I'll take a hot tea," I finally said.

"And you, good sir? Another vino?" Lance asked Tim. Tim peeled his eyes from the doorway. "What's that?"

"Can I get you another vino?" Lance repeated.

"No." Tim placed his hand over his glass. "I have to drive home."

"One hot tea coming up. I'll let you two kids chat about master plans."

Tim blinked hard twice. "Sorry, Juliet. I don't want to sound rude, but could we talk about food and wine pairings after the holiday? It's been a long night."

"I absolutely agree. I'm wiped out." I waited for a second and decided to use these few minutes alone with Tim to see what his reaction would be to the news that Francine was missing. "Did you hear about Francine?"

He blinked rapidly. Was he really tired or was that an involuntary reaction? "Francine? You mean the singer Francine?"

I nodded. Why was he acting like he didn't know Francine?

"What about her?"

"She's missing. The police were just upstairs. They think that someone might have harmed her."

Tim almost tipped over his wineglass. He caught it with one hand. "Francine's missing? Who told you that?"

"Didn't Nate come down here looking for her?"

"No. I haven't seen Nate all night."

"Really?"

Tim tipped the empty glass and swirled a drop or two left on the bottom. "Nate hasn't been around much at all. I heard that he was arrested or something."

"He's upstairs right now."

"Huh." Tim shrugged.

One of them was lying. But who?

"Why would someone want to hurt Francine?" Tim asked.

"The police are looking into that now. It could be connected to Cami's murder or it could be a false alarm."

"That's weird, but she's not exactly loved around here."

"What?" This was news to me.

"I mean she's fine, but she has a diva streak in her. She's always demanding extra hot tea and had a habit of sneaking off with expensive bottles of whiskey. She would say she was going to pour herself a shot to soothe her throat and bring the bottle back to the bar, but she never did. One of the housekeepers told me she found four empty bottles in Francine's room upstairs."

I couldn't get a read on Tim.

"Did you tell Jon or Emma that Francine was stealing bottles of whiskey?" Again I wondered who was telling the truth. Tim had told me that day I bumped into him at Torte that he took Francine a glass of whiskey, but she had said she didn't drink.

"They didn't seem to care. They said that she and the singers were welcome to free drinks and meals during their performances. It was part of their contract. I told them that Francine was abusing their generosity, but they shrugged it off."

That sounded like the McBeths.

"What was really interesting to watch was her and Cami. They hated each other. I think it was a power thing. Francine's been the star at the Winchester for many years. She couldn't handle Cami coming in and usurping that power. I've kind of been wondering if she killed Cami."

I wanted to steer the conversation to wine and Tim had given me the perfect opening. "Do you keep track of the inventory of wine, beer, and hard alcohol?"

"Yep, everything related to the bar falls under me. I'm responsible for every aspect of the bar and wine cellar, from making sure our cocktail menu is constantly being updated to ordering and seeking new wine vendors."

"So you must have extensive spreadsheets on your wine and alcohol inventory."

The edges of Tim's eyes creased. "Yeah. I keep those records. Why?"

"Well, I was thinking that you could probably check the inventory record and get an actual count of how much Francine has taken during the season, right?"

"I could," Tim agreed. "But like I said if the McBeths don't care, I'm not going to lose any sleep over it."

"Do the McBeths look at the inventory much?"

The crevices near his eyes deepened. "That's my job."

"Right, but they own the inn. They must go over reports with you to see how sales are doing and to budget for each season."

"Not really. That's what they hired me to do."

I glanced toward the bar. Lance waved to me with his finger. I decided that now was my chance to press Tim.

"I don't understand. As a small business owner, it's my job to know where every dime is spent, from napkins to flour and equipment to marketing. My mom and I spend hours going over every line item to know where we can cut products that might not be selling as well and where to bulk up on products that are flying off the shelves. I can't believe that the McBeths aren't involved in that process with you. You must have a year-end inventory meeting, right?"

Tim swirled the drops of wine in his glass at a dizzying pace. "I do. I'm in charge of inventory and I give the

McBeths a big-picture view of how the bar is performing financially but they've never been interested in the minutiae."

I found Tim's words nearly impossible to believe. The McBeths hadn't built a successful inn, restaurant, and bar by being completely clueless about their finances. Something wasn't adding up.

"Maybe it's time to call a meeting with them," I suggested. "If Francine was stashing expensive bottles of whiskey in her room, who knows what else could be being skimmed from the Winchester. I'll have to offer Jon and Emma my services. I've mastered reviewing inventory spreadsheets over the years. Maybe we'll be able to figure out if Francine was stealing even more."

Tim's face blanched. He dropped his glass and it shattered in tiny pieces on the floor.

I waited for him to respond, but he jumped to his feet and went to find a broom. I had hit a nerve for sure. Tim was sweating and there could only be one reason why—he had to be the one stealing from the McBeths.

Chapter Twenty-five

By the time Lance returned with my hot tea and a Christmas martini, Tim had vanished. "Do tell, darling, how did it go? I intentionally hung back because I could see sweat dripping from the poor man's brow from twenty feet away. You went for the jugular, Jules. Well done." He lifted his glass to me.

"He has to be lying, Lance." I gave him a recap of our conversation.

"Agreed. He's making the McBeths out to be fools—like Falstaff. They might be ready to set sail for warm sandy beaches, but they are hardly bumbling."

I sipped my tea. "Exactly. Tim is either lying or exaggerating. I need to follow up with Nate or his parents tomorrow."

"An excellent plan. For a moment I thought you might ruin my grandiose plan this evening. I do adore you, Juliet, but sometimes I want to tap some sense into that beautiful skull of yours. No menu planning—please—I was setting up the perfect entry for you, and you nearly missed the opportunity."

"Sorry. It's late." I wrinkled my brow. "Come to think of it, how did you know that I was going to talk to Tim tonight?"

"I didn't."

"Lance."

"Fine. I have my sources and a gentleman never divulges. However, I will tell you that I heard a rumor from a credible source that Tim might be padding his own coffers. I decided to come down for a nightcap and you happened by. Quite synchronistic timing if you ask me."

Thank goodness Thomas and Detective Kerry had left. Thomas would never forgive me if he thought that I had roped Lance into joining me.

"The question of the hour is, why are you here?"

"Same reason."

"And you didn't call yours truly?"

"It's complicated."

"A shabby excuse." Lance glared at me in jest. He polished off his martini. "Count yourself lucky, I won't hold it against you this time. I can see your eyes are beginning to droop. Let's get you to bed. Ashland's pastry muse needs her beauty sleep."

I didn't argue. Nothing sounded better than my bed at the moment. Lance agreed to stop by the bakeshop in the morning with an update.

"The night is still young for me." He kissed both of my cheeks. "I think I'll trot down to Pucks Pub for the second act of the tubas. Perhaps the rumor mill will keep running through the night. See you in the morning. Rest those baby blues."

* * *

I must have crashed the minute my head hit the pillow because the next thing I knew I was woken by the sound of my phone ringing.

What time was it?

I fumbled to turn on my nightstand light and find my phone. By the time I got out of bed and dug through my purse it had stopped ringing. The screen flashed a picture of Carlos's face next to the missed number.

He had left me a message. "Julieta, I am sorry if I have woken you. I know it is still early, but I wanted to say hello before I must go and put on the show for dinner service. The festivities on the ship, they are not the same without you. I am wishing you were here, *mi querida.*"

The message cut out.

I tried to call him back, but he had either been called away to the kitchen or service was spotty on the ship.

My bed suddenly felt cold. What would it be like to have Carlos and Ramiro here now? I would be brewing a pot of coffee for two and making a cup of velvety hot chocolate for Ramiro.

Ramiro would love the plaza's holiday lights, skiing on Mount Ashland, ice-skating in Lithia Park, a day trip to historic Jacksonville to ride the Christmas trolleys around town. There was so much to experience in the area, I wished they could see it with me, I thought as I pulled on a pair of jeans, a fleece sweatshirt, and a thick pair of wool socks. Instead of making a pot of coffee at home, I decided if I was up I might as well get a head start on the day at Torte. Today was the day before Christmas Eve. I knew that it would be a mad rush of last-minute shoppers. I could get the pastry cases stocked this morning and put the finishing touches on my surprise cake for Mom and the Professor's Christmas Eve dinner.

Another round of snow was falling outside. The plaza in its winter slumber cast a cheerful glow with its dazzling display of lights.

I unlocked the basement doors and fired up the ovens before starting my first pot of coffee. Soon the kitchen was warm and smelled of our special Christmas blend packed with nutmeg, cinnamon, cardamom, and pepper. I poured myself a steaming mug and retrieved my fondant ornaments and cake from the walk-in.

Next, I heated milk and butter on the stove. Once the butter had melted into the milk, I removed the saucepan from the stove and added a pinch of sugar and packets of yeast. While the yeast was rising I opened a vat of buttercream. We always kept buttercream reserves in the refrigerator, but during the holidays we had tripled the amount we kept on hand. Buttercream can be saved in an airtight container and left in the fridge for up to two weeks. It was important to keep it away from anything fragrant like onions, as the frosting might absorb the smell. Whenever we needed more frosting we would simply remove a tub from the fridge and let it come up to room temperature before using.

My yeast had bubbled with its first rise, so I mixed in sugar, flour, and salt and kneaded the dough into balls. I covered the balls with dish towels and let them rise again.

The cream cheese buttercream had come up to room temp, so I placed the cake on a spinning stand and used a flat spatula to spread a second layer of frosting. Since I had iced the cake last night and allowed it to chill, the frosting went on with ease. Soon the cake looked like the snow piling up outside.

I paused for a minute to check on my bread dough. Each ball had doubled in size, so I patted them into greased bread pans, brushed them with an egg wash, and slid them into the ovens to bake.

It was nearly six. My team should be arriving soon. I wanted to pipe the cake and get it back in the walk-in on the off chance that Mom would decide to come in early this morning.

I piped red and green trim on each layer of the cake. Then I used buttercream as the glue for my fondant cutouts. When I was finished, I stood back to appraise my work. The cake had come out even better than I had imagined it in my head. It was elegant yet simple, with a hint of whimsy and a touch of a design one might have found at a Jane Austen dinner party.

Pleased with my work, I hid the evidence in an oversized delivery box and stashed it in the back of the walk-in.

As I removed the first trays of sweet bread from the oven, Sterling, Marty, and Andy all arrived. Their coats were covered in snow. Andy stomped on the mat at the basement door. "It's blowing like crazy again. Night skiing is going to be off the hook later."

"Did you go last night?" I asked, sipping the spiced coffee.

"Did I go last night? Boss, come on. Of course. We closed the lifts down." Andy shook snow from his parka and showed off the ski lift pass attached to his zipper.

Marty's nose was bright red. He tugged off a stocking cap. "I haven't ventured up to the mountain yet. Not that I would ski." He patted his belly. "But my wife and I loved to sit in the lodge and drink spiked cider while watching the kids fly down the slopes. Is there a lodge at the mountain?"

Andy gave him an enthusiastic nod. "Yeah, they just revamped it. It's awesome. You could totally come spend an entire day. There's a bar upstairs with huge windows to watch the skiers and a big old fireplace. They serve pizza and all kinds of yummy grub."

"I'll have to add it to my holiday list," Marty said as he traded his coat for an apron.

I couldn't believe I hadn't thought to invite Marty to Christmas at Mom's. This was his first year without his wife.

Sterling and Andy helped themselves to coffee.

I pulled Marty aside. "Do you have plans tomorrow night?"

Marty smiled, but his eyes held a sadness. "I found a midnight candlelight service. I thought I would go and light a candle for Maureen."

"That's wonderful." I squeezed his hand. "Would you consider coming to Christmas Eve dinner with us first? Mom is planning dinner at seven, so we'd be done with plenty of time for you to make a midnight service."

Marty's eyes welled. "That would be wonderful. What can I bring?"

"Just yourself."

"Hey, wait a second, boss. Are you extending invitations to dinner at Mr. and Mrs. The Professor's new place?" Andy asked. "How come me and Sterling aren't invited?"

"I . . . uh . . ." I started to try and explain, but Sterling interrupted.

"Don't worry, Jules. Andy is messing with you."

"That's right, boss." He winked. "My Christmas Eve plans involve shredding the slopes until they kick me out."

"What about you, Sterling?"

Sterling looked at his feet. "Me and Steph are making dinner. Don't tell her I told you this, because she'll kill me, but she planned a five-course meal from her favorite reality baking show. We're going to attempt our first turkey and chestnut stuffing."

"That's awesome, man." Andy clapped him on the shoulder. "I'll stop by on my way home from Mount A. That's cool, right?"

Sterling's piercing blue eyes lit up. "Sure, just ask Steph."

"No way." Andy threw his arms up. "Time to get upstairs and fire up the espresso machine."

Marty took over bread production and Sterling began chopping onions and garlic for a creamy butternut squash soup. I should have given more thought to my staff. Once the others arrived, I was going to double-check and make sure no one else was going to be alone on the holiday.

The morning vanished. We cranked out tray after tray of butter stollen and rum fruitcake. I must have logged ten miles running between floors to restock the pastry case and bring up boxes of holiday cookies packaged and ready to go.

During a spare minute, I stopped to check in with Sequoia and Rosa about their holiday plans.

"I'm not really into Christmas," Sequoia said. "I'm more of a solstice girl, but I'm happy to have a day and a half off so I'm taking a long winter hike and some friends are having a potluck."

"That sounds fun," I said.

Rosa smiled. "My family is huge. The celebrations will begin tomorrow evening with an authentic Mexican feast. My sister and I will make over a hundred tamales. Last year they were gone in an hour."

"Tamales. Maybe we can do a tamale feast for our January Sunday supper. You could teach the team how to make them."

"Yes, that would be good. They aren't hard. Lots of rolling."

"Let's plan on it."

I left them to the line of customers eager to get their hands on our bourbon pecan and apple cranberry pies.

Bethany and Steph were piping dozens of snowflake cupcakes. "What are you doing for the holiday, Bethany?" I asked, watching as she dotted the top of the fluffy white frosting with a shimmering chocolate star.

"I'm having a pajama party. It's girls only because all men are jerks. We are baking Christmas brownies and watching cheesy Hallmark movies in our pjs."

"Love it." I felt relieved knowing that everyone on my staff had friends or family to be with.

Mom showed up mid-morning. "Sorry, honey, I would have been here earlier, but I had my own shopping to finish and a few secret errands to run."

"No problem. We have things surprisingly well under control.

"What were you shopping for?" I teased.

"Wouldn't you like to know? You'll have to wait until Christmas morning to find out."

I glanced around the kitchen. Marty had gone to take the last of our bread deliveries to our local clients. "Hey, I invited another guest to dinner tomorrow. Marty. I hadn't even thought about the fact that this is the first year without his wife."

"How wonderful. We'd love to have him. In fact, I had mentioned it to him a while ago, and I'm not sure if he realized that no formal invitation was necessary. You should see my pantry. I bought enough to feed a small army, because you never know who might arrive." Her eyes twinkled.

"Are you expecting someone else?" I couldn't tell if she was being funny or if she was serious.

"Honey, this is Ashland. You should always expect extra guests. You know Doug, he's already invited everyone we know and plenty of strangers we've never met. Better to be prepared than not."

"Speaking of being prepared. How can I help? Do you want me to come over tonight to help with prep or as soon as we close tomorrow?"

"You have plenty to do with Torte. Tomorrow is fine. Doug and I are going to pop open a bottle of wine tonight and do as much of the prep as possible." She frowned. "At least that is if he can get away from the case."

"Oh yeah, did you hear anything about Francine?" I gave her the condensed version of what had happened last night. As I recalled the strange turn of events, I couldn't stop thinking about Francine. She had motive. Her career was on its way down, a long, slow slide into oblivion as Lance would say. The Winchester had become her bread and butter. Without the ongoing Dickens gig she was left to play small venues and open mic nights. Cami had posed a major threat to her stability and perceived star status. Plus, she had the means to pull it off. She knew the historic inn as well as any of the staff. Her room was just at the top of the stairs. She easily could have snuck away between sets, killed Cami, and returned to the feast without being seen. The only issue was what I had witnessed in the Victorian house's window last night. I was sure I had seen Francine. But there was no way someone could have injured—or worse, killed—her and dragged her away that fast. Nate and I had gotten upstairs within minutes. What was more likely was that Francine had staged the scene for me and then made her getaway.

"Yes, I heard. Thomas and Detective Kerry came by late. They searched Francine's place and couldn't find her."

"So do they think that someone harmed her?" As I asked the question, I felt like I already knew the answer.

Mom curled her lip. "Doug is there now having a look for himself, but Thomas said that her apartment was a mess, and it looked as if she had packed in a hurry. I think they're leaning toward wondering if she was involved in Cami's death and has made a getaway."

Suddenly the pieces of the puzzle began to fall into place. Could I have mistaken what I had seen last night? Had Francine put on a brilliant Tony-award-winning performance?

Chapter Twenty-six

"Francine killed Cami," I said aloud. I thought about everything I knew about the case—the red nails, the whiskey bottles in the passageway, the fact that she knew the inn from top to bottom. She must have been the woman Bethany had seen Jon talking to in the cellar. The only thing I couldn't reconcile is what I had seen in the window last night.

Mom nodded. "It's Doug's current working theory. He's put out an APB for her. He sent Thomas and Kerry to interrogate the members of her singing group. And he's searching her apartment right now."

"Wow."

"Doug thinks that Francine was terrified that she would lose the income from the Dickens feast. He had already been looking into her financial records and discovered that the Dickens-Feast money sustained her for the winter. She must have gotten desperate."

"But that doesn't explain what I saw in the window last night or why the secret passage was reopened."

"Oh, you sound like Doug. He said this case has led to

so many dead ends, but for the moment Francine is at the top of his list. He'll be by later. You can ask him yourself."

We returned to baking. The afternoon flew by. My fingers were stiff, and my feet ached. By the time we were ready to close we had sold out of every item in the pastry case. Not a single crumb was left anywhere.

I called the team together after we had finished cleanup. "Amazing work today, you guys! I'm so impressed with your effort. Tomorrow will be even busier, but we're closing at noon so come ready to run around for a few hours and then you all can take some much-deserved time off."

Everyone clapped.

"It's still early enough for you to get some last-minute shopping in, so everyone get out of here. I'll finish closing up."

"Forget shopping. Who's hitting the slopes with me?" Andy asked.

"We have a turkey to stuff," Sterling said, grabbing Stephanie's hand. I couldn't believe it. She looped her hand through his and gave him a genuine smile. "Chestnut stuffing, here we come." She turned to Andy. "Why aren't you taking your date up to the mountain?"

"Nah. I ditched her. She was kind of . . ." He searched for the right word.

"Vapid?" Stephanie offered.

"No. Dumb." Andy blushed.

Stephanie shot Bethany a triumphant look and then she and Sterling left hand in hand.

"Marty, you want to tag along with me tonight?" Andy offered.

"Thanks for the offer, but I have some shopping to finish." He gave me a wink. I hoped he didn't feel obligated to bring a gift to Mom's.

Sequoia and Rosa made their departure. Andy tried Bethany. "What do you say, Beth? Wanna come slay it with me?"

"Can't. I have a hot date." She flipped her curls.

"A date?" Andy stuck out his tongue. "With who?"

"With someone." Bethany flung her hair to the opposite side and walked away.

"She's dating someone?" Andy asked me.

"Don't ask me. Talk to her."

Andy looked taken aback. "Yeah, right." He gave a half shake of his head and then raced after her. "Hey, Bethany, wait up."

I smiled to myself. I was pretty sure that Bethany's hot date was literal—as in a pan of brownies—but a little jealousy never hurt.

After everyone had gone I realized that the Professor had never come by, nor had Lance. Oh well, maybe it was better for me to stay out of the investigation and focus on baking. I did a final walk-through and made sure that everything was in order for the morning. I couldn't believe that Christmas was almost here. I had a couple last-minute gifts of my own to purchase, so I turned off the lights and locked up for the night.

The energy on the plaza was like that of a kid waiting to see Santa. People spilled out from every shop and restaurant. I crunched through the snow to my favorite shop, London Station. The two-story shop housed everything from kitchenware to clothing. Every time I stopped in, I discovered something new.

London Station, more than any other shop in the plaza, embraced the holiday spirit. Intricate snowflake cutouts hung with invisible fishing line covered the ceiling, giving the effect of snow falling from above. There were more than a dozen Christmas trees inside along with a huge holiday display in the front of the store.

"Merry Christmas." A woman dressed in an elf costume greeted me at the door with a cup of mulled cider. "Welcome to London Station, can I help you find anything?"

I took the cup of cider and explained that I was looking for a few last-minute gifts for friends. I wanted to get something extra for Lance and a little gift for Marty. She pointed me in the right direction and told me to holler if I needed anything.

I browsed through the aisles while carolers sang on the upstairs balcony. The space was so packed with shoppers that I had to squeeze my stomach in to fit between racks of cashmere scarves and plaid throw pillows with reindeer.

I found a stainless-steel martini set for Lance and a collection of dish towels with an assortment of breads embroidered on them for Marty. On a whim, I added a couple packages of Christmas Party crackers to my basket. They would be a fun addition to tomorrow night's dinner. I made my way to the register with my gifts and bumped directly into Emma.

"Emma, what are you doing here? Shouldn't you be at the feast?"

Emma's brow was damp with sweat. Had she run here from the Winchester? "Oh, Juliet, you have no idea. Francine is a no-show. I know you've heard the saga on that, but we had expected that her singing troupe would perform without her, but none of them have arrived. We are serving the first course as we speak. I made a call to Peachie. You know Peachie, right? She's owned London Station as long as I can remember." Emma took a quick inhale. "In any event, I called Peachie because I knew that they've been having rotating choir groups singing on the balcony. I told her about our predicament and she said to come down. The choir is finishing now and I'm going upstairs to beg them to come sing at the inn."

"Let me go check out and I'll come with you."

"You don't need to do that." Emma tapped nervously at her watch. "I hope I can convince them. Jon told me to give them an extra bonus—whatever it takes."

"I get it. You go talk to the choir. I'll pay for my gifts and meet you back here in a minute."

"Thank you, Jules." Emma hurried upstairs.

The choir must have agreed to her terms because by the time the clerk had packaged and gift-wrapped my purchases, Emma was leading them out the front door.

I had to sprint to keep up with her.

At the Winchester, she directed them to the first dining room. They were already in black choir robes. "That will have to do," she said. "There's no time to change and we don't have enough costumes for each of you."

The professional choir didn't miss a beat. Soon their melodic voices carried into the lobby. "Is there anything I can do?"

Emma glanced to the dining room where we had been seated for our party. "Would you mind going down to the wine cellar to check with Jon and Nate how the ornaments are coming along? After last week I'm so nervous about it. I'll go check with the kitchen on the second course."

"No problem." I hooked my bag around my arm and went downstairs. A strange sense of déjà vu came over me as I descended into the basement.

The cellar door was shut. I knocked and then turned the handle. It opened. "Jon, it's Jules, Emma sent me to check on you."

Please don't let this be a repeat of the night Cami was killed. I was beginning to think the Winchester was cursed. Every time I'd been at the hotel recently, something creepy had happened.

When I stepped into the cellar I wished I hadn't. Tim stood in front of a wall of wine. Every bottle had been removed and laid in piles and boxes on the floor.

"Tim? What's going on?"

He whipped around. "Jules."

I looked to the corner where Jon's desk and the ornament seating chart sat. Neither Jon nor Nate were here. This was bad. A sick feeling welled in my stomach. What was Tim doing? Why was he dismantling the wine wall?

I started to back up. Had I gotten it wrong? Maybe Francine wasn't the killer. I didn't like the way Tim was staring at me with wild, almost manic eyes.

"Stop. Where are you going?" He held a bottle of merlot in his hand. Did he plan to use it as a weapon?

"I'm looking for Jon and Nate." I tried to keep my voice as steady as possible.

"They're not here."

"I see that. I'll go look upstairs."

"Why are you staring at me like that?" He stood the bottle on top of an empty crate.

"What are you doing with the wine?"

How was Tim going to explain this? He was either looking for something or getting ready to clear out the wine cellar. Then again why would he try to steal everything now? In the middle of dinner service when everyone was around? That didn't make sense.

"No, wait. Stop." He held up both hands with such force that I startled. "Please. Let me explain."

"I don't know what's going on, but I don't want to be in the middle of this." I took another step backward.

"Stop." Tim's voice was demanding. "It's not what you think. I mean it kind of is, but I swear I didn't hurt anyone."

I considered my options. I could make a run for it. The stairs were right behind me and the kitchen was buzzing with staff. Emma knew I was here. Tim couldn't do anything rash. And there was something about the pleading look in his eyes that made me want to hear what he had to say.

"You were right about skimming. I realized last night that you had figured it out. It's fine. I've been in over my head for too long. It's actually a relief that you know." He set a bottle of wine on a wooden crate. "But it wasn't me. At least not at first."

"Okay." I wasn't sure where this was going, but at least the crazed look in Tim's eyes had subsided.

"Things got out of control fast. I feel terrible and I think I know who killed Cami."

Chapter Twenty-seven

"Who?" I asked, keeping my distance from him. If I had to make a fast break I could.

Tim picked up a wine cork and flipped it between his fingers. "It will be easier if I start from the beginning."

"Go ahead." I stayed in the doorway.

"You see, I realized a while ago that Francine wasn't just taking expensive bottles of whiskey to her room. She was taking a lot more. It was subtle at first. A bottle of wine here and there. The McBeths had given me full control over the wine cellar, so they didn't notice it either, but one night I caught her stealing."

"Stealing wine?" I asked, not wanting to give away any of my suspicions about Francine to Tim. "Did you tell the McBeths?"

He hung his head. "No. I know I should have, but I had already told them about the whiskey and they weren't worried about it. They wanted to keep Francine happy. The guests love her, and the Dickens feast is the inn's biggest moneymaker of the year."

"I don't understand. So you caught her stealing and

looked the other way?" Tim couldn't be entirely blameless in this. I wanted to keep him talking.

"Not exactly. She had a plan. She already knew about the sale of the Winchester. She made a point that we wouldn't really be stealing from the McBeths. Cami was going to inherit the inventory as part of the sale and I was in a position to fudge the books, so no one would be the wiser."

"How?"

"That part was easy. Bottles get broken, damaged, and returned all the time. I can comp bottles to guests and staff or special contractors like Francine. We formulated what I thought was a foolproof plan. You have to understand that I would never do anything to hurt the McBeths. They've been amazing to me over the years, but Cami was a different story. She was horrid and was planning to bulldoze the inn anyway. Francine made a compelling argument. She said that we had a unique opportunity to make some extra cash and stick it to Cami. It's not like Cami cared about any of our jobs. She was going to fire everyone anyway."

"So what was the plan?" I felt calmer the longer Tim spoke. He wasn't acting like a killer who had something to hide.

"The plan was that I would fudge the books. Francine would stockpile the wine inventory in the secret passageway attached to her room. She had discovered the door in the back of the closet and came to me with her supposedly 'foolproof' scheme. She said it was the perfect hiding spot for our stockpile. Once we had amassed enough product, we would work together to resell the wine and alcohol to other restaurants and pubs, at a discount to them but full profit to us." He broke a piece off the cork. "Look, I know when saying this out loud how terrible it sounds, but you have to believe me that I didn't think it would do any harm to the McBeths and I was about to be out of a job. You know what they say—desperate times call for desperate measures."

I wanted to point out that Tim was a certified sommelier. Any restaurant in town would have been happy to scoop him up.

Tim tossed the broken cork in the crate. "Things started out okay, but Francine got greedier and greedier. She decided that taking a couple dozen bottles here and there wasn't going to give us enough profit fast enough, so she came up with a plan to trash the wine cellar the night that Cami was murdered. She wanted it to look like someone was breaking in and have it seem like the break-in was connected to the Dickens feast. Then we were going to come back and take all of the wine."

"Whoa." There was probably a minimum of one hundred thousand dollars of inventory in the Winchester's wine cellar.

"I know. It's bad. I told her that was taking things too far. She wouldn't listen. She was crazed. She had it out for Cami and by the time I realized that things were out of control I was too involved. Francine threatened to go to the McBeths. She told me that everything implicated me, and nothing involved her. If I didn't help her she was going to blame the entire thing on me."

He sounded sincere, but I couldn't let my guard down. He could be lying. I wondered where Nate and Jon were. Hopefully one of them would show up soon.

"It was supposed to go down last night."

"What was?"

"The cellar break-in. Francine called me up to her room after they finished the set for the evening. She sent her group home and we took down the board in the closet. The plan was that we would stash the product in the passageway and that every night Francine would load up as much as she could in her suitcase. She would be performing through New Year's Eve, so we had over a week to get everything out. She loved the idea of hiding the wine at the inn."

"Why did you take down the boards to the entrance at the library? Wouldn't that have given more of an opportunity for someone to find the stash?"

"That was Francine's idea. Occasionally I host special wine tastings for guests in the library. Francine thought it would be another opportunity to smuggle more bottles out. I could pack them in with the empty bottles after the guests departed."

"That is quite the plan." I stared at the disassembled bottles. "I don't understand what you're doing now though."

"I'm sure that Francine staged what you saw in the window last night."

My breath caught in my throat. Had I been right? Could what I had witnessed in the window have been a ruse for Francine to make her great escape?

Tim continued, "And I know she's going to try and pin this on me. I was hoping maybe she screwed up and left something down here. She's the one who destroyed the seating chart. She's big on hidden rooms, and I just thought maybe I could find a tiny shred of evidence to prove that I wasn't the mastermind behind this scheme."

"Tim, you have to tell the police and the McBeths." Suddenly I felt certain that we were on the right track. It all added up. If Francine had realized that her plan was in danger, then she probably got spooked and decided to act fast. It made even more sense that she had pretended to be struck on the head. I wondered how long she had waited in the window for someone to come up the walkway. I had been in the wrong place at the wrong time. Or, maybe the right place at the right time depending on your perspective.

"I know." He pounded his fist on his head. "I hate that I'm ruining everything I worked for over a stupid mistake. I never should have agreed to any of this. Now I've made a deal with the devil."

"Did Richard Lord hire you?"

His eyes widened. "How did you know?"

"It wasn't hard to figure out. The other morning at the bakeshop you said you were heading to an interview and I watched you cross the street to the Merry Windsor."

He looked dejected.

"The Professor is fair. He might be willing to be more lenient if you cooperate now." That wasn't a lie; I knew that the Professor would take whatever Tim told him into account. That didn't mean that Tim would get off without any consequences, but it did mean that he would receive straightforward and reasonable treatment.

"Yeah. That's true."

"Should I call the Professor?" I reached for my phone.

Tim crouched next to the crate of wine, picked up a bottle and cradled it to his chest. He whispered yes but couldn't meet my eyes.

I placed the call. The Professor said he would be over within minutes. True to his word, he arrived shortly with Thomas and Detective Kerry in tow. He called the McBeth family downstairs as well. I sat with Emma, Jon, and Nate while Tim repeated his story.

The McBeths, in true Christmas spirit, embraced Tim with a hug when he finished. "I don't condone your choices," Jon said. "But I also understand that we all make mistakes and have regrets. We'll support you in any way we can."

Tim broke down at their gift of forgiveness and kindness.

The Professor motioned to me. I followed him upstairs. "Thank you, Juliet."

"For what? I didn't do anything." I wanted to kick myself for not putting it together sooner.

"Ah, but indeed you did. You listened. Tim had a heavy heart and conscience. He needed a listening ear to release his burden and guilt. You provided that for him without judgment."

"What's going to happen to him?"

"That will be up to the McBeths to decide. My sense is that they're unlikely to press charges. I would wager that they'll find another way for Tim to repay them."

"And what about Francine? Do you think she killed Cami and that what I saw last night was just an act?"

The Professor stroked his beard. "Quite likely. Ms. La Roux was not financially stable. That we've proven with bank statements. And Thomas was able to get one of her fellow singers to admit that he helped set up her getaway."

"So we know for sure that she wasn't hurt?"

He tapped the corner of one eye. "No. Your eyes did not deceive you when you saw Francine in the window. However, what you didn't see was that it was merely a farce. She convinced her friend to pretend to be about to hit her with the candlestick and intentionally scattered drops of red wine to make it look like blood. She wanted us to think that she was dead. I'm guessing her intent was to disappear."

"The drops on the carpet were wine?"

"A lovely Bordeaux. The lab report came back this morning."

"If she was broke, how was she funding her getaway?"

The Professor stared upstairs. "The wine cellar wasn't her only target. It appears that the cash register in the bar and at the front desk were cleaned out last night."

"What about the power outage?" I asked. "Thomas had mentioned something about the fact that whoever cut the power would have had to have knowledge and a background in that line of work. How did Francine cut the line and not end up electrocuting herself?"

"Ah yes, another mystery solved." The Professor ran his fingers through his beard that was streaked with gray. "Most astute question, Juliet. It turns out that those two events—Cami's murder and the severing of the power line—were not connected."

"Who cut the power then?" As I asked the question, I answered it at the same time. "It was Nate, wasn't it?"

The Professor reached into his tweed jacket and removed a pair of reading glasses. He placed them on the tip of his nose to read a framed menu hanging on the wall by the staircase. It was from the first Dickens feast. "Indeed. Nate, if you recall, worked a variety of construction jobs on and off while working at the inn over the years. It turns out that he knew how to shut off the meter to the main house, then cutting the line was no problem. That was one of the first things that led to his initial arrest. We didn't believe that he had killed Francine, but he was the only person well versed in electrical knowledge."

"And he wanted to get back at Cami and his parents for selling the inn, so he decided to sabotage the dinner?" It made sense. That explained Nate's absence and remorse upon returning that night.

"Exactly." The Professor ran his finger down the list of items on the original Dickens menu. "Not much has changed, has it? A few additions like that lovely pumpkin risotto I had, but otherwise it appears that the McBeths know something about the power of long-standing traditions."

"Why mess with perfection, when you have a winning menu?" I agreed.

He returned his reading glasses to his pocket.

"Do you think you'll be able to catch Francine?"

"I'm confident that she will be found. She's a woman on the run. Likely she panicked when she realized that Tim was going to crack. She made a hasty getaway and, my dear, this is the twenty-first century. We have many, many ways to track a suspect down."

"Does this mean you'll be able to enjoy the holiday?"

"Absolutely." His eyes danced. "Your mother and I have a feast fit for kings prepared. I must go and finish my work. We'll see you tomorrow." He kissed the top of my head.

I clutched my bag filled with presents and headed for home. For the first time in days I could sleep easy knowing that Cami's murder had been resolved. The only problem was that it was the night before Christmas Eve—how could I possibly sleep?

Chapter Twenty-eight

Working Christmas Eve morning at Torte didn't feel like work. We handed out peppermint sticks and hot chocolate. Everyone who walked through our front door was treated like family and given samples of our eggnog fudge and cranberry strudels. The morning flew by and before I knew it I was hugging each of our staff, handing them checks for their holiday bonuses, and sending them on their way with Merry Christmas greetings.

I went home to change and gather my gifts. Mom and the Professor had invited me to spend the night, so I packed a bag with my cozy fleece pajamas and slippers. Christmas Eve dinner was casual, but I couldn't resist wearing a red skirt, matching tights, and a cream sweater with holly berries. I dusted my cheeks with blush, added a touch of silver eyeshadow, mascara, and shimmery lip gloss. Then I tied both sides of my long blond hair back with two silver barrettes. Happy with my appearance, I loaded my suitcase, gifts, and the special cake into the car.

The drive to Mom and the Professor's new house took me out to Emigrant Lake. The mountains on every side were covered in snow. Andy must be loving this, I thought as I pulled into their driveway.

They had decorated the front walkway with garlands of evergreen boughs and pinecones. "Merry Christmas!" I called, stepping inside. The open-concept living room, dining room, and kitchen allowed for great flow and conversation. A fire burned in the fireplace that connected the living and dining rooms. A twenty-foot tree draped in strands of popcorn and cranberries stood in front of the wall of windows that looked down to the lake.

"Juliet!" Mom waved from the stove. She had a green apron tied around her waist.

The Professor tended to the fire. "A jolly holiday eve to you!"

I greeted them both with a kiss. Then I unloaded my bag of presents, adding them to a large pile under the tree. I went back to the car for the cake. "I brought a surprise," I said, setting the box on the counter.

"I told you not to bring anything," Mom scolded.

"I know, but I wanted to bake something."

The Professor came over to see the unveiling. They both cheered with delight when they saw the cake. "The Bard would write a sonnet for this masterpiece. We must display this. Don't you agree, Helen?"

Mom painted homemade rolls with melted butter. "Yes. It's gorgeous, honey."

The Professor picked up the cake and walked it to the dining room. Their long table had been draped with red and green plaid tablecloth and set for the occasion with china, silver flatware, and crystal wine goblets. He made room for the cake on a side table. "What do you think? Dessert here?"

"Works for me."

Holiday jazz played on a vintage record player. The house smelled like roasting turkey and herbed gravy.

"Put me to work. What can I do?"

"You, young lady, can help yourself to a glass of wine and sit right here at the island and chat while Doug and I put the finishing touches on dinner."

"No way. I came early to help."

Mom's eyes twinkled. "That's why we got an even earlier start. We're basically done, aren't we, dear?"

The Professor nodded. He pointed to bottles of wine waiting at one end of the counter. "Your mother is right. Red or white?"

"I'll take red, please."

He poured me a glass of wine and topped off Mom's.

"How many people are coming to dinner?" I pointed to the bag I'd brought the presents in. "I found some Christmas party crackers that might be fun to pop before dinner, but before I set them at each place I should probably make sure I have enough."

"There's the three of us, and Lance, and Marty. Thomas and his parents, and Detective Kerry."

I took a sip of the wine. It was smooth and had notes of cherries and a hint of smoke. "That's nine," I said, counting the places at the table. "You have two more place settings."

"Oh right." Mom glanced at the Professor. They shared a cryptic look. "The McBeths might drop by. I wanted to make sure we had a spot for them in case they do."

"How are they doing?" I asked the Professor.

He poured himself a glass of chilled white wine. "I would say much better than expected, all things considered. In a happy turn of events they have decided to stay on half-time and help Nate and his wife transition to full owner-ship of the Winchester over the next few years. It seems that the Dickens feast will live on."

"That's great to hear. Any news on Francine?" I got up to set the colorful paper crackers on each plate. My dad, who, like the Professor had been a huge Shakespeare buff, had fallen in love with the English tradition of Christmas crackers. The festive snap of the party crackers always signaled the start of Christmas Eve dinner at our house growing up.

"Indeed. It is a holiday miracle. The authorities in Santa Monica pulled her over during a routine traffic stop and identified her. As I said, it is nearly impossible in this mod-ern age to escape the ever-watchful eyes of 'big brother.' There are cameras everywhere." He glanced at the ceiling and chuckled. "Not to worry, your mother insisted that I did not have permission to install cameras here."

"I wouldn't think otherwise."

He smiled. "In any event, Francine is being held in Cal-ifornia until after the holiday and then will be transported here to be arraigned. We have a solid case against her from physical evidence at the crime scene to Tim's con-fession on his involvement, and her financial records. I'm very confident that justice will be served in this case."

"That's even more good news. One thing that's been bugging me is Jon's tainted whiskey. Bethany saw him toasting with a woman who had red nails. I'm assuming that must have been Francine. Why didn't Jon say anything, or did he really not remember?"

"His memory was greatly impaired by the substance she slipped him."

"I'm confused. Why would she have needed to drug him? Wasn't she already planning to make a getaway?"

"Indeed. I believe that Jon likely came upon her when she was down in the cellar attempting to stockpile more wine and cash. She acted on impulse, but must have done some plotting since she had the drug. She was probably hoping that if she could knock Jon out, she would be long gone by the time he came to or had any memory of what happened." He swirled his wineglass. "Yes, it's a shame. Jon and Emma are so trusting, and Francine took advantage of that. We learned that they often kept extra cash from the bar in the top drawer of the desk in the wine cellar. Francine intended to take the cash and anything else she could load into her getaway vehicle."

The doorbell sounded. Thomas, Detective Kerry, and his parents were the first to arrive. Detective Kerry wore a pair of black slacks, ballet flats, and a red and white striped sweater. She brought her own stack of gifts to add to the tree. Thomas looked handsome in a pair of khakis and a red checkered shirt. I went to hug his parents as the door sounded again and Lance swept in.

"Happy, Happy Christmas!" Lance's arms were loaded with bottles of champagne and silver and gold gift boxes. I helped him with the gifts.

Marty arrived next. I gave him an extra-long hug. "So glad you could join us."

He brushed away a tear. "Thank you for the invitation.

I'm happy to be surrounded by happy people on a night that might otherwise feel lonely."

I squeezed him again. "It's okay to be sad too. After losing my father I've always found the holidays and every other milestone in my life to be bittersweet. You are among friends and no one here is immune to loss. If you want to feel sad tonight, we'll join you in that sadness too."

Marty blinked away more tears. "I sure wish you could have met my Maureen. She would have loved you."

We walked to the kitchen together where Mom immediately embraced him in another hug. I couldn't take away his grief, but I was glad that he was surrounded by people who would love and support him.

Wine flowed freely, and the conversation turned to tales of holidays past. Like the year that Thomas, who used to sleepwalk and eat as a kid, ate two entire pies in the middle of the night on Christmas Eve.

He patted his trim stomach after his mom finished recounting her surprise to find two empty Torte pie tins and a fork on the counter on Christmas morning. "Hey, blame Jules and Helen. They shouldn't make pies that are so tasty."

"Two pies?" Detective Kerry was incredulous. "That's impressive."

Thomas laughed and looked around the kitchen. "Guard your pies, ladies. I'm in the house."

Mom swatted him with a dish towel.

Lance popped open a bottle of the champagne that he brought. "I say let's raise a glass to Christmas, friends, and our beloved Ashland." He filled fluted glasses with the bubbly.

Everyone toasted.

The Professor cleared his throat. "Shall we be seated?"

Mom opened the oven to reveal a golden turkey, a honey-glazed ham, and a prime rib. "We couldn't decide on a main course since this is our first official Christmas together, so we decided on all three." She gave the Professor a sheepish smile.

"Yes, you, our most beloved guests, will have to help us decide what tradition we'll have to continue." He took off his green apron to reveal a navy blue British Christmas jumper with a snowflake pattern across the chest.

Thomas found his spot at the table. "I don't think there's any question. Once you start with three you can't go back."

Mom laughed. "I had a feeling that might be the consensus."

"No complaints from moi." Lance loosened his belt. "I wore my baggy pants."

I wrinkled my brow. "You don't own a pair of baggy anything, Lance."

He tugged at the waist, revealing an inch. "You stand corrected, darling. Wait until I get my fork on that roast beast."

Everyone laughed.

Mom and the Professor stood at the head of the table. She started to speak but before she could get a word out tears spilled from her eyes. "I can't do it, you go, Doug. I'm too happy to see everyone I love here in our new house." She placed her hand on her heart.

Her emotion made me teary. Lance placed his hand on my knee in a show of solidarity.

"Tonight words from Hamlet are rattling in my head:

'Love is begun by time . . . time qualifies the spark and fire of it.' We could interpret this passage to reference the burning flame of love, but for me as I stand next to my beautiful wife by the warmth of our new hearth, surrounded by family and friends, I am struck by the endurance of love. New love, old love, and the loves we have lost but who always remain in our hearts." He paused and cleared his throat. I looked around the table. There wasn't a dry eye.

"This is the message of Christmas," the Professor continued in his rich, resonant voice. "The message we hold in our hearts throughout the year. When love is present there is never anything to fear."

Mom choked up.

The Professor raised a glass. "To love! Merry Christmas!"

We clinked glasses.

"Juliet." Lance leaned close to whisper in my ear. "Joking and jesting aside, you know that I adore you. You are my best friend and I would be lost without you."

"Same here." I kissed his cheek.

Mom and the Professor delivered platters to the table, the turkey, ham, and roast, along with tureens of soup and gravy. Ceramic bowls of varying shapes and sizes were filled to the brim with mashed potatoes, stuffing, green beans with toasted almonds, roasted Brussels sprouts, cranberry sauce, salad, and buttery rolls.

We each held up our Christmas crackers. "Everyone grab both tabs and pull hard to pop them," I instructed. It sounded like firecrackers on the Fourth of July as the paper crackers burst apart and toys and colored tissue-paper crowns spilled out.

Lance placed his purple crown on top of his head. "How fitting. Purple is my signature color, you know."

The doorbell rang.

Mom was in the middle of bringing a tray of raspberry and cherry jams to the table. The Professor was carving the turkey. "Can you get the door, Juliet? That must be the McBeths. Right on time."

I stood and walked to the door. As I was about to open the handle I turned around because everyone had gone silent. They were staring at me. "What?"

"Just open the door, honey. We don't want to leave the McBeths waiting in the cold."

I turned the handle and nearly dropped to my knees. Carlos and Ramiro stood in the doorway holding packages and suitcases.

"Carlos? Ramiro?" I looked to them and then to Mom and the Professor and then back to them again. Was I dreaming?

"Julieta." Carlos stepped inside and planted a memorable kiss on my lips.

Everyone broke into laughter.

"Is it really you?" I reached to put my hand on Ramiro's cheek.

"*Sí*, it is a surprise. Are you surprised?"

"Stunned." I glanced at Mom again. She beamed with delight. "But you called from the ship?"

"No. We were at the airport. I wanted to throw you off the scent." Carlos's grin made my knees feel like they were about to buckle.

"Let them inside, Juliet," Mom called.

I laughed and made way for them to come inside. Once

they had set their bags down I wrapped them both in giant hugs. "I can't believe you're really here."

"We would not miss Christmas in Ashland, with you *mi querida*." Carlos reached for my hand.

His touch sent a jolt through my body.

Ramiro was equally excited. "It's snowing on Christmas. Like in the movies."

Everyone laughed. They joined us at the table, regaling everyone with stories of their travels. I pinched myself most of the night. Ashland held a piece of my heart and Carlos held the other. To have them together at Christmas was the very best gift of all.

Mom's Antoinettes

Ingredients:

Cookies:
1 cup butter
½ cup sugar
1 egg
1 ½ teaspoons almond extract
2 ½ cups flour
½ teaspoon salt

Frosting:
1 cup butter
¾ cup cocoa powder
2 1/2–3 cups powdered sugar
1 teaspoon vanilla
1 tablespoon heavy cream

Filling:
1 jar raspberry jam

Directions:
Cream butter and sugar together in a mixer. Add egg and almond extract and mix well. Slowly incorporate flour and salt. Roll dough into a large ball and chill for one hour. Preheat oven to 375 degrees F. Make small balls (half inch) and place on cookie sheet. You should be able to get four to five balls per row. Then use the palm of your hand to press balls into circles (approximately the size of a quarter). Bake for six to eight minutes. Allow to cool.

For the chocolate frosting—whip butter in mixer. Slowly incorporate cocoa powder, powdered sugar, vanilla, and heavy cream. Then mix on high setting for five minutes, or until frosting is creamy and light.

Assemble cookies by spreading a thin layer of raspberry jam on the flat side of two cookies. Sandwich them together. Spread a generous layer of chocolate frosting on the top. Pop in your mouth and enjoy!

Chicken Cordon Blue Crescent Pie

Ingredients:
  2 ½ packages of crescent rolls
  2 chicken breasts, cooked and shredded
  6 slices of bacon, fried and diced
  6 slices of ham
  6 slices of Swiss cheese

1 tsp onion powder
1 tsp garlic powder
1 tsp pepper
1 8 ounce package cream cheese, softened
2 tbsp butter, melted
Italian seasoning

Directions:
Preheat oven to 375° F. Mix cream cheese, chicken, garlic powder, onion powder, and pepper. Arrange one of the packages of crescent rolls on a pizza stone (leaving each roll in two rectangle strips) in a cross shape. Then overlay the next package of rolls so that there aren't any gaps. Spoon chicken mixture into the center of the dough. Sprinkle bacon on top of the chicken mixture. Press ham around the side of the chicken mixture, and then cover with slices of swiss. Fold the edges inward to form a round pie. Use two to four crescent rolls from the remaining package to close the top of the pie. Brush with melted butter and sprinkle with Italian seasoning. Bake for 25 to 30 minutes with a cookie sheet underneath the pizza pan to catch any juices that might spill out.

Torte Sugar Cookie Cutouts

Ingredients:
    Cookies:
    1 cup butter, softened
    ½ cup sugar

1 egg
2 teaspoons almond extract
¼ teaspoon salt
2 ¼ cups flour

Frosting:
½ cup butter
1 teaspoon vanilla extract
1 tablespoon heavy cream
1 1/2 cups powdered sugar

Directions:
Preheat oven to 325 degrees F. Make the cookie dough
by mixing butter and sugar on low speed until they cream
together. Add egg, almond extract, and salt. Slowly incorporate flour. Chill in the fridge for one hour. Lightly flour
a cutting board and divide dough into two balls. Roll first
ball until it's 1/8 inch thick. Cut into fun shapes, place on
baking sheet, and bake at 325 degrees for seven to eight
minutes or until the cookies are golden brown.

Allow cookies to cool completely. While cookies are
cooling, whip butter in mixer until smooth and creamy.
Add in vanilla and heavy cream. Slowly add in powdered
sugar. Once the powdered sugar has been incorporated
mix on high for five minutes.

Frost cooled cookies and decorate with sprinkles or
fancy sugars.

Chocolate Shortbread with Peppermint Pudding

Ingredients:

For the crust:
½ cup butter, chilled and cubed
1 cup flour
¼ cup sugar
¼ cup cocoa powder
1 tsp vanilla

For the filling:
1 package vanilla pudding
2 cups heavy cream
1 tsp peppermint extract
1-2 tsp red food coloring
For the topping
1 ½ cups whipping cream
1/3 cup sugar
1 tsp peppermint extract
White chocolate peppermint candies and sprinkles for
    decoration

Directions:
Preheat oven to 325 degrees F. Use a food processor to
combine butter, flour, sugar, cocoa powder, and vanilla.
The dough will be crumbly—almost like sand. Press
firmly into a 10-inch tart pan. Bake at 325 degrees for 20
minutes and allow to cool completely.

Meanwhile, whisk the vanilla pudding, heavy cream,

red food coloring, and peppermint extract until it's smooth and creamy. Set aside.

Whip cream, sugar, and peppermint extract until it forms stiff peaks. Carefully remove shortbread crust from tart pan. Layer with peppermint pudding, whipping cream, and decorate with peppermint candies and sprinkles. Serve cold.

Cranberry Ginger Christmas Cake with Cream Cheese Frosting

Ingredients:
- ¾ cup butter
- 1 ½ cup sugar
- 3 eggs
- 1 tsp vanilla
- 2 ½ cups flour
- 2 tsps. baking powder
- 1 tsp salt
- 2 tsps. ginger
- 2 tsps. nutmeg
- 1 tsp cinnamon
- 1 ¼ cup buttermilk
- Fresh cranberries (2 cups chopped—save remaining berries for the top of the cake)
- 2 cups chopped walnuts
- Fresh rosemary (for top of the cake)

Frosting:
- 2 cups butter (at room temp)

1 eight-oz package cream cheese (at room temp)
1 tsp vanilla
4 ½ to 5 cups powdered sugar
Fresh whole cranberries for decoration

Directions:

Preheat oven to 350 degrees F. In an electric mixer, cream butter and sugar together, and add eggs and vanilla. Sift dry ingredients together in a separate bowl. Alternate adding dry ingredients and buttermilk until batter is smooth. Stir in walnuts and cranberries by hand. Grease three eight-inch round cake pans and fill equally with batter. Bake at 350 degrees for thirty minutes or until cakes are golden brown.

Allow cakes to cool completely. Meanwhile, make the cream cheese frosting. Whip butter, cream cheese, and vanilla on medium speed until blended. Slowly incorporate powdered sugar, beat for another three to five minutes on medium high speed, until frosting is smooth and creamy.

Stack cakes by spreading a thin layer of cream cheese frosting between each cake. Use remaining frosting to cover the top and sides of the cake. Adorn with whole cranberries and sprigs of fresh rosemary.

Andy's Ode To The Bard Latte

Andy's holiday creation is sure to put you in a festive spirit and give you a taste of the old world with touches of winter pine.

Ingredients:
    2 shots of espresso
    1 cup milk
    1 tbsp ginger syrup
    Fresh pine needles (finely chopped)
    Gold dust (optional)

Directions:
Prepare espresso and steam milk. Once milk is steamed, pour over espresso. Add ginger syrup and stir together. Sprinkle with finely chopped pine needles and gold dust. Serve hot.

Lance's Hot Buttered Rum

Lance knows his cocktails and his hot buttered rum is no exception. You'll be the hit of the party with this winter warmer.

Ingredients:
    1/2 cup butter
    1/2 cup brown sugar
    1 tsp nutmeg
    1 tsp vanilla
    1 tsp cinnamon
    ½ tsp salt
    4 shots of rum (1 shot per drink)
    4 cups hot water (1 cup per drink)
    Cinnamon sticks, for garnish

Directions:

Whip butter, sugar, nutmeg, vanilla, cinnamon, and salt in a mixer until well combined. Scoop mixture (in four even portions) into four large coffee mugs. Add a shot of rum to each glass. Lance prefers spiced rum. Pour one cup of hot water into each mug and stir until the mixture dissolves. Finish with a cinnamon stick garnish.

Read on for an excerpt from

NOTHING
BUNDT TROUBLE

—the next Bakeshop Mystery from Ellie
Alexander, coming soon from St. Martin's
Paperbacks!

They say that the future is mutable. That our choices and actions influence every outcome. That could be true, but the only way I was going to be able to embrace my future was to understand my past. Moving into my child-hood home had quickly acquainted me with years of long-forgotten memories. Like the fact that the hallway floorboard squeaked with the lightest touch. It was a good thing I had never tried to sneak out when I was a kid. There was no chance I would have been successful. Maybe that's why my dad had never bothered to fix the creaky floor. After he died, I guessed that a loose piece of hard-wood was low on Mom's priority list. So here I was al-most twenty years later, tiptoeing down the hallway in my slippers, trying to avoid the squeaky sections of the floor.

My parents' house—now my house—was tucked in amongst towering Ponderosa pines, sequoias, aspens, and blue spruce trees on the aptly named Mountain Avenue in Ashland, Oregon. The view from the back deck offered a panorama of Grizzly Peak and the sepia-toned hillsides across the valley. As a kid, I had always felt like I lived in a tree house. I would fall asleep watching the spindly branches of the pine trees waving in the window and staring up at the star-drenched sky.

When Mom and her new husband, the Professor, had offered to pass the house on to me, I had been resistant. It wasn't because I didn't love the house. Quite the opposite. It was that I didn't want to take advantage of their generosity. They had done so much for me since I had returned home to Ashland. However, they had made it clear that keeping the house in the family was important to them. After their wedding last summer, they had opted to leave both of their old worlds behind and start a new life together on the wind-swept banks of Emigrant Lake. I hadn't seen Mom this happy in years. Her enthusiasm was contagious. For the past week she had been over every day helping me unpack boxes and rearrange some of the furniture she had left behind.

The holidays were behind us, which meant that I actually had time to focus on organizing my new space. Ashland is a tourist destination and mecca for theater lovers. When the Oregon Shakespeare Festival is in season there's never a dull moment at Torte, our family bakeshop. Most small business owners in town (myself included) know that there is a small window of time each year to plan a tropical getaway or tackle the list of tasks that fell by the wayside during the rush of the tourist season. Rather than jetting off to a sunny island or trekking through the snowy Siskiyou Mountains, I had decided to use the down time to officially move in.

Since I had spent nearly a decade sailing from port to port in my position as head pastry chef for the Amour of the Seas, I hadn't had a need to accumulate things, which made unpacking a breeze. My move had consisted of packing my clothes, collection of cookbooks, and kitchen tools. The apartment I had been renting above Elevation, an outdoor store on the plaza just a few doors down from the bakeshop, had come fully furnished. My challenge now was finding enough furniture to fill the four-bedroom house.

Mom had left a few pieces of mission-style furniture, including a large dining room table and chairs, a couch, side tables, coffee table, and a desk. I'd been sleeping on my old twin bed in what used to be my childhood bedroom. Mom had converted it into her sewing room when I left for culinary school. I figured it was probably time to graduate to an adult bed, so had ordered a custom queen-size four-poster bed and mattress. It was due to arrive this afternoon, and I couldn't wait.

As if on cue, the doorbell rang. I went down the oak staircase to answer the door.

"Hello, darling." My friend Lance stood on the porch, holding a bouquet of pale white roses dotted with greenery in one hand and an expensive tool kit in the other.

"You're early." I greeted him with a kiss on the cheek and showed him inside. Lance had offered to come help me set up the bed and dressers.

"Better early than late." He handed me the flowers as I shut the door behind him. "I figured I should be here to oversee the delivery. We wouldn't want the delivery crew to ding up your walls, would we?"

"No." I chuckled. "Imagine the horror."

Lance set his tool kit in the entryway and tugged off

his charcoal gray wool coat. Beneath the coat he wore a pair of perfectly cut khaki slacks, a cornflower blue shirt, and boat shoes. He hung the coat on a rack by the door. "You jest, Juliet, but you'll thank me later."

"I'm sure I will." I pointed down the hallway to the kitchen. "Come on in. I'll put these in some water."

We walked to the kitchen where sunlight flooded the room. The original pressed glass windows reflected a greenish glow from the trees outside. I had planted a row of herbs above the sink that were just beginning to sprout.

"I see you've wasted no time getting the kitchen organized," Lance noted, pointing to the display of cookbooks near the six-burner gas stove and my copper pots hanging on a wire rack above the butcher-block island.

"It's my happy place. I had to start here." I filled a vase with water and arranged the roses.

"Trust me, we are all the better that the kitchen is your happy place." Lance lifted the lid on my canary yellow Dutch oven. "My lord, what smells so divine?"

"That's meatball soup for later. I couldn't beg for your assistance without feeding you. I made a batch of butter rolls, a simple Italian salad, and a bitter chocolate cake. If your handyman skills are really as good as you claim, then I just might feed you when we're done." I tried to wink.

"For a spread like that, you can work these muscles to the bone." Lance flexed. He was naturally lanky with a thin frame and angular features.

I rested the vase of roses on the island. "How are things at the theater? Are you ready for the new season?"

Lance undid the top button of his pale blue shirt and

rolled the sleeves up partway. "It's fine. Have you heard the news about the Cabaret? That's where the *drama* is these days."

"No." I poured us cups of French press that had been steeping. "What's going on?" Despite Ashland's small population at around twenty-thousand residents the entire Rogue Valley was ripe with talent. There were dozens of theaters (large and small), music venues, and countless pubs and restaurants that offered a range of entertainment from open mic night to stand-up comedy and poetry readings. Our little hamlet was truly an oasis of entertainment. On any given night you could take in a fun and raucous musical at the Cabaret or catch a serious production of Shakespeare under the stars on the Elizabethan stage.

"The new owners have taken over. Truly wonderful people. Such great vision. They're a young couple from LA. They've been on the scene for years and I can't wait to see how they transform the cabaret over the next few years."

"Cream?" I asked, pointing to a pitcher resting on the island.

"Always." Lance looked miffed that I had even asked.

"What's the issue, then?" I poured a generous splash of heavy cream into Lance's coffee and swirled it into the dark brew.

"Where to start? The stage has been rife with emotion. I never should have agreed to provide my expertise. I blame it on my benevolent nature."

"You're so kind, and so humble." I poured myself a cup of the French press.

"I am. I truly am. Sometimes I astound myself at my

generosity." Lance raised his coffee mug in a toast to himself. "I mean after all it is my duty to give them a lay of the land here in Ashlandia, so to speak. But I hadn't counted on the fact that I would be spending so much time hand-holding and refereeing petty arguments. I've been burning the midnight oil running back and forth between campus and the Cabaret."

"You should have told me that you've been busy. I wouldn't have asked you to come help me put furniture together."

Lance dismissed me with a flick of the wrist. "Nonsense, darling. I never would pass up an opportunity to spend a day with you. Plus I need a reprieve from *Mamma Mia* for a few. If I hear that song again, I might have to bloody my ears."

"Gross." I shuddered at the thought. The Cabaret had been running its latest production, *Mamma Mia*, to sold out audiences for a month. I had read in the paper that they had extended the show due to demand. "Don't ruin it for me. I bought tickets for Mom and me for next week."

"You'll love it. It's a fabulous production and Amanda, the new artistic director's, use of space and set design is nothing short of brilliant. If you've seen it fifteen times though, those catchy musical numbers begin to stick in your head." Lance shoved a finger in his ear and pretended to try to rub away the lyrics.

"I can't wait. I scored front table seats and I'm surprising Mom with dinner too." The Cabaret served a full dinner menu and drool-worthy desserts and cocktails as part of the show. It added to the ambiance of its intimate setting in an old refurbished church. Seeing shows at the

Cabaret had been a family tradition. My parents were friends with the original owner and had helped launch the new theater when I was young.

"As long as the cast and crew don't implode in the next week, you'll be fine."

That sounded ominous, but the doorbell sounded again, interrupting our conversation.

"That must be my furniture." We left our coffees and went to show the delivery crew where everything went.

Lance removed a tape measure from his tool kit and proceeded to direct the poor delivery guys as if they were actors in his company. Fortunately they had a good sense of humor and played along when he stopped to measure each door frame before allowing them to load my bed upstairs. It didn't take long for the crew to unload the boxes. When they were done, I offered them homemade Amish sugar cookies, and then Lance and I got to work on the hard part—assembly.

"These floors are magnificent," Lance commented as he placed pieces of painter's tape to mark the spot where each of the four-posters would be placed. "They don't make hardwood like this anymore. It's all manufactured and processed laminate now. Is this oak?" He massaged the smooth surface of the shiny floor.

"Yeah. It was already here when my parents bought the house, but they had the floors sanded, resurfaced, and stained. The house was not in great condition when they bought it, but guess what they paid for it back in the 1980s?"

Lance made an "x" with the tape and moved near the window. "Do I even want to ask?"

"Probably not. Mom showed me the original deed and I thought she was pranking me. They bought this house which is over two-thousand square feet on a ten-thousand square foot lot for fifteen thousand dollars. Can you believe that?"

"No. I can't. Don't even ask me what I paid for my place." He made a chocking motion.

Lance's house was on Scenic Drive, one of the nicest streets in Ashland. Given its size, ornately manicured grounds, and views, I would guess that he paid close to a million dollars. Housing prices in Ashland had skyrocketed in the last decade. Even cute cottages in the railroad district were selling for half a million dollars or more. Many of Ashland's restaurant and hotel workers had been priced out of the city. They couldn't afford the rising cost of rent or buy a tiny two-bedroom fixer-upper for prices that would normally be found in a city like San Francisco or Seattle. It was an ongoing source of stress for Mom and me. We paid our team at Torte a fair wage, but even with that many of our staff had been priced out of Ashland's rental market.

"I think we're ready to start arranging the slats for the base," Lance announced, balancing a stack of narrow pieces of wood.

Surprisingly the bed went together easier than I had expected. In less than hour we managed to assemble the bed, two dressers, and a nightstand. I stood back to observe our work. The master bedroom was good size with two rectangular windows on either side of the bed, a skylight, and an adjoining bathroom with a claw-foot tub and basin sink.

"What do you think?" Lance brushed dust from his hands.

"I love it." The four-poster bed had a romantic vibe with its white finish, raised panel detailing on the head and footboards, and tapered legs. I had painted the bedroom in a bright slate gray. The contrast of the white bed with the oak floors and gray walls gave the room an almost coastal feel. I planned to drape sheer fabric across the posters and accent the walls with art from my global travels.

"It feels like you," Lance agreed. "You need a large floor rug though, and you should replace that light fixture with a romantic chandelier." He pointed to a basic light fixture above the bed. "Something black with candles to add a touch of drama, yes?"

"Yeah. That's a good idea."

"And, plants, darling. For the love of God, please get yourself some plants."

"Deal." I piled up the cardboard boxes to recycle. "Are you ready for a dinner break?"

"I thought you would never ask."

I punched him in the shoulder. "Just for that I'm going to make you take this stack of recycling down."

Lance hauled the cardboard outside while I went to finish dinner. I ladled the hearty meatball soup into bowls and removed the rolls from the oven. Then I poured us glasses of white wine and tossed the salad in a garlic vinaigrette.

"Thanks for your help. I couldn't have done that without you." I set our dinner on the island.

Lance raised his wine glass to me. "Don't sell yourself short. There's nothing you can't do, Juliet. We both know that. But, here's to new beginnings."

"To new beginnings." We clinked our glasses together.

"This house suits you," Lance noted, glancing around the warm kitchen with cheery yellow accents.

I blew on my soup. "I know. I thought it might be weird at first. You know, coming home, literally, but I love it. It feels right."

"What are you going to do with the rest of the empty rooms upstairs?"

"No idea. Do you know anyone looking for a room to rent? I've been thinking about renting out a couple rooms to SOU students." The truth was that the house was too big for me. The main floor had a living room, dining room, kitchen, half bath, and office. Upstairs was the master, plus two additional bedrooms, and there was a full unfinished basement. My former apartment could probably fit in the kitchen and dining room alone.

"Don't do that yet. Who knows what will happen with your talk, dark, and devilishly handsome husband. Wasn't there talk at the holidays of him coming to Ashland for a more permanent trial?"

Permanent and trial seemed to be in opposition to me. In some ways that summed up my relationship with Carlos. When I had left him on the ship, I didn't look back. I had thought that my decision to leave was likely the end for us. But Carlos hadn't given up that easily. He had been trying to convince me that we weren't star-crossed lovers. I still wasn't sure. There was one thing that I knew—Ashland was home for me. I had put down roots and had no intention of leaving. I loved Carlos, too. So much so, that being apart from him had left a lingering ache that I wasn't sure would ever fully heal.

I knew that we couldn't drag things out forever. It was time for us to make a decision about our future and the only way to do that was for him to come to Ashland and stay. I desperately wanted things to work with us. Having Carlos and his son Ramiro in Ashland would be perfection. But was it a pipe dream?

My inner voice had been nagging me for a while now. I wasn't sure that Carlos was meant to be somewhere small. He was made for the world. Maybe it was one of the reasons I had been living in limbo. If Carlos was away at sea, I could pretend like he still belonged to me. If he came to Ashland and didn't love it then I was opening my heart to breaking all over again.

Mom had told me once that love was always worth the risk. I had a feeling I was soon going to learn the depths of that risk.

I brushed the thought aside and focused on my conversation with Lance. After he left, I made quick work of the dishes. Then I returned upstairs to finish decorating my new bedroom. A fluffy tangerine down comforter and matching down pillows softened the gray tones. Prints from my global travels framed the far wall. Mom had mentioned that she had left a few boxes of assorted vases, artwork, and a lamp in the basement, so I went downstairs to see what I might be able to salvage. Otherwise, I had agreed to donate whatever I couldn't use.

The basement was partially finished with dirt floors and exposed duct work. It had been a great hiding spot for childhood games of hide-and-seek. Two large wooden shelves stood near the washer and dryer. I dug through boxes of old Christmas and Halloween decorations, tubs

with dishes, towels, and silverware, and found two bedside
lamps that would work perfectly. With as much as Mom
had saved for me, I might not have to go furniture shopping after all.

I set aside the things I wanted and began to restack the
boxes. The last box wouldn't fit back on the shelf. I tried
shoving it harder. No luck.

Odd, I thought as I made space on either side to try and
squeeze the box back into place. The box still wouldn't fit.

I removed the other boxes and decided to restack the
entire shelf. Once I had taken all the boxes down, I realized
what the issue was. A broken piece of wood had fallen
from the shelf above and gotten lodged at the back of the
rickety shelving unit. I tossed the wood on the dirt floor.

Dust tickled my throat. I coughed and waved tiny par-
ticles of dirt from my face. I considered calling it a night,
but then decided that if I was already this far into reorga-
nization I might as well give the entire shelves a good
cleaning.

I went upstairs to grab a rag and cleaning supplies. Then
I proceeded to remove every cardboard box and plastic tub.
Mom had labeled most of them, but some of the labels
were faded and hard to read, so I sorted through each
box and placed new labels on them. A wave of nostal-
gia washed over me as I discovered pictures from Torte's
early beginnings, family vacations, and even some of my
baby clothes. Mom had mentioned that she had was leaving some memorabilia for me, but I hadn't seen many of
the pictures in years. Tears welled in my eyes as I leafed
through photos of my mom, dad, and me at the beach and
Lake of the Woods. My favorite photo was of my parents

in front of Torte on the day they opened the doors to the public for the first time. They were holding hands and beaming.

I'll have to frame this one and put it on my nightstand, I thought, adding it to my "keep" pile and returning the tub of memories to the shelf. Another box caught my eye. It was stuffed at the very back of the shelves and covered in a half inch of dust. This box clearly hadn't been touched in years.

In order to free it, I had to move the unit a few inches from the wall. The thin cardboard box dropped to the ground. I picked it up and peeled off yellowing masking tape. At first glance, there didn't appear to be anything in the box other than some old newspaper clippings, but when I removed the faded newsprint, I found a leather-bound journal.

My heart rate quickened as I unwound the leather string on the journal and let it fall open. I recognized my father's handwriting immediately. It had been years since I had seen his cursive scroll. Seeing it made my eyes well again. I ran my finger over the words as if the touch of the ink on my skin would connect us again.

Miss you, Dad, I whispered, flipping through the pages of the journal. He had practically written a book. Every page was filled completely. Were these his personal thoughts, and should I read them?

I didn't want to violate his privacy, but he'd been gone for so many years now that the thought of reading his words in his voice was too enticing to pass up. I finished organizing the boxes and took my newfound treasures and Dad's journal upstairs.

It wasn't terribly late, so I made myself a steaming hot mug of apple cinnamon tea, put on my pajamas, and tucked myself into my new cozy bed with my father's journal. Was it a bad idea to venture into his past?

What if the journal contained details about my parents' relationship? What if he had intentionally hidden it in the basement? Maybe it contained a long forgotten secret. Was it fair to dredge up the past?

In the same breath, I knew had to read it. Because my dad had died in my formative years there were so many things I wished could have asked him. So many questions left unanswered.

Not the big things. I knew that he loved me—deeply, unconditionally. I knew that he loved Mom too. Their story could have graced the pages of Shakespeare. On the rare occasion that they had fought, they quickly mended things with a love note left at the coffee bar or a bouquet of wildflowers left on the dining room table. They had been steadfast supporters of each other. At least through my eyes.

What if my memories weren't true?

There's only way to find out, Jules. I took a long sip of my tea and flipped the journal open to the first page.

It was dated June 14, 1988.

Some quick math informed me that I would have been five at the time.

Beneath the date were the words: "Feeling conflicted."

I almost flipped the journal shut, but I couldn't stop myself. I read on.

"What should I do? I should have told Doug no when he asked for my help, but he's a trusted friend and I never would have imagined that a small favor would lead us here."

My heart thudded in my chest. Doug, as in the Professor, Doug? As in Mom's new husband?

I had known that Doug was good friends with both my parents. He had said as much himself when he asked for my permission to marry Mom. I'll never forget our conversation, when he had confessed that he had loved her from afar for many years. He had barely admitted it to himself at the time because he and my father were best friends. His revelation had made me admire him even more. To have never acted on his desires and stand by Mom in the years after Dad's death, offering support and comforting shoulder for her grief, was the true test of enduring love, in my opinion.

I continued to read.

"The 'pastry case' as Doug and I have agreed to refer to it, has spun out of my control. I fear for Helen, for Torte, and for Juliet. Yesterday when I returned to the bakery a man was seated in a booth at the front window. He wore a baseball cap to shroud his face from view. I asked Helen how long he'd been there. She said he'd been drinking the same cold cup of coffee for at least forty-five minutes. I knew right away something was off about him. He didn't meet my eyes when I offered a refill. I could barely hear his response. I think he mumbled something about being done anyway. Then he vanished. I made my rounds in the dining room and when I walked past the booth again, he was gone. Thank goodness Helen was in the kitchen. When I picked up his coffee cup, I noticed that he had written something on his napkin. I thought maybe it was a tip, but the words on that napkin have shaken me to my core. 'Stop now, or you and your family will be the next to die.' What have I done? How could I have put Helen and Juliet at risk? I'm going to talk to Doug tomorrow and tell him that I have to get out of this—now."